"I lied to ~~y~~
you much. ~~~~

Her gaze rose to his. "Really? Why?"

He smiled. "Because I'm curious. I wanted to know one thing before I left." He tugged her closer.

"Yeah?" She stopped when they were toe to toe. "And what's that?"

"Just how good you taste." He started his descent, his mouth angling toward hers.

She planted a finger on his lips. "I take it you tend to live up to your name, Casanova. Do you always get your way with women?"

He hesitated only a moment, pushing his memories to the furthest corner of his mind. "Mostly." He gave her his sexiest smile. And again he swept in for the kiss. That was all he wanted. Then he could leave and never look back. Relationships were too complicated and he wasn't staying. "Is it working?"

Her free hand slipped behind his head and pulled him down so that their lips could meet in a wordless response.

Dear Reader,

Cape Churn is becoming such a part of my life through the three stories I've written in this setting and the one I'm writing now. The more I write about it, the more I would love to visit this town and experience the Devil's Shroud for myself. Alas, the town is fictional and all the characters exist only in my imagination. But I love them all and want to go along on their adventures and be with them when they finally find their happily-ever-afters.

This book takes you back to the McGregor bed-and-breakfast and gives you a little history on the original owners of McGregor Manor, where you will learn about the heartache and unrequited love of the man who built it.

For those who don't believe in ghosts, suspend your disbelief and immerse yourself in the story. Whether you believe in ghosts or not, the living, breathing characters have a lot to learn about love, each other and themselves. And maybe they're getting a little help from those who came before.

Perched on the rocky Oregon coast, this quiet little vacation town will see more troubles. Molly McGregor and Casanova Valdez will struggle to find the source of the problems before someone dies. The past comes back to haunt the guests of the B and B, where we hope good will overcome evil.

Join me on a dark, stormy night when the Devil's Shroud envelopes the land and sea. Perhaps we'll have a ghostly encounter....

Happy reading!

Elle James

DEADLY LIAISONS

—

Elle James

HARLEQUIN® ROMANTIC SUSPENSE

ISBN-13: 978-0-373-27867-1

DEADLY LIAISONS

Copyright © 2014 by Mary Jernigan

Printed in U.S.A.

Books by Elle James

Harlequin Romantic Suspense

Harlequin Intrigue

ELLE JAMES

A Golden Heart Award winner for Best Paranormal Romance in 2004, Elle James started writing when her sister issued a Y2K challenge to write a romance novel. She has managed a full-time job and raised three wonderful children, and she and her husband even tried their hands at ranching exotic birds (ostriches, emus and rheas) in the Texas Hill Country. Ask her, and she'll tell you what it's like to go toe-to-toe with an angry 350-pound bird! After leaving her successful career in information technology management, Elle is now pursuing her writing full-time. Elle loves to hear from fans. You can contact her at ellejames@earthlink.net, or visit her website at www.ellejames.com.

This book is dedicated to my family, whose loving support has encouraged me to continue to pursue my writing career. My husband, who believes in my abilities and asks, "Why aren't you writing?"; my sister, with whom I brainstorm and share my successes; my father, because he taught me the value of hard work; my mother, who is my first line of defense beta reader; my oldest daughter, who reads my work and always looks forward to the next story; my son, who is proud of his mom and her writing; and my youngest daughter for keeping me on my toes. I love you all!

Chapter 1

"You should have seen the look on Nova's face when Tazer face-planted him on the mat at the gym." Creed Thomas clapped a hand on Casanova Valdez's back.

Casanova chuckled, remembering that day. "Hey, no one told me she was a black belt in judo. And look at her." He pointed to Steele. "She looks like a damn powder-puff model."

Nicole Steele, also known as Tazer because most people didn't know she'd hit them until they were lying flat on their backs, glanced at the tips of her fingernails. "Looks can be deceiving." That was the dichotomy who was Tazer. Completely at ease, but ready for anything.

As he sat at the table filled with his teammates and a select few residents of Cape Churn, Oregon, Stealth Operations Specialist Casanova Valdez was surrounded by people he liked and trusted. His teammates. They meant the world to him. He liked his job, the people he worked with, and he felt he was contributing to the greater good of society. But something was missing.

His gaze followed Molly McGregor as she served the other occupants of the dining room at the McGregor Bed & Breakfast, where the team had chosen to gather with members of the local community to celebrate victory.

He and Tazer should have been on their way back to D.C. The next flight out would be the following morning. They hadn't even left Cape Churn when they'd received the news. Thank goodness. They'd been having lunch at the Seaside Café when their flight from Portland had been canceled due to a mechanical issue with their plane. At that point, Gabe had invited them to a victory dinner at the McGregor Bed & Breakfast his sister operated. It gave Nova the chance to see the pretty bed-and-breakfast owner again. He couldn't seem to get her out of his mind.

Molly's movements were quick and efficient, her every greeting accompanied by a sunny smile. Light blond hair swung about her shoulders, falling in long loose curls down her back, her green eyes sparkling as bright as the crystals dangling from the chandelier that hung from the center of the spacious dining room. She treated every guest like family, making them welcome and including them in her happy disposition. Nova liked being around her. She made him feel as if he'd come home when he walked into McGregor Manor. He hadn't felt that way since his grandparents had died.

"Bet you think twice when you flirt with a woman,

huh, Nova?" Creed elbowed him in the arm, bringing him back to the conversation and his friends gathered around the table. Their hostess, Molly McG., ducked out of sight through the swinging door to the kitchen.

His lips twisted in a wry grin as he recalled the first day he'd met his teammate in the gym at headquarters, the beautiful and deadly Nicole Steele, or Tazer as they'd nicknamed her. "Tazer schooled me," he admitted.

"Damn right." Tazer's lips curved in a sensuous smile as she leaned back in her chair, so beautiful she could easily have graced any glossy magazine cover. Instead, she, too, was a member of the elite SOS team, sworn to protect the country and step in when other federal agencies weren't enough. "And what did you learn?" she asked in her smooth, husky tone.

"Never underestimate a beautiful woman." Unfortunately, he hadn't learned the lesson well enough the first time around. A trip to the jungles of Bolivia, falling in love with the daughter of a drug lord, and losing her and almost losing his life had been the lesson he'd learned the hardest. A face-plant on a gym mat didn't even compare.

"Well, no matter how you met, I'm glad we're on the same team," Creed said. "Without your help, the entire Western Seaboard might not be here today." Creed raised his glass. "To success."

Everyone at the table raised their glasses to toast.

Nova lifted his glass of water. What they'd done had been deemed a preemptive strike against a terror cell planning to attack and devastate major cities on the West Coast, including Seattle and Los Angeles.

"To success." Nova sipped the water, wishing it was

whiskey. Alcohol and driving on a foggy night didn't mix, and he had a long drive ahead of him to get to Portland. The rescheduled red-eye flight departed in the early hours of the morning and he didn't want to get up at zero dark thirty to try to make that drive from Cape Churn in a hurry.

As soon as he could bow out gracefully, he'd be on the road. In the meantime, he enjoyed visiting with his coworkers and new friends. Especially the owner of the B&B, who was as nice to look at as a field of white daisies. Molly McGregor, that perpetual smile on her face, breezed in from the kitchen carrying a pitcher of water. She topped off glasses around the dining room.

Sure, he'd sworn off commitment a long time ago. But that didn't mean he'd sworn off women. A man would have to be blind not to appreciate her.

Molly was the sister of Gabe McGregor, the local cop who'd helped them find and neutralize a very dangerous man. The man responsible for trafficking uranium into the United States. Their target had been in the market to sell the uranium to a warped individual creating dirty bombs with enough explosive power to blow Los Angeles and Seattle off the face of the planet.

A backhand to his chest woke Nova out of his musings, yet again.

"Hey, now, don't be getting any ideas about Gabe's sister," Tazer said. "I might get jealous."

"Since when have you ever been jealous of another woman?" Creed asked.

Tazer pouted. "I was jealous of one last week in the airport. Her Jimmy Choo shoes had me ready to knock her over and rip them off her feet."

"And who's Jimmy Choo?" Gabe asked.

Sitting beside him, his wife, Kayla, laughed out loud. "A designer, silly."

Gabe glanced around at the others. "Am I missing something? Since when are shoes worth killing for?"

Kayla rolled her eyes. "You're such a man."

"Tazer has a fetish for shoes." Nova glanced at his female teammate. "I'm surprised you restrained yourself."

She admired her fingernails. "They didn't look my size, or I'd have found a way."

"Everyone all right here?" Molly stopped by their large table, her hair escaping the clip holding the sides up and back away from her face. "I'm sorry, we're just packed tonight." She pushed a loose strand behind her ear. Her hand drifted down the long column of her throat to where her shirt came to a V over generous breasts.

Nova's pulse beat a little faster and he shifted in his chair. He hadn't been this attracted to a woman in a long time. Not since…

"What's the occasion?" Kayla asked.

"Tonight is the first night of the First Annual Ghost Hunting Weekend at the McGregor B&B." Molly glanced around at the packed dining room. "I never dreamed a ghost hunt would draw such a crowd. I had a group from Seattle sign up a month ago and then a couple more joined at the last minute. One from Portland and the other from Eugene. And I only posted it online, no other advertising."

"People love their ghosts and legends," Gabe said. "Supposedly, this house is haunted."

"Shh." Molly pressed her finger to full, luscious lips

and winked. "You'll steal my thunder. I'm telling the legend as part of the event."

Nova found himself wishing he could press his lips where her finger was. He shook himself. Now wasn't the time to be enthralled with a woman. As soon as he could catch a plane, he'd be on his way back to D.C., to headquarters to see what his boss, the head of SOS, had up his sleeve for his next assignment. Perhaps it would take him to another part of the world.

The more he moved, the better. It was all part of his plan to stay ahead of his demons. Stay busy and don't stagnate. New places, new people, new assignments involving lots of action helped him to forget.

Creed leaned close to Nova. "You're thinking about her again, aren't you?"

His jaw tightened. "How could you tell?"

"One minute you're staring at a pretty girl, the next, your face gets darker and your eyes narrow. You're scaring the locals."

Nova made a conscious effort to maintain control over his face and expressions. No use bringing everyone down just because he couldn't forget what happened two years ago.

As easily as slipping into the shower, Nova slid into the past. He and Sophia Cardeña had been swimming naked in a spring-fed pool surrounded by the jungle. He'd been deep undercover for four months and had fallen for the drug lord Alfonzo Cardeña's daughter he'd been using as his *in*. His liaison with Sophia had smoothed the path to the leader's confidence and allowed him inside the compound hidden away in the darkest jungles of Bolivia.

At first he'd faked being in love with the beautiful

Sophia. But after being in her presence and learning that she was as innocent as her father was corrupt, Nova had fallen for the dark-haired beauty.

Unfortunately, on their way back from the pool, through the trees and bushes, Nova had pulled Sophia to a stop. He'd twirled her around in front of him and kissed her. Knowing he'd be leaving soon, his intelligence-gathering mission coming to a close, he didn't want things to end between them. He'd made the mistake of daring to dream he could have a life with a woman in it.

The DEA would have taken over with the information he'd compiled and sent back to SOS. He'd been about to ask Sophia to go with him, to get away from the jungle, claiming he had to make a trip back to the States to visit a sick grandmother.

He'd prayed she'd go along with him and trust his lie until he had her away, and before the DEA moved in and the war on drugs commenced.

Only, the bullets started prematurely. When he'd turned her around in front of him, the loud crack of a rifle shot split the air.

Sophia fell against him, her eyes wide with her surprise, her mouth open on her last gasp.

The bullet had gone straight through her heart. Within seconds, she was dead, her hand in his, dragging him to the ground.

More bullets flew overhead. Though he'd covered her body with his, it had been too late.

One shot. That was all it took.

"Want a shot?" Creed nudged him, holding a bottle of tequila and a glass in front of him.

Nova pulled himself back to the present, the coppery scent of Sophia's blood still clinging to his memories. "What?"

"I asked if you'd like a shot of tequila, but you were obviously somewhere else."

"I'm back."

"Good, because for a moment there you looked ready to kill. You really aren't here tonight, are you?"

No, he wasn't, but he'd wallowed long enough. A drink might take the edge off the painful memories. Just one wouldn't impair his driving skills. He nodded. "Nothing a shot of tequila won't cure."

Before Creed could pour the shot, Tazer reached across and placed her hand over the shot glass. "No way. He's driving me to the airport tonight. I need him sober."

"Right." Creed set the empty shot glass on the table. "Not all of us are staying for some R and R." He glanced across at his fiancé, Emma Jenkins. "Thankfully, I am. And I know I can use a few days of downtime."

Molly moved away from their table and back to the crowd on the other side of the room. "If you all are done, I'll bring out dessert and we can begin with the legend of McGregor Manor."

The group of young and older people set down their forks and knives and offered up empty plates to Molly.

When she teetered under a stack of dishes almost as big as she was, Nova leaped to his feet and offered to help.

"No, no, I've got them," she said, her face pink from the strain.

"Yeah. I can see that." He took half, his fingers brushing against hers, sending a shot of adrenaline skimming through his body, and something more. Awareness—powerful, hot and completely arousing.

Molly's eyes flared, the green irises darker, the color in her cheeks deepening. Had she felt it, too?

Rather than drop the dishes and explore this phenomenon further, Nova gathered the remaining plates from the nearby tables, stacking them on top of the ones he'd taken from Molly, and followed her into the kitchen.

"You can set them beside the sink. I'll wash them later." She waved a hand toward the sink, refusing to lock gazes with him.

He moved around the center island, close enough to touch her, but avoiding contact. Unfortunately, he couldn't avoid his body's reaction to being alone with Molly.

As directed, he set the plates on the counter beside a sink full of water frothing with suds.

Molly washed her hands, making even that routine action sexy. Then she gathered a large tray of key-lime tarts and hurried backward through the swinging door into the dining room.

Left to himself in the kitchen, and too turned on to risk reentering the dining room with his friends, Nova scraped the leftovers off the plates into the trash can, rolled up his sleeves and started washing the enormous stack of dirty dishes. His mother had always said empty hands were the devil's tools. For some reason, he was on edge and in need of something to keep him busy. Maybe a little mindless dishwashing would calm him.

He was halfway through the plates when Molly entered, calling over her shoulder, "I'll be right back with coffee."

When she spotted him, she yelped and pressed a hand to her chest. "Oh, my. You scared a year off my life. What are you still doing in the kitchen? You're a guest."

He shrugged, his shirt damp with water he'd splashed onto it. "I thought you could use an extra set of hands."

"I would have done them later." She bit her bottom lip, the green of her eyes sparkling in the overhead light. "But thanks. You didn't have to do that."

"I know." He wanted to bite that lip and suck it into his mouth. Nova fought the urge to reach out and pull her into his arms, shocked by the raw need coursing through him.

Molly grabbed a full coffeepot and backed toward the swinging door, pausing as she pressed her shoulder to the door. "You should be out there enjoying your dessert with the others."

"I'll sit when you join us."

Before he'd finished his words, she was shaking her head. "Not possible. This is my busiest time of the day, besides breakfast. I rarely sit."

He dried his hands, gathered a second pot of coffee and turned toward her. "Then let me help you."

With a smile that lit up the room, she said, "Thanks. It is a little busier than I'm used to."

Together, he and Molly made it around the room, pouring coffee into mugs and then gathering the dessert plates as the guests polished off the last of the miniature pies.

The ghost hunters and Nova's own table of friends pushed back and stood, moving toward the dining-room door.

Molly made one more pass to collect the last of the dishes and asked if anyone wanted anything else. "If you're ready, you can step into the lounge. I'll be there in a moment."

Gabe McGregor took the plates from Molly's hands. "Go on. Kayla and I can finish up the dishes while you see to the guests."

Nova let Kayla take his plate and he followed Molly into the study along with Creed, Tazer and the ghost hunters.

Molly stood in front of the fireplace and waited for everyone to take a seat, then she began.

When she started, her smile was bright, her face open and frank.

"Ian McGregor came to this country from Scotland in the late eighteen hundreds to escape political oppression and make his fortune. Not long after he arrived, he signed on with the Burlington Northern Railroad Company and helped build the rail system that spanned the United States from coast to coast.

"He worked his way up the chain until he was a highly paid supervisor over a thousand men. His keen business sense allowed him to amass a significant amount of savings, which he used to buy land and businesses.

"In his late thirties, he retired from the railroad and settled here in Cape Churn, where he met the prettiest girl in town, Rose Engelmann, a beauty whose family had fallen on hard times. He courted Rose and asked her to marry him, but she had fallen in love with a pirate and had secretly been seeing him without her parents' knowledge. Rose refused to marry Ian McGregor.

"Unbeknownst to her, Ian paid the pirate a visit to

gauge the man's intentions toward the lovely Rose. The
pirate laughed about his affair with the beauty, claiming he left a woman in every port.

"Ian paid the man a hefty sum to leave and never return. As Ian had anticipated, the pirate took the money
and left Cape Churn.

"Rose was heartbroken and, with her family in dire
straits, agreed to marry Ian." Molly's brows lowered,
the gleam disappearing from her eyes as she enthralled
her listeners with her tale.

Nova was no exception. He leaned forward, clinging to every word, caught up in her story, almost feeling the pain of Ian's unrequited love.

"Ian knew she didn't care for him, but he set out to
do everything in his power to make her fall in love with
him, to woo her heart over to him by building her this
mansion fit for a princess. He surrounded it with rose
arbors and gardens so beautiful she couldn't help but
fall in love with the place as well as him. He was a kind
and gentle lover, not asking more than any man would
ask of his wife and treating her with respect and love."

Molly's gaze slipped to Nova.

His heart flipped over and beat faster, his groin
tightening.

Then she lowered her lashes, hiding her emerald-
green eyes as she continued, "She bore a single son,
but alas, Rose couldn't or wouldn't fall in love with
Ian—her heart still belonged to a pirate who never
loved her in the first place.

"Ian was proud of his son and loved him dearly.
For years he tried to gain the love of his wife, but finally gave up, growing more despondent, until one
day he caught pneumonia and didn't want to fight his

way back to good health. As his physical condition de-
clined, a ship sailed into Cape Churn, carrying Rose's
pirate. He learned of the pirate's return from his loyal
servant and valet.

"Calling Rose into his bedroom, he told her what
he'd done all those years ago. If she was still in love
with the pirate, and if the pirate shared the same feelings, she was free to go.

"Rose hurried to the village, anxious to be reunited
with the pirate. When she arrived at his hotel, she hurried up the stairs to the room they'd shared in secret and
found him in the arms of another woman. She begged
him to take her back and leave the woman he was with.
He laughed and told her to go away.

"Rose returned to McGregor Manor sad, angry and
disappointed. Ian dragged himself out of his bed to
soothe her. But she would not be consoled. Instead, she
ran outside during a night when the devil had cloaked
the land and cliffs in its ghostly shroud—when the fog
had gathered at its thickest.

"Ian followed her, weak and sick, stumbling toward
the sounds of her sobs. He found her at the edge of the
cliff and tried to talk her into returning to the mansion. She refused, blaming him for driving her lover
away. When he grabbed her arm to lead her back to the
house, she pushed him away. He staggered backward
and fell over the cliff onto the rocks below.

"Horrified, Rose finally realized what a fool she'd
been. Ian had loved her and wanted nothing but the best
for her. She'd thrown his love away and then pushed
him to his death. Distraught and grieving for all her
mistakes and for destroying her chances at love, she
threw herself over the cliff to join Ian in death.

"The legend says that because neither found love in life, they wander the gardens and the mansion's halls—Ian searching for Rose, and Rose searching for Ian. Neither ever quite finding the other.

"Many times, I've heard Rose's sobs in the middle of the night." Molly's eyes were filled with tears at the end of the story, her voice dropping to a sad whisper. "And when the Devil's Shroud blankets the cliffs, I swear I've heard the echo of Ian calling to Rose and Rose's sobs in the sound of the waves splashing against the cliffs."

The crowd of onlookers, including Casanova, remained silent for a full minute after Molly finished, mesmerized by Molly's storytelling and complete believability. Whether the story was true or not didn't matter. Everyone believed.

The room erupted in applause.

"Wow, that was beautiful." Emma Jenkins wiped a tear from the corner of her eye. "Not that I'd want to run into the pair in a dark hallway." She shivered. "Ghosts give me the creeps just thinking about them."

"You sure Rose didn't kill Ian on purpose?" a woman with auburn hair asked. "Ian did send her lover away."

Molly's brows knit. "You're Talia, right?"

The woman hesitated, then nodded.

"No one knows for sure," Molly continued. "If she did kill Ian on purpose, why would she have joined him?"

"Unless someone pushed her," said a big guy with pale blond, wispy hair and glasses. He'd sat near Talia all evening, his gaze rarely leaving her.

Nova concealed a smile. The man had a thing for the

dark-haired woman, and by the looks of it, she didn't know he existed.

Talia's gaze shifted to Nova as if she could sense his thoughts. Nova's glance returned to Molly's clear, green gaze.

"What happened to Ian and Rose's son?" a man asked.

Molly grinned. "That would be my great-great-grandfather. He was raised by an elderly aunt who came to Cape Churn from Philadelphia."

Another guest raised her hand. "Have you ever seen Ian and Rose's ghosts?"

Molly nodded. "Once I saw Ian on the upper landing late in the night, wearing his nightgown and carrying a candle."

"What about Rose?" she asked.

"I've seen her by the cliffs. Not that I recommend anyone go out there tonight. Because, you see, while you were enjoying the evening meal, the Devil's Shroud crept over the cliffs and cloaked McGregor Manor in thick fog."

As one, the roomful of people moved, everyone leaping to their feet to crowd through the door onto the wide front porch of the mansion.

Nova remained behind. "Beautiful."

Molly's cheeks flushed and she looked at her hands. "Thank you. And thank you for helping with the dishes." She collected coffee cups from tables and started for the kitchen.

Not wanting to let her get away, he followed, picking up dessert plates and glasses as he passed through the dining room and into the kitchen. He shouldn't start anything with the McGregor woman, especially when he was about to leave, but something about her touched him and made him want to get to know her better. Was it the way she empathized with the former owners of the grand mansion? Or the perpetual smile that remained permanently affixed to her lips?

Molly was already elbow deep in the sudsy water when Nova entered the kitchen, carrying more dishes.

"Really, you didn't have to do that." She blew at a strand of hair falling over her forehead.

Nova set the dishes on the counter beside her and brushed the strand of hair behind her ear. "Better?"

He stood so close, he could see the tiny flecks of gold in her green eyes. She blinked, her lips parting.

Before he could think better of the idea, he lifted her chin with the crook of his finger. "I imagine you are as beautiful as Ian's Rose."

"I'm sure she was much prettier," Molly replied, her voice breathy, her gaze dropping to his mouth.

"I seriously doubt it."

When her tongue darted out to wet her lips, Nova was drawn to her, wanting a kiss to taste those damp lips. He bent toward her, his breath mingling with hers.

When their gazes met, her green irises flared. She raised a wet, sudsy hand to his chest, the warm water penetrating the fabric of his shirt.

Nova wondered what it would feel like to have her soap-covered hand running across his bare skin. His pulse leaped and he closed in on those luscious lips.

"Molly, your guests are ready for their tour." Gabe McGregor swung the kitchen door open and backed through, carrying a tray of mugs and glasses.

With great reluctance, Nova stepped away from Molly.

"I'll be right there." Molly's gaze dropped from his and she went back to work, scrubbing furiously at the already clean dish.

Nova faced the intruder.

Gabe grinned when he spotted Nova and Molly. "Ah, Casanova, thanks for helping out. I should have jumped up when you did. Molly always seems so capable, I forget she could use an extra hand now and then." Gabe set the tray on the butcher block in the middle of the kitchen. "Why don't you two take a break while I finish up the dishes?"

Molly refused to look up as she rinsed a pot and reached for a towel.

Gabe handed one to Nova. "I'll be right back with the last of the glasses, then I'll finish up the dishes." He pointed at his sister. "No excuses."

"You heard the man. No excuses." Nova took the pot from Molly, dried it and then dried her hands. "Come on, you've been working all evening. I'll bet you didn't even eat dinner."

Molly glanced around the kitchen as if gauging the amount of work still needing done. "I sat down at your table."

"You didn't touch the food on your plate." He gripped her hand in his and tugged her toward the door, knowing he needed to get going, but not until he finished what he'd started with a real kiss.

Her cheeks turned a deeper shade of red. "Have you been watching me?"

"Not much. But enough to tell when a beautiful green-eyed blonde, with cheeks that can blush as brightly as a ripe peach, isn't eating her meal."

Her hand flew to her face. "I'm not blushing. It's hot in here."

He smiled, knowing better, but seizing an opportunity wherever he could find it. "Then we should step outside so that you can cool off. Come, *cariña.*"

By the time they emerged onto the porch, the ghost hunters and Nova's teammates had reconvened in the lounge around a blazing fire.

Refusing to release Molly's hand, Nova leaned against the rail, his back to the wall of fog that had crept in on the McGregor B&B. Like a cocooning, impenetrable shroud, the fog blocked the beautiful view of the cape. The only residual evidence of the ocean nearby was the soft splashing sound of waves slapping the rocks far below the cliffs.

Molly didn't pull free, allowing him to lace his fingers with hers.

"I lied," he began.

She stared at where their fingers wove together. "Oh? When?"

"When I said I didn't watch you much."

Her gaze rose to his. "Why me?"

He smiled. "I'm *curioso.*"

"Curious about what?" she whispered.

"I wanted to know one thing before I left." He tugged her closer.

"Yeah?" She stopped when they were toe-to-toe. "And what's that?"

"Just how good you taste." He started his descent, his mouth angling toward hers.

Before he could get there, she raised a finger and planted it on his lips. "I take it you tend to live up to your name, Casanova."

"On occasion." His thumb brushed the hair from her cheek, then slipped across her lips.

"And you expect me to fall in with a little flirtation?"

Nova's brows dipped. "A woman who is as *bonita* as you must have great passion."

The color heightened in her cheeks. "Pretty words, Casanova. Do you always get your way with women?"

He hesitated only a moment, pushing his memories to the farthest corner of his mind, forcing his shoulders to lift in a casual shrug. "Mostly." He gave her his sexiest smile. Again he swept in for the kiss. That was all he wanted. Then he could leave and never look back. Relationships were too complicated and he wasn't staying. "Is it working?"

"Almost." She pressed a finger to his lips again. "Except I know your type. Kiss and leave."

"I never make promises I can't keep. No strings, no false words of love or commitment. Just the truth. I find you hard to resist, and I want to kiss you. *Tiene un problema* with just one kiss?"

She tipped her head. Her gaze locked with his and then slid down to his mouth. "I guess I don't have a problem with just one kiss. You're leaving. As long as we're both in agreement that a kiss means nothing, what do I have to lose?" Her free hand slipped behind his head and pulled him down so that their lips could meet. At first her mouth brushed lightly against his, then she flicked her tongue across the seam of his lips.

He opened to her and she swept in. His arms rose around her, pulling her against his body, rubbing her pelvis across the ridge of his fly. A groan rose up his throat and blended with her own.

A sound pulled Nova out of the kiss and he glanced in the direction it had come. The porch swing on the end of the veranda swayed on its chains as if a ghostly hand had set it in motion.

He tipped his head toward the swing. "I think your ghosts approve."

Molly gazed that way, still standing in the circle of his arms. "Or disapprove." She moved out of his arms, straightening her blouse. "Are you and Nicole heading to Seattle soon?"

"Trying to get rid of me already?" Nova checked his watch. "We'll have to go in a few minutes."

She nodded and stared toward the parking area, where cars lined up in front of the B&B, blurred by the murky mist. "Be careful on the drive up the coastline. The fog is wicked tonight. There's bound to be a number of wrecks by those crazy enough to drive in it." She stepped back and shoved a hand out. "Well, it was nice to meet you."

Nova lifted her hand to his lips and kissed her open palm, then curled her fingers around it. "Save that for a lonely day. My plane flies out early in the morning. I have to go." *No commitment, no strings,* Nova reminded himself when he wanted to pull her back into his arms and kiss her again.

Gabe stuck his head out the door. "Oh, there you are. Nicole was looking for you."

"Tell her I'm ready when she is."

Tazer, Creed, Emma, Kayla and Gabe stepped out onto the porch.

Creed held out his hand. "Sorry to see you go. I'm sure there's more work piled up than we have people to work it. But duty calls."

"Yes, it does." Nova grabbed Creed's hand and shook it, then dragged him into a bear hug. No time for anything but duty. Relationships were inadvisable, given the secrecy of their band of brothers. He shook hands with the men and hugged the women, saving Molly for last.

Gabe glanced around. "Now, where did Molly go? I'll go get her." He turned toward the door.

"Don't. She's busy and I need to get on the road." Although he would have liked to see her one last time, with all the people around, it wouldn't have been enough. One kiss should have sufficed. It had sparked a hunger for more instead of quenching his thirst. He'd be better off leaving than hanging around to see Molly again. What good would it do?

Tazer slung the strap of her purse over her shoulder. "Ready?"

"Ready."

He held the door for Tazer, then rounded the rental car, climbed in and strapped his seat belt over his lap.

Tazer leaned her head back against the headrest and closed her eyes. "I'd hoped to sleep on the trip to Seattle, but I think you're gonna need my eyes as well as yours to find the road."

"So it seems." Nova pulled onto the highway, or what he could see of it, and picked up a little speed, his headlights reflecting back at him, little help against the blanketing fog.

"The locals weren't kidding when they called this stuff the Devil's Shroud." Tazer leaned forward, her hand gripping the armrest. "I hope it's not this bad all the way to Portland."

"It should clear when we drive farther inland."

"Sheesh, we haven't even made it to town." Her nose practically pressed to the passenger window. "I can't even see the side of the road."

"I know. I'm going to slow down. No use getting ourselves killed. We have all night to get to Portland." Nova eased his foot against the brake pedal. The vehicle didn't slow. He pushed his foot harder and harder until the pedal was all the way to the floorboard, and nothing happened.

Tazer shot a nervous glance his way. "I thought you were going to slow down."

Nova's hands gripped the steering wheel as the road curved around the side of a cliff and started the long descent toward the town of Cape Churn. "Uh, sweetheart, we've got a problem."

"Don't call me *sweetheart*." She held on to the dash, her eyes wide, nervous. "And slow the hell down."

"I would, but there are no brakes."

As the incline grew steeper, the car's speed increased.

Nova shifted into low gear, hoping to use the engine to reduce their speed. And it did, for an eighth of a mile when the grade dropped to 10 percent. What had seemed like a nice, scenic drive along the winding coast now felt more like riding a giant rattlesnake, twisting and gyrating out of control.

Nova jerked the wheel at the last minute before the vehicle would have plunged off the edge of a cliff he couldn't see.

Tazer gasped. "Holy crap, Nova! Watch out!"

"The fog's too thick. I can't see the curves," he called out.

"Drop off, drop off, drop off!" Tazer pointed, screaming.

Jerking the wheel hard to the right, Nova nearly hit the rising cliffs on his left. "I can't hold it on the road. We have to bail."

"Bail? Are you out of your—" Tazer squealed again.

Nova swerved to avoid driving off the edge of another cliff.

The road leveled out and started up a slight incline.

His hands on the wheel in a white-knuckled grip, Nova steered the car as close to the cliff as possible. "If I'm not mistaken, around the next curve starts a descent into the town on the curviest and steepest part of the road."

"Curvier than this?"

"If we're going to abandon ship, it's now or never."

"Crap, and these were my favorite shoes." Tazer reached for the door handle.

A voice in Nova's head urged, *Jump!*

"You go first. I'll hold it steady," Nova said, his jaw tight, his stomach knotted.

Jump!

"We don't have time." Tazer unfastened her seat belt. "On the count of three.

"One…" Nova released his belt.

"Two…" Tazer joined the count.

"Three!"

Nova flung his door open and threw himself out of the car, hit the ground hard, tucked and rolled to a stop.

The car continued forward until it reached the curve in the road and launched itself over the edge of the cliff.

Without wasting a breath, Nova staggered to his feet. "Tazer!"

No answer.

"Tazer!"

"Damn."

"You all right?"

"No."

"Keep talking until I find you."

"I'm over here."

"What's wrong?"

"They're broken. Damn."

His heart in his throat, Nova yanked his cell phone out of his pocket. The screen was cracked, but it still worked. Or would work, if there was any reception at this point on the highway. "Any bleeding?" he asked, still angling toward her voice.

"Yes."

"Apply pressure, I'm almost there."

"Yeah, you are. Look out!"

He practically tripped over Tazer before he saw her pushing to her feet against a solid cliff wall. He shone his cell phone in her face. "Stay down until I can get some medical assistance."

She held up a hand and grimaced. "I don't need assistance."

"I thought you said you broke something."

Frowning, she shoved her hands out in front of her. "I broke every one of my freakin' fingernails." Her knees were scuffed, her elbows, too, and she had a scratch on her face.

"We almost died on this road, and all you're worried about is your manicure?" Nova chuckled as he helped her to her feet. "One of these days I hope to understand women."

"And one of these days, and I'm thinking *very* soon, I want to understand why your brakes didn't work. And when I get my hands on whoever ruined my nails, I'll kill him."

Chapter 2

Molly promised a tour of the mansion the following day, offered coffee and turned her ghost-hunting guests loose for the night to settle in with a word of caution about wandering away from the house in the fog. "Don't tempt fate."

"Well, we'll be on our way, too." Gabe bent to press a kiss to her cheek. "Take care, little sis."

"Are you sure you don't want to stay the night?" She glanced around at Emma, Creed, Gabe and Kayla. "One of the guests canceled and I have a spare bedroom available. Gabe, you and Kayla could sleep there—it's a king-size—Emma and Creed can have my room and I can claim a couch. For that matter, the one in the lounge is a fold-out double bed."

"Thanks, anyway," Kayla said. "Dakota's babysitting Tonya. I don't want him to have to watch her all night."

"How's that going?" Molly asked.

Kayla smiled. "He loves his little sister and she adores him."

Molly's glance shifted to the driveway, where she could barely see the outlines of the cars parked there; the light from the porch bounced off the fog rather than penetrating it. "I hate for you to get out in that."

"If Kayla has her way, we'll crawl." Gabe hugged Kayla close to his side.

"I don't think so." Kayla swatted his chest. "But we will go very slowly."

"What about you two?" Molly asked Creed and Emma, who hadn't been able to get their hands off each other all evening.

Seeing how happy they were gave Molly that pang of longing she'd been experiencing all evening long. Her family and friends were finding the loves of their lives and she was still mooning over a man she would never see again.

Emma yawned and leaned into Creed's side. "My dog needs to be let outside before he goes to sleep for the night, otherwise I'd take you up on the offer."

"I understand he's doing better since the terrorist threat was…what's the word you used?" Molly asked.

"Neutralized," Creed finished.

"Moby's doing great." Emma's lips twisted. "But he still cringes when he hears loud noises."

"A dog with PTSD." Creed shook his head.

"Hey, you knew what you were getting into." Emma leaned back, her brows narrowing. "Love me, love my dog."

"And I love both." Creed kissed the end of her nose. "You more than Moby."

Emma's frown cleared and she leaned against him. "That's better."

Molly forced a laugh past the lump in her throat. Creed and Emma had almost lost their lives in the struggle to capture the terrorists. Emma was one of Molly's closest friends, like the sister she never had. "You two be careful in the fog."

Emma hugged her. "You bet we will. And don't go walking near the edge of the cliff tonight. Can't have the ghosts of McGregor Manor pushing you over the edge."

Molly laughed. "Hardly. As thick as the Devil's Shroud is tonight, I'd miss seeing the edge and fall over sooner than being pushed. I'm not worried about the ghosts."

Kayla shivered. "Personally, I'm more concerned about the ghosts than the fog."

"See what you've done?" Gabe chucked his sister beneath her chin. "You weave a spooky tale, Molly McGregor. Kayla will be up all night imagining every little sound is the ghost that inhabits the lighthouse."

Kayla shook her head. "Will not. I'm at peace with them. However, I've had an eerie feeling since I walked into the B&B this afternoon. Something feels different."

A trickle of apprehension slithered down the back of Molly's neck and she laughed, the sound less than confident. "It's all hocus-pocus to entertain the guests."

"Was any of it true?" Emma asked.

"The story is as true as hearsay. Ian and Rose did live here in the mansion. Ian built it for her, but how they died is all speculation. Their bodies were found at the base of the cliff. No one knows what really happened."

"You mean the accident could have been a murder and the murderer got away?" Kayla hugged Gabe tighter. "Now, that's something I'd rather I didn't know."

"I'd read about the McGregors when I was researching the history of Cape Churn, and you're right," Emma said. "Some of the letters written in that time talked about finding the couple at the base of the cliff. Nothing was mentioned about a murder or marital strife."

"I found Rose's diary hidden in a secret compartment of an old secretary desk in an upstairs room. She was very unhappy, fancying herself in love with the pirate. Now, whether or not she'd had an affair with him wasn't mentioned in the diary. But it all makes for a great story."

"You mean you really haven't seen any ghosts?" Kayla asked.

Molly shrugged. "I've felt pockets of chilled air and thought I saw something once along the cliffs and twice in the house. I don't know if it was power of suggestion or the real deal. I like to think I have an open mind."

Kayla's face paled. "As long as they aren't malevolent."

Molly laughed. "I don't think so. So far, I haven't experienced anything more dangerous than stubbing my toe on a piece of furniture. I like to think of them as my friendly ghosts."

"I feel better already," Kayla said. "Let's go home, Gabe. I've done enough ghost hunting for the evening."

Molly touched Kayla's arm. "I'm sorry if the story disturbed you."

"Oh, no, I just seem to feel things more. I never could watch scary movies or walk through graveyards."

"And after you were attacked by a serial killer, I can imagine you're even more sensitive." Emma hugged Kayla. "You're safe among friends now."

Kayla smiled. "It's nice to have friends. Well, Dakota and Tonya are waiting." She turned toward the parking area, took one step and screamed.

Shadows moved and forms materialized out of the fog.

Molly's heart leaped into her throat and she was just short of screaming herself when Casanova and Nicole emerged, rumpled, with their clothes torn and their skin scratched and bruised.

The five people on the porch rushed forward, Emma Jenkins, the nurse among them, pushing to the front. "What happened?" she asked, taking charge of inspecting their injuries.

"Brakes gave out," Casanova said. "The fog was so thick it was too dangerous to navigate the road at breakneck speed. When we got to even steeper parts of the road, we decided to bail."

Molly pressed a hand to her chest. "Dear Lord, you could have rolled off a cliff."

Nova raked a hand through his dark hair. "I'm glad I couldn't see what was off to the sides of the road. I remember sheer drop-offs along the way out here." When Emma tried to look at the scrape on his elbow, he shook his head. "Check out Tazer first. She has more scrapes than I do."

Emma moved on to Nicole. "Molly, do you have a first-aid kit with bandages, alcohol and gauze?"

"I do." Molly turned and fled into the house in

search of the things Emma would need. In the downstairs powder room, she leaned over the sink, staring at herself in the mirror without seeing her own reflection. They could have been killed.

She jerked open the cabinet door beneath the sink and retrieved the kit she kept on hand for emergencies like bug bites, cuts and scrapes, not bailing from vehicles speeding down a curvy road along a foggy cliffside. Her breath caught.

Footsteps behind her forced her to pull herself together. She turned, with a smile plastered to her face. "Here it is—"

Casanova stood in the doorway, an angry road burn on his cheek and chin, making him even more attractive and rugged than before. Almost dangerous. "You okay?" he asked, his voice warm and sexy.

She laughed, the sound more hysterical than she'd intended. "You're asking me? You and Nicole jumped out of a runaway vehicle and you're worried that *I'm* all right?" She shook her head. "I should take you straight to the hospital and have them examine your head."

"I take that as a yes, you're okay." He grinned and took the kit from her shaking fingers. "I'm fine. Just a little bruised."

"Thank God." She touched her hand to his arm and jerked it back as the spark of electricity she'd experienced earlier jolted through her arm and down to that place that hadn't been stirred in three long years.

What was it about Casanova that made her blood run hot and her body ache to touch him? Was it all in his name? He was charming, attractive and a smooth talker. And he probably broke hearts around the world with those dark eyes, big hands and sexy accent.

Her breathing became more labored, her body flushed with warmth, pooling at her core. The bathroom walls seemed to close in around them, making it even more intimate than a bathroom ought to be.

"I should get this out to Emma." She ducked past him, her hip brushing against his, sending a rush of longing through her.

How long had it been since she'd dated? Since before her fiancé's sailboat had disappeared in the Devil's Shroud. His boat had returned to shore in pieces. Bill's body had never been recovered. Three years had passed since then. Three years in which she'd thrown herself into refurbishing, remodeling and making McGregor B&B into the viable operation it was today.

"Oh, good." Emma entered the house, leading Nicole. "I need to run water over the wounds to clean out the gravel and asphalt."

"In here." Once again, Molly passed Casanova to enter the bathroom. "You can use the sink or the bathtub."

"I can do this myself," Nicole protested.

"Yeah, but you have a trained nurse right here," Molly argued. "Why not let her take care of it for you?" She held out a washcloth to Emma.

Nicole took it. "She's off duty and I can do it myself." She stepped into the bathtub and went to work cleaning the wound while Emma ripped open packages of gauze and the medical tape. Emma had Nicole's wounds cleaned, treated and bandaged in minutes.

Nicole rose. "I'll call the boss and let them know we won't make it back in the morning."

"I can take you both to Portland," Creed offered.

Casanova shook his head. "I don't think we should risk it. You haven't been out on that highway."

Kayla shot a glance at Gabe. "Should we stay?"

Gabe shook his head. "I have to get back. If something happens—and it always does on nights like this—I'm on call with the police department. We'll take it slow." He looked across at Nicole and Casanova. "I could drop you off in town at the hotel, or one of you could sleep on my couch and the other on the floor in my living room. It's a little closer to town."

"I'd offer to let you stay with us," Emma said, "but I'm having the cottage remodeled, the bed in the guest room was dismantled and I got rid of my old couch."

"Don't be silly." Molly waved her hand. "I can accommodate Casanova, Nicole, Emma *and* Creed. And I'll provide breakfast."

"We don't want to add to your burden," Casanova insisted.

"Then you can help cook breakfast." Molly smiled brightly. "Gabe and Kayla, call me when you get to your place so that I know you're okay."

"We will." Gabe kissed Molly, and the couple departed, leaving the remaining folks standing on the porch.

Molly led Emma and Creed to the guest room and then stopped in the hallway to gather sheets and blankets from the linen closet. As she carried them to the first floor, her heart beat faster with each step that brought her closer to *him*.

Nicole came in from the front porch. "Could I use your landline? I'm not getting any reception on my cell phone."

"Sure, it's in the dining room." Molly pointed the

way. "I'm making a bed for you in the old servant's quarters if you don't mind. It's only a single."

"I'm not picky," Nicole said. "Thank you for putting us up."

"It's the least I can do after your near-death experience."

Nicole ducked into the dining room, leaving Molly alone with Casanova. Her voice murmured through the open doorway, the sound muffled by distance.

Molly's pulse hammered through her veins as she pulled the cushions off the couch and reached for the handle to unfold the hidden bed beneath. A bed Casanova would soon be sleeping on. Did he sleep naked? Her stomach fluttered.

"Let me." Casanova's hand closed over hers and all her good intentions flew to the four winds.

She stepped back so quickly she nearly tripped on the cushion she'd tossed to the floor behind her.

Casanova grabbed her arm and yanked her against his chest to keep her from falling.

With her breasts smashed against him, she couldn't breathe. Or was it just because he stole her breath away?

"What is it about you that makes me want to kiss you?" he whispered, his head dipping toward her.

"I don't know." Molly's eyelids swooped low and her chin tipped upward, her lips tingling even before his touched hers.

"The boss is okay with our delay," Nicole said, the words louder as she stepped through the doorway. "Nothing urgent on the docket…"

Molly leaped over the cushion and scrubbed her

palms over her jeans, her face heating as if she stood too close to a raging fire.

And wasn't that what she'd done? Stood too close to Casanova, a man who flirted and left a woman at every stop? If she kept it up, she'd get burned.

"Uh, did I interrupt something?" Nicole's lips turned up on one corner. "I'm sure I can go back into the dining room and call someone else or make a snack or something, if you'd like to be alone."

Pressing her damp palms against her cheeks, Molly shook her head. "No, no. I can show you to your room now, if you'd like."

"Are you sure?" Nicole turned to go back into the kitchen.

"Yes." Molly grabbed the twin-size sheets and hurried past Nicole. "If you'll follow me, I'll show you the room. It's not much."

"Honey, don't let my Jimmy Choo shoes fool you. I've slept on the ground in the cold rain before. Nothing can be as bad as that."

As she left the room, Molly could hear a soft chuckle from one hot agent who'd managed to turn her inside out in a matter of minutes. What was she thinking? The man was temporary, at best.

So? What was wrong with a temporary fling?

Molly flipped the switch on the old maid's quarters she'd converted into an office. She'd left the twin-size bed in there on the off chance she had to rent out her own room should the B&B fill to overflowing. "You could have my bedroom, if you want."

"No, this is great. A mattress and pillow are all I need. And I presume I can use the shower in the bathroom we were just in?"

"You certainly may. The towels are in a cupboard beside the sink."

"Thanks."

When Molly turned to leave, Nicole caught her arm. "And, Molly…"

"Yes?"

"Be careful with Nova."

Molly's brows narrowed. "I'm sorry, I don't know what you're talking about."

"You two were in a clinch, and it wasn't about wrestling." She loosened her grip Molly's arm. "I'm just saying, he's a flirt, but there's something more beneath that bravado. I suspect he got hurt once."

Molly laughed. "And here I thought you were worried about me having *my* heart broken."

Nicole frowned. "That, too. He hasn't taken an interest in anyone in a long time."

"And you think I have the ability to hurt him again?" Molly shook her head. "I barely know the guy."

"Love doesn't take years to grow."

"And lust shouldn't be confused with love." Molly glanced down at the hand on her arm. "If there's nothing else I can get you…"

"Just so you know—" Nicole's hand tightened on Molly's arm before she finally let go "—I look out for my team."

"Casanova is a big boy." *Boy* hardly described the hulk of a man. "He can look out for himself."

Nicole smiled, her face as lovely as any model's. "Men can be fools when it comes to women. Casanova may be a crack agent, but he's a little soft when it comes to matters of the heart."

"Unlike you?"

Nicole dipped her head. "Unlike me."

"Don't worry," Molly said. "I'm not out to prove he's a fool." She backed through the doorway, spun on her heels and ran.

She couldn't believe Nicole had warned her off Casanova. As if Molly could be a threat to Nicole. She was stunningly attractive and could no doubt hold her own in any catfight. Then why warn Molly to back off?

Unless she had a stake in the handsome agent. Was Nicole in love with him? If so, why hadn't she owned up to it or shown any sign?

Molly pressed a hand to her flushed cheek. As she blew through the kitchen, she checked the settings on the stove to make sure it had been turned off properly. Passing through the dining room and into the front lounge where Casanova would be sleeping, she paused.

He wasn't there.

The bathroom door was open, the light off inside. She checked the study; the door was open, the light was off and nothing stirred inside.

Which left the front porch.

Molly lifted the flashlight from the charger by the door and gripped the handle, shivering. Butterflies crowded her belly as she stepped out. The porch light had been turned off and the only light to see by was shining through the window of the front lounge from a small lamp. It barely diffused through the thick fog creeping in at the corner of the long, wide porch.

Molly looked right then left and saw no sign of Casanova. A soft sound penetrated the cloak of mist surrounding the house.

Molly strained to make it out. It sounded like someone sobbing.

"Help me."

More sobbing. The sound, like that of a child or young woman, came from toward the rocky cliffs, more a faint whisper, almost nonexistent. At first she thought she might be imagining it, after all the talk about ghosts. Or that the sea splashing against the rocky shore below had somehow created its own echoing call. Molly's heartbeat kicked into high gear.

"Help me."

There it was again. Molly stepped down the porch steps, breaking every rule she'd ever given her guests. If someone was in danger, she couldn't just leave that person alone out there.

When her feet touched the ground, she switched on the flashlight, the beam bouncing back at her against the wall of pea-soup fog.

If she were smart, she'd march her butt right back into the house and get someone else to help her.

Then again, everyone was settling in for the night. What if she were wrong and the sound was just her overactive imagination?

Maybe, if she walked to the end of the house, keeping the porch and walls within sight, she'd hear the sound more clearly and determine if it was out by the cliffs or close to the house. Or not there at all.

She inched her way alongside the railing, her flashlight pointed at the ground in front of her. She knew the yard was safe, but once a person stepped outside the glow of light, she'd be lost in a fog. Had one of her guests gone on her own personal ghost hunt alone and wandered too far away from the house?

Sheesh, maybe telling the story of seeing Rose by

the cliff had been too tempting to one of the members of the tour group.

"Help me."

The cool, damp night air pushed through the threads of her cardigan, chilling Molly. "Who's out there?" she called out, her voice cracking. She cleared her throat and moved to the end of the house, toward the sea. "Hello?"

Molly took another step, taking her away from the safety of the structure. She turned and shone her light at the porch. The fog swirled between her and the porch, but it was still within sight.

She took another step and another. On the third, she turned back and shone her light at the wall of fog.

Her heart leaped to her throat and she stepped back in what she hoped was the direction she'd come. For a moment she didn't see the deck; when it came into sight, she wanted to throw her arms around the railing. Instead, she stood for a moment gathering her wits. "I'm going to get some help," she called out to the fog.

"Please. Hurry."

The plaintive cry made her turn away from the house, torn between going for help and leaving the lost soul alone for a few moments.

As if led by her own feet, she walked back out into the fog. "Where are you?" As soon as the words left her mouth, she knew how stupid they were. If the lost person knew where she was, she wouldn't be calling out for help. "Keep talking so I can find you."

"Here. I am here. Hurry."

Molly stepped out, following the sound of the voice. "Who are you?"

"Here."

"I'm coming."

This time when she turned back to shine her light at the porch, all she saw was exactly what had been in front of her—more fog. Her head spun as she struggled to keep her balance in a world that had lost its spatial references. Fog surrounded her, pushing in to consume her.

Heart pounding against her ribs, Molly swallowed a sob, unsure of where she was and which way to go. "Hello?" she called out, her voice wobbling. "Hello!" Her voice grew stronger, louder.

The voice she'd been following didn't respond. The fog had swallowed her so completely she no longer knew which way to go to reach the house. She took one step, then another, shining her light at the ground, hoping to recognize a bush, grass, anything to bring her back home.

Tears pooled in her eyes, making it harder to see. "Hello?" The word caught on a sob. "Anyone?"

A pebble skittered across the ground.

Molly spun one direction, then another, unsure which direction the sound had come from. When she made a one-eighty, she ran face-first into a wall with arms that wrapped around her.

She fought, opening her mouth to scream, but a hand clamped over her lips, and another trapped her arms against her sides.

Chapter 3

She fought like a little hellcat, kicking, twisting and scratching, landing a hard kick against his shin.

Nova grit his teeth and held on. "Shh. It's me, Casanova."

Immediately, her struggles ceased and her stiff body relaxed, melting against him.

Molly's fingers curled into his shirt. Her lips pressed into the fabric, making him wish he wasn't wearing a shirt so that he could feel those lips against his skin.

"Thank you," she whispered.

He chuckled. "For what? Scaring you half to death?" He leaned her back to arm's length, her flashlight providing enough light that he could see the expression on her face, one of receding terror, tracks of tears glistening on her cheeks. "What are you doing out here?"

"I thought I heard a voice," she said, her body beginning to tremble beneath his fingertips.

"I did, too." He smoothed her hair back off one cheek and tucked it behind her ear.

"You did?" She looked up at him, her gaze hopeful.

"Yes." He smiled. "I heard your voice calling out."

Her shoulders slumped. "No, another voice. Someone calling out for help."

"Maybe we should go back in and do a head count of your guests?"

"Yes, please. Just to be sure."

"Come on."

She shone the light around them, unable to see past two feet in front of the beam.

"This way," he said confidently.

"Are you sure?"

He nodded and pointed at the ground. "Gravel and grass. We're on the edge of the parking area. I was out at Creed's rental car, trying to charge my cell phone, for what it's worth."

"You won't get a signal."

"I gathered that." He hooked an arm around her waist and guided her slowly across the boundary of grass and gravel to the walkway that led to the front porch.

"Would it be undignified to hug the porch rails?" she said with a nervous laugh.

"If it makes you feel better, go ahead."

She hesitated, then slipped her arm around his waist and hugged him. "No, really. I'm okay now." But she didn't move out of his embrace.

He was glad. Nova liked how she felt against him, her body warm, curvy and soft in all the best places.

After a quick accounting of persons in each room, starting with Nicole, Molly was finally satisfied that all her guests were tucked in bed or in the shared bathroom, not out wandering around in the fog.

"See? All here and accounted for." Casanova stood at the top of the landing, reluctant to leave her.

She twisted her fingers together, not making a move to go to her own bed. "I guess I was hearing things. Who else would be out there at this time in the fog?"

"Perhaps it's your ghost."

She smiled, the light absent from her eyes. "I never really saw any ghosts."

"You said you had an open mind. Perhaps it was picking up on someone from the past."

"I hope so. If someone really did fall over that cliff…" Her body trembled. "I'd hate to think I did nothing to help."

"Well, try to get some sleep." He bent and brushed his lips across hers, thinking only a little taste and he'd head to his own bed on the fold-out couch below. As soon as his mouth touched hers, he realized how wrong he was. As it was before, one little kiss wasn't enough.

Her arms circled behind his neck, drawing him closer, her tongue darting between his teeth to claim his. He didn't fight it, falling into her without thought of tomorrow or all the demons that had plagued him since his time in the jungle. For the first time in years, he didn't think about Sophia, his focus on Molly and her delectable tongue, her shapely body pressed against his.

He ran a hand down her side, cupping the full, rounded flesh of her bottom, melding her pelvis to his, rubbing her against the stiff erection straining to be free of his jeans.

When at last he raised his head to stare down at the

beautiful blonde, her green eyes shone up at him in the dimly lit hallway, her lips swollen from his kiss. He didn't want it to end there. Nothing short of taking her could be enough and he doubted that would take the edge off this particular hunger.

Part of him prayed she'd turn and walk away. The other half silently screamed *hallelujah* when she took his hand and led him into her bedroom.

Another door slammed in the hallway as Molly closed her door behind her.

"I just want you to know I don't usually invite strange men into my bedroom." She leaned against the panel, biting on her lower lip, as if not sure what to do next.

Casanova knew exactly what to do next. "So noted." He swept the back of his knuckles along the curve of her jaw and down the length of her long, smooth neck, the path continuing to the swell of her breasts beneath the cardigan. With quick, efficient movements, he released the buttons one at a time and pushed the heather-gray sweater over her shoulders.

Following his lead, she unbuttoned his cotton shirt and, standing on her toes, shoved it over his shoulders, tugging the tails free of his jeans.

His groin tightened, and his member throbbed against the long, hard zipper pushing against it. He wanted to rip his clothes off and then hers, and slam into her, riding her like a wild man until his thirst was slaked and he regained control.

But those deep green eyes looked up at him with heated lust and a great deal of trust. If he wanted this woman—all of her—he'd have to take it slow or else he'd scare her off like a skittish deer in the woods.

Biting back the urge to plunge into her, he tugged the hem of her silky rose-colored blouse out of her pants and lifted it up over her head, tossing it to the side.

She wore a lace demi-bra that half covered each breast, pushing them up into luscious mounds, ripe for tasting.

He bent to kiss one rounded swell, cupping his hand beneath to lift it, squeeze it and pinch the budded nipple beneath the fabric.

"You're beautiful," he whispered, nipping the tip of her breast through the lace.

"Shh. Don't talk. Just feel." She reached behind her and unclasped the catch, releasing the ends and letting the straps slide down her arms.

Casanova leaned back far enough to let the garment drop to the floor, then swooped in to take the tasty bud between his lips and suck it into his mouth.

She gasped, drew in a quick lungful of air and held it, her body stiff as he lavished his tongue across the bud, flicking, nipping and teasing it even tighter before he switched attention to the other.

Molly pulled at the rivet on his jeans, releasing the metal button. Slowly, she slipped the zipper down over the hard ridge, careful not to catch his skin in the metal teeth.

Since he preferred going commando, his erection sprang free into her hand, hard, straight and pulsing. When she wrapped her hands around it, he moaned and pushed into her grip.

All thoughts of taking it slow rushed from his head. Nova slid his hands over her rounded bottom, cupped the backs of her thighs, lifted and carried her to the bed in the middle of the room, settling her on the edge.

He hesitated, though it killed him to. "Are you sure?"

She pressed a finger to his lips. "Remember? Don't talk." Molly lay back, unbuttoned her jeans, and shimmied out of them and the skimpy panties she had on beneath.

Nova frowned, trying to understand her reasoning until the jeans hit the floor. With her naked body lying on the mattress in front of him, reason became the last thing on his mind as he leaned over her, pinning her wrists above her head.

He claimed her lips in a searing kiss she returned with equal intensity that sent fire burning through his veins to culminate in his groin. His member stiffened and he nudged her opening, anxious to enter her, but not too mindless to not think of protection. When he came up for air, he let go of her wrists and reached into his back pocket for his wallet, flipped it open and removed the foil packet he always carried.

Molly took the packet from his hands and laid it to the side on the bed and then sat up, pressing her lips to his chest, her hands gliding down his back to cup his buttocks. She slipped out of the bed and dropped to her knees, her mouth making a slow descent to the throbbing evidence of his raging desire.

His hand threaded through her golden hair, his fingers digging into her scalp as she took him into her mouth. He marveled at this gift he'd discovered in the wilds of the Oregon coast.

Nova sucked air into his starving lungs and held it as she worked magic with her tongue. When he could stand it no longer, he pulled her to her feet and lay her back on the comforter, determined to bring her to the same level of excitement she'd taken him to before he took this madness any further.

She lay back, her legs dangling over the edge of the bed. Her tongue swiped across her lips.

Nova kissed her, thrusting past her teeth, tasting himself in her mouth. He trailed kisses across her cheek, her jaw and down her neck to the gentle swells of her breasts, capturing first one and then the other. He rolled the nubs between his teeth, nipping softly.

Her back arched off the bed, pressing her breast deeper into his mouth. But he wasn't stopping there. He continued his exploration of her body down her torso, dipping into her belly button and lower, his fingers leading the way for his mouth to follow.

Molly writhed against the comforter, her hands twisting the fabric. Finally, she reached for his hand, and guided it to the furry mound over her sex, pressing one of his fingers into her damp entrance. So warm, wet and ready.

Holding on to his control by a thread, he parted her folds and touched his tongue to the narrow strip of flesh between.

She moaned, her fingers rising to cup the back of his head, threading through his hair, tugging him closer as her hips bucked off the mattress. "Please," she cried.

"Shh," he whispered, blowing a warm stream of air across her damp flesh. "Don't talk. Just feel." He licked her again, this time settling into a steady, sensuous rhythm that had her squirming and crying out his name.

When she jerked to a halt, her body tense and stiff, he knew she was there.

He rose to his feet, ripped open the packet, slid it down over his hard shaft and drove into her, hard and fast.

Her slick channel tightened around him, contracting to draw him deeper. She wrapped her legs around his waist and dug her heels into his buttocks, urging him to go faster, pump harder. He complied, driving in again and again, until he burst over the edge, a flash of mind-blowing sensations inundating his body, wave after wave.

When he returned to reality, he was buried inside her, still hard, still standing and thoroughly satiated. He slipped free, scooted her farther up the bed and lay down beside her, gathering her into his arms.

Nova wondered what had just happened. Since Sophia, he hadn't been that out of control with a woman. And he'd been quick to leave as soon as they'd had sex. With Molly, he felt no compelling desire to leave her. Instead, he wanted to hold her, to feel her body against his through the night, driving away the cold, erasing the memories, renewing his faith in humanity. He could get used to having her around.

He had to remind himself that wasn't an option.

The arm around her middle tightened, pulling Molly back against Casanova's hard body. She reveled in the warmth, the sense of security and the feeling of completeness, forgetting for a few crazy moments that this would not last. By tomorrow, he'd be gone, and she'd be running the B&B by herself, alone as usual.

Why she'd invited him into her room, she didn't
know. Perhaps seeing her brother and Kayla and Emma
and Creed interact so happily with the ones they loved
had sparked something inside that she'd been careful to
keep buried. For the past three years, she'd told herself
she didn't need a man in her life. Relationships were
too difficult. They hurt too much.

But there was the physical side of having someone
there that she couldn't forget. The warmth of a body
lying next to her, the feel of a man driving deep inside, filling all those empty places she'd thought long
forgotten.

What had come over her to invite a stranger into her
bed? Her hand curled around his brawny arm. Was it
the way his gaze had followed her around the room?
She'd never understood the phrase *undressing her with
his eyes* until she'd met Casanova. Every move she'd
made in front of him, fully clothed, she'd felt exposed,
naked and desirable. Her body had reacted before her
brain engaged.

When he'd found her in the fog, she'd reacted like
any female grateful to him for saving her and bringing her back to the house would. But gratitude had
nothing to do with her opening her bedroom door and
her body to him. She could only attribute that to the
rampaging desire flaming through her, too long sup-
pressed. She'd invited him in, telling herself it was just
a night, he was just a man, not a relationship, and he'd
be out of her life before the sun rose on the next day.
No strings, no regrets.

But the warm reality of his body spooning hers was

so much more than what she'd imagined. The warmth faded as she remembered what came next. Morning, daylight and his departure from the McGregor B&B.

Her heart lodged in her throat and her eyes ached, a precursor to the tears she refused to shed over a stranger. She pushed his arm away and sat up. "I need to check the kitchen. I think I forgot to turn off the burner on the stove."

He sat up, too, his lips curling. "I'll check it. I'm headed down, anyway."

"No, take your time. I always do a last pass before I call it a night." She jumped out of the bed, slipped a silky pink robe over her nakedness and ran for the door.

His chuckle followed her to the end of the dark landing, where she stopped to gather her wits and a breath before her descent to the main floor. As she took the first step, a ghostly white figure flashed in her peripheral vision.

Molly teetered on the top step, remembering too late that the lightbulb over the landing needed replacing. Then a firm pressure on her back sent her tumbling down the steps. She didn't have time to scream. Her arms and legs flailed as she scrambled for a grip on something, anything, to slow her fall. Pain shot through her where her body and limbs banged against risers and rails on her wild trip plummeting downward. When she came to an abrupt stop at the bottom, she lay still, breathing hard and mentally accounting for all her body parts, each of them reminding her where they were with a fresh wash of pain.

As she lay there, her vision fading in and out, she wondered what the hell had happened. Her mind whirled around the voice in the fog and the ethereal aberration on the landing. But what stood out most was the pressure on her back as she'd taken that first step.

As a wall of fog surrounded her, one thing was very clear. Whether it had been man or ghost, she'd been pushed down those steps.

Chapter 4

Nova had just jammed his legs into his jeans when loud thumping noises sounded outside the door.

Molly.

Barefoot and shirtless, he ran to the door and onto the landing overlooking the lounge area below. Nothing moved.

He hesitated a moment, then a low moan rose from the bottom of the stairs.

"Molly!" Nova ran to the top of the landing. What he saw below made his stomach churn.

Molly lay crumpled at the bottom.

He took the steps two at a time, leaping over Molly to the floor, where he bent to check for a pulse.

"What's going on? Why all the noise?" Creed appeared at the top of the landing, buttoning his jeans.

Emma peered around him, pulling her shirt closed

about her. "Oh, my God, Molly." She pushed past Creed and raced to the bottom. "Is she—"

The steady flow of blood moving through her jugular thumped against Nova's fingertips, sending a flood of relief over him. "Alive. Thank God."

"Someone call 9-1-1," Emma ordered. She glanced up at Creed descending the stairs. "Get me a blanket."

Molly stirred. "I'm okay." She rolled to the side, wincing. "Really. No need to call an ambulance."

Nova crouched beside her and slipped an arm around her, afraid to move her and aggravate her injuries further. "What happened?"

"I wish I knew." She leaned against him, resting her head on his chest. "One minute I was standing at the top of the stairs, the next I'm seeing things and tumbling down the stairs." She blinked and frowned up at Nova. "I swear a ghost pushed me."

Nova's insides tightened. "A ghost pushed you?"

Molly swayed and pressed a hand to her cheek. "The fall must have scrambled my brain. Forget it."

Not likely. Hell, Nova didn't believe in ghosts. And if ghosts existed, they didn't push people down stairs. People pushed people down stairs.

Emma's hands skimmed over her arms and legs. "No compound fractures, but that doesn't mean there aren't any broken bones or a concussion. We're taking you to the hospital. No argument."

"Okay." Molly pressed a hand to her head. "Just don't yell. For some reason, I have a splitting headache." She touched her forehead where a nasty bruise was purpling. "Ouch. Anyone get the number of the truck that hit me?" She glanced up at her guests gathered on the landing. "I'm all right, just a little clumsy," she called out, then whispered to Emma, "Tell them everything's okay. I don't want them to leave. I can't afford to refund their money."

Emma shook her head. "They're the least of your worries."

"I beg to differ." Molly's brows furrowed and she winced.

Creed turned to the onlookers. "Show's over. Miss Molly will be fine. You can all return to your beds."

The guests left their perches, moving slowly back to their rooms, murmuring among themselves.

"Help me to my feet." Molly leveraged herself against Casanova's arm.

"Stay put," he said in his sternest voice. He softened it to add, "If you've sustained any spinal injuries, you could exacerbate the problem."

"Exactly. Let the medics get you to the hospital on a backboard and check you out before you start turning somersaults." Emma touched Molly's arm when she tried again to rise. "Please."

"Okay. I'll go to the hospital, but I have to be back in time to make breakfast for everyone. It is a B&B. They will be expecting a meal."

"I'll take care of breakfast," Nova offered.

"Thank you, but it's my responsibility." Molly stared stubbornly ahead, tugging at the short robe to cover her naked body. "I don't even know if you can cook."

He chuckled. "How hard can scrambled eggs and pancakes be?"

Emma snorted. "Here we go."

Molly grinned at Emma. "The menu calls for maple-pecan scones, strawberry-shortcake French toast and salmon croquettes." Her brows rose challengingly. "You up for that?"

Nova scratched his head, wondering if she was being serious, but not ready to back down. "Maybe. Let's get you to the hospital to get checked out and then we'll take it from there."

Twenty minutes later, the ambulance arrived, emergency lights off at Molly's insistence. The driver had driven slowly through the treacherous fog to get there. Two paramedics strapped Molly onto a backboard and loaded her into the rear of the vehicle.

Emma rode with her, Nova following behind in Creed's car. When Creed volunteered to ride with him, Nova asked him to stay and oversee the guests, not wanting to leave the B&B unattended with guests there.

Fortunately, no one asked why Molly was running around with only her robe on, and no one had seen him leave her room barefoot and wearing only his jeans. The way Molly had run out of the room indicated she was regretting making love with him. And that she'd fallen down the steps in her rush to get away from him had him feeling guilty. He should have used his head instead of following his other body parts into a lusty tumble in bed with a virtual stranger.

Molly didn't strike him as a woman who would want a one-night stand. But she had to know he was only in town for the night and that he'd be leaving the next day.

On the slow drive into Cape Churn, Nova thought back through Molly's words. She'd said she'd seen a ghost and that it had pushed her down the stairs.

No way. As far as he was concerned, there was no

such thing as a ghost. But who would want to hurt Molly?

At the hospital, Nova was relegated to the waiting room, while Molly disappeared with Emma down a hallway to go through a battery of X-rays and tests to make sure she didn't have any fractures from her fall or a concussion and swelling in the brain.

Nova paced for what felt like hours until Molly came out wearing a pair of scrubs and limping on crutches, assisted by Emma.

Nova hurried forward.

Emma smiled. "No broken bones, thank goodness. Just a sprain. The doctor wants her to stay off her foot for a week."

"A week." Molly's face was bruised and worried. "I have guests. I can't stay off my feet for a week. This weekend means the difference between paying the mortgage and electric bill, and going broke. I have to take care of my customers."

"You can hire someone in to do all that," Nova said. "You need to keep your foot up."

"If I hire someone, it eats all my prof—"

"I'll do it," Nova cut in. He raised his hand when she opened her mouth to protest. "Not for free, but in exchange for room and board for the weekend."

Why he volunteered, he didn't know. Royce Fontaine would be waiting for his return, and probably already had another assignment lined up for him. He pushed those thoughts aside, concentrating on convincing Molly to let him stay.

"I won't have an extra room tonight."

"When Nicole heads back to D.C. in the morning,

I can take her room or the one Creed and Emma are using tonight."

Molly frowned. "Nicole's room is not much of a bargain room."

"I don't need much. I've always wanted to see more of the Oregon coast and you could use the help. It's a win-win."

Already, her head was shaking. "I don't know."

Emma jumped in. "I can help out this week, but I work Saturday and Sunday on a couple of twelve-hour shifts here at the hospital. If Casanova wants to help, let him."

Nova held his breath and waited for Molly's response.

Finally, she gave a less-than-enthusiastic "Okay."

He released the breath he'd been holding, wondering why he cared so much. Molly was only a one-night stand. He wasn't in the market for a long-term relationship. However, after he'd scared her into running, he felt to blame. Finding out who might have it in for her was the right thing to do. If she hadn't run out on the landing, she might not have been pushed.

Staying the weekend would give him the opportunity to find out who was responsible for almost killing her.

Light, muted by the dense fog, shone from what seemed like every window in the mansion. Molly's pulse raced. "What's going on?" The pain medication had finally kicked in and she thought she might be able to stand on her own.

When Casanova pulled Creed's car to a halt in front of the house, she threw open the door and stepped out on her good leg. When she put weight on her other ankle, pain shot up her leg and she bit down on her lip to keep from crying out. She would have fallen if she hadn't been holding on to the car door. How would that look to her guests? Assuming her guests hadn't packed up and left as soon as she'd been taken away in the ambulance. "Did we leave all the lights on?"

Emma shook her head. "No."

"Then what the hell's going on?"

Creed emerged from the front door and descended the steps. "About time you guys got back. I was almost ready to come looking for you on the road. Not that I would have seen anything."

"We took it slow. I'm still a little punchy about driving in that stuff after crashing one car earlier." Casanova rounded the vehicle and stood beside Molly. "Ready?"

Heat rose up her neck into her cheeks. Then she realized he meant to help her into the house. She nodded and reached out to take his arm.

Before she could take one step, Casanova scooped her up and carried her to the house.

"Put me down. I can use crutches to get in."

"I know." He grinned. "But this is much easier, *si?*"

Emma laughed. "Oh, Molly, let him play the he-man. It's kind of nice for a change."

"As if you'd let anyone haul *you* around like a child."

"Oh, honey. Can you honestly say you feel like a child with a big, burly guy like Nova holding you in his arms?" Nicole descended the stairs, not a hair out of place, like a model on the runway, except for the bruises and scrapes on her arms and legs.

Molly could only imagine how ratty she looked after

falling down the stairs, and now wearing a set of faded scrubs, which she was very glad to have, considering she'd tumbled down the stairs in nothing but a flimsy silk robe. A hairbrush and lipstick would have been nice. But then she wasn't trying to impress anyone. Was she?

"Did everyone leave?" Molly asked.

"On the contrary." Nicole smiled. "The ghost-hunting group got all excited about possible contact with a ghost. They've been busy setting up their cameras and equipment, hoping for a chance to catch the ghost on video."

"You're kidding." Molly's ankle throbbed, the bruises all over her body hurt, and she'd been worried the entire time she'd been at the hospital that her guests would demand a refund.

"Nothing like exploiting a bad situation. A woman almost dies and they're excited." Casanova's jaw tightened and a muscle ticked in the side. "I think I might have to have a word with them."

"Why? I couldn't be more thrilled." Molly grinned.

"Are you insane?"

"No. I just can't afford to refund their money if they decide to leave. I've spent almost half of their deposits on the food I'll be serving."

"Woman, maybe you don't understand the severity of the situation." Casanova stared down at her, his brows furrowed. "Someone pushed you down those steps."

"We don't know that. I'm not sure what happened. I was in a hurry." To escape the man she'd made love to and her growing desire to do it again. "I could have tripped, slipped or just misplaced my foot on the first step. It could happen to anyone."

"Then, sweetie, you better have good liability insurance," Emma said, "and have the ambulance on speed dial."

When Casanova stepped through the door, the group of ghost hunters lined the staircase and stood in the great room. They all turned to face her and gave her a round of applause.

"What the heck?" Casanova muttered, setting Molly on her good foot, his arm remaining around her waist.

Molly was glad for the support as Josh Steiner, the group's tall and lanky leader, stepped forward and grasped her hand.

"We're glad to see you're going to be okay and we'd understand completely if you want us to leave."

"Thank you. And no, the event will continue. And don't worry, my assistant, Mr. Valdez, will be helping out during your stay." She shot a glance at said assistant.

He nodded. "Miss McGregor will still be in charge. I'll be her gofer."

"Oh, good." Josh's pale, freckled face was suffused with an excited pink and he waved his hand toward the equipment set up throughout the room and at the top of the stairs. "I hope you don't mind, but since the poltergeist manifestation occurred on the landing above, we've set up the cameras in hopes of recording any more signs of it. We've already captured evidence of orbs on video when we turned out the lights. This place is full of them."

Molly almost laughed at the excitement Josh exuded. "I don't mind at all as long as you don't create a tripping or fire hazard for my guests."

"We've taped the wires down on the upper landing

and the cameras are placed out of the way of the main traffic. If there's anything else you'd like us to move, we'd be happy to," Josh assured her. "This will be an awesome addition to my *Ghosts of the West Coast* series."

"Great." She shifted, her ankle throbbing, all the bruises on her body reminding her that she'd taken a pretty bad tumble. "If you all don't mind, I'm going to take one large pain pill and hit the sack. But I'll have breakfast ready at eight o'clock in the morning." She gave Casanova a sheepish grin. "Correction, my assistant and I will have breakfast ready for you all in the morning."

"We can fend for ourselves," Josh said.

"I wouldn't dream of it. I've prepared a special menu and activities for each day you're here." Molly straightened, determined to see the long weekend through, though her body felt as if it had been through a rock tumbler. "Well, then, good night all."

Molly took a step toward the staircase.

"There's no way you're making it up there on your own," Nova muttered in her ear.

"I can do this," she gritted out.

"Don't be ridiculous." He swung her up into his arms and carried her up the stairs as if she weighed nothing at all. He didn't even break a sweat.

Molly's heartbeat pounded against her ribs as he neared her bedroom door. Hadn't it all begun there? It seemed a long time ago when she'd made love with him and then run out the door like a scared rabbit faced by a big, bad, sexy wolf. Now they were back to the starting point, only this time the spirit was willing but the body was in too much pain to go along with a romp in the bed.

It didn't stop her skin from flushing with desire and her face from heating at the sight of her rumpled sheets.

"I can take it from here," she insisted.

"What's wrong with letting me help? It's not as if I haven't seen you naked." His mouth twitched as if he fought a grin.

"Yeah, but you haven't seen me naked *and* beat up."

His grin faded. "All the more reason for me to stick around."

"No."

"If someone pushed you down those stairs, they might try to hurt you again. I'm staying."

"No, you're not."

"I'm not the one you need to be afraid of."

"You're not." She was more afraid of herself and that she was far too attracted to a man who wasn't going to be around after the long weekend ended. "Look, Casanova, I've been running this B&B by myself for several years now. Other than my brother's occasional assistance, I've done it on my own. I'm not used to having someone else help out."

"With your ankle sprained, you'll have to get used to it. At least for the weekend."

She knew he was right.

"Now, I'm going down to get you a glass of water. Would you like me to send Emma up to help you into your sleepwear? Or would you prefer me to do the honors? Or do you sleep naked?" He waggled his brows wickedly.

The movement warmed Molly's heart at the same

time it reminded her he was only living up to his name. "Emma, please."

He settled her on the bed and turned toward the door.

"And, for the record, I don't sleep in the nude when I have guests in the house."

When Casanova shot a quick glance over his shoulder at her comment, Molly let a half smile curl onto her lips and her brows rose, daring him to ask if she slept nude when there were no guests in the house.

He hesitated, then grunted, "I'll send Emma up."

Perhaps she was playing with fire, flirting with Casanova. He was probably used to women vying for his attention. His massive biceps and that wickedly sexy smile could turn any woman's knees to jelly. Molly knew there was no future in a relationship with him and her body wasn't up for more of what they'd shared earlier. The pain didn't stop the slow burn of longing in her core.

The next few days could be either really difficult or she could look at the situation as a much-needed fling to get the kinks of abstinence out of her system. Perhaps it was time to start dating again and she was way out of practice, having only had one man in her life since high school.

The temporary nature of Casanova's presence might be just what the doctor ordered. She'd practice her flirting skills, he'd leave and she'd be ready to find a partner who'd stick around.

Granted, it would be difficult to find one quite as tempting as the handsome Hispanic secret agent. Molly made a note to herself not to give her heart away.

"I told Casanova I'd come help you out." Emma entered her bedroom. "I can only stay a few minutes, then I have to be on my way back to town."

"I thought you were staying."

Emma grimaced. "The hospital called and wants me to pull a double starting now. Seems the E.R. is full of victims of the Devil's Shroud." She helped Molly out of the scrubs with a nurse's attention to pain points. She was especially careful not to disturb the swollen ankle.

"Other than my ankle, I'm not that bad off. I should be getting around fine by morning."

"You might be getting around, but you're going to feel every one of those bumps and bruises, too. It takes a day for the aches and pains to kick in full force and even more time for the pain to go away."

Molly lifted the bottle of pain meds. "I hope I don't have to use these. I need a clear head to manage the guests for the weekend."

Emma gave her a stern look. "Don't be a hero. If it hurts so much you can't sleep, take a pill. You'll be of no use to anyone if you're walking around in a sleep-deprived haze."

"Yes, ma'am." Molly gave her friend a mock salute. "Thanks, Emma."

Emma hugged her. "Don't go falling off things again. I only have a few friends around here, and I'd hate to lose one."

"You have more than a few friends. The whole town loves you. You're everyone's favorite nurse."

"There are a lot better nurses at the hospital than me." She tugged the scrub shirt over Molly's head. "Wanna tell me why you were running around the landing in nothing but a skimpy robe before you fell?"

Molly's face burned. "Not really."

"Wouldn't have to do with one tall, dark and sexy hunk, now, would it?"

If her face could catch fire, it would have burned. Molly pointed to the dresser. "Could you get a pair of panties out of the top drawer?"

"Avoiding my question because I'm right?"

"Avoiding your question because it's none of your business," Molly snapped, then regretted her short response as soon as it was out of her mouth. "I'm sorry. I shouldn't bark at the hand that undresses me."

"I'm used to cranky patients." Emma returned from the dresser with a light green, frothy nightgown and a pair of lacy black panties. "Did I hit a sore spot?"

"I have so many sore spots, I lost count." Molly purposely misconstrued Emma's question.

"Since when have you played coy with me? You're always the one who is open and up front about people and their feelings. What's different?"

"Nothing's different."

Emma slipped the nightgown over Molly's head and chuckled. "I know. It's because you're the one in the spotlight now."

"I'm not in the spotlight. No one's feelings are being exorcised here. Casanova will be gone by Monday, if not sooner."

"And you're afraid to like him too much, aren't you?"

Molly bent to slip her panties on, jostling her sore ankle in the process. She winced, more from Emma's comment that was spot-on than the pain from bumping her injury. She sighed and scooted back in the bed. "I haven't been on a date since high school. When

Bill died, I didn't think I ever wanted to be with another man. He was my high-school sweetheart. I really haven't dated."

"And now?"

Her cheeks burning again, Molly looked away.

"You've been with him." Emma's words were a statement, not a question. "Which would explain why he ran down the stairs wearing only his jeans." She nodded her head, her lips twisting, then spreading into a big grin. "About damned time, girl." Emma hugged Molly and stepped back to inspect her. "You need a life besides this old monster of a house."

"It's not a monster. It's my family home, left to me by my parents."

"Sometimes what we inherit from our families is more of a burden than a gift."

"I love this place. I never wanted to live anywhere else." Molly glanced away. "It was part of the reason my relationship with Bill had hit a rocky point even before he disappeared."

"I didn't know you two had been through rough times."

"We had. He'd gone out sailing that afternoon because we'd been in a fight about finances. My teaching paycheck wasn't enough to keep McGregor Manor. Even with Gabe pitching in before he moved back to Cape Churn, we knew it was only a matter of time before we had to sell the place or do something drastically different to keep it afloat."

"What did Bill want?"

"To sell." Molly picked at the hem of her nightgown. "I didn't want to. We argued, he sailed and he never returned. The Devil's Shroud crept in before he could get back to shore."

"I'm sorry."

"I was, too. But it was a long time ago."

"Three years isn't that long."

"Yeah, but I couldn't help but think that if I had just agreed to sell, he'd still be here."

"You don't know that. He might have gone sailing, anyway, to celebrate winning the argument." Emma gave Molly a gentle smile and patted her arm. "You can't live in the past or carry guilt for something that was never your fault."

"I know."

"Then take your moments of joy where you find them."

"I feel like you're giving me permission."

"If that's the way you look at it, yes." Emma crossed her arms over her chest. "I hereby give you permission to flirt with Casanova."

"Did I hear my name?" The man in question appeared in the doorway carrying a gallon-size plastic bag full of ice. "Thought you'd like one of these to reduce the swelling."

"You're just in time." Emma winked at Molly. "I have to get to town. The hospital is overrun with Shroud victims. I've been recalled. But since I'm leaving Molly in good hands, I don't have to worry."

"I'll take good care of her."

"I'm counting on it."

As Casanova bent to lay the bag of ice on her swollen ankle, Molly glared at her friend.

"Gotta go." Emma blew her a kiss and winked as she left the bedroom.

With only Casanova in the room, Molly felt exposed in her almost-sheer nightgown. She pulled the blanket up to cover her breasts, leaving her injured leg on top of the comforter, the ice barely chilling her desire for the man whose fingers were touching her leg.

She wanted to jerk her leg back out of his reach, while at the same time she wished he'd run his fingers up a little higher....

She closed her eyes and gritted her teeth to keep from moaning aloud. It was going to be a long weekend.

Chapter 5

When Nova had entered the room, he'd stood transfixed, his gaze on Molly lying on the bed. She wore a pale green nightgown that only covered her to just below her hips, leaving her shapely legs exposed. The fabric was so light and sheer, her taut nipples made little points, the rosy-brown areolas a tempting shadow beneath.

His groin tightened. He wanted to leave before he embarrassed himself. Emma scooted out the door so fast, he had no choice but to stay and administer the ice bag. "Are you going to be all right in here by yourself?"

"I'll be fine."

"I'll lock the door on my way out."

She worried her lip. "I'd rather you left it unlocked."

He shook his head. "Not happening."

"What if there's a fire and I can't get out fast enough? If I call for help, no one will be able to get to me."

"Do you want me to stay?"

"No."

"Don't worry, I'm not planning on climbing in bed with you and ravaging your body, no matter how sexy you are in that." He pointed at her nightgown she'd all but covered with the comforter. "Besides, call me prejudiced, but I prefer women who aren't blue and purple." He brushed his finger across an angry bruise on her cheek and ground his teeth together. "Look. I'll leave the door unlocked, but I'll bed down outside your room."

"On the floor?" Her brows shot up into the hair swooping down over her forehead. "You can't sleep on the floor."

"I've slept on worse." He forced a smile. "A floor will be great compared to some of the foxholes filled with water I've slept in."

"You slept in a foxhole filled with water?" She chewed on that damned lower lip again, making his insides bunch and other places grow harder.

"Can you handle this?" He nodded toward the ice bag.

"I thought so," she whispered, and then louder she added, "I can manage."

"Good night, Molly." He turned toward the door, paused and faced her again. "Just for the record, why did you run out of the room earlier tonight? Was it something I said?"

She glanced down at her hands, her pearly-white teeth still worrying that lip, making Nova want to gather her in his arms and suck it into his mouth. He bunched his fists to keep from reaching out to her.

"I was afraid." Molly looked up, her mouth quirking upward.

"Afraid of me?"

She shook her head. "No. I was afraid of *me*."

He frowned. "Why?"

"Despite your namesake, and against my better judgment, I could like you a whole lot." Her voice faded off into a whisper.

"You know I'm not going to—"

"Stay," she finished. "Exactly." Molly glanced away. "But that's neither here nor there. And I won't let you sleep on the floor outside my room. What would the guests think?" She glanced around the room, her gaze settling on the wingback armchair. "I suppose you can sleep in the chair. There's a blanket in my closet."

He retrieved the blanket from the shelf, noticing a gun case beside it. "You have a gun?"

"Oh, that." She snorted. "Gabe made me get one back when there was a serial killer in Cape Churn. He even taught me how to use it. I'm pretty good."

"Why do you keep it on a shelf instead of by your bed?"

"I don't want someone to use it on me."

"It will do you no good for protection if you can't get to it fast enough."

"That's why I have this." She reached for a spray can on the nightstand. "Wasp killer. It has a ten-foot spray distance. If someone breaks into my room, I spray him in the eyes. Kayla's alive today because of her wasp spray. She used it on the serial killer."

"I'm impressed. But I'd feel better if you kept both nearby."

"I really think it's overkill."

"Better over-prepared than dead."

"Yeah, and I won't be prepared for tomorrow if I don't get some sleep. It's past midnight and my alarm goes off at five."

Casanova nodded. "Get some rest. I'll sleep in the chair, but I want to do a final security check before I turn in."

"You make it sound like we're under lockdown or in a prison."

"Trouble is I'm not sure if the bad guys are on the inside or the outside."

"Or if there really are any bad guys."

"There are always bad guys."

"That's pretty pessimistic of you."

"I prefer to call it being realistic and being ready."

Molly yawned. "I think my pain pill is kicking in." She closed her eyes. "I'll be asleep before you return."

Casanova straightened the ice bag on her ankle.

"Nova?" Molly's eyes opened halfway. "Do you mind if I call you that?"

"Not at all. My friends call me Nova."

Her eyes closed again. "That's nice. I guess that makes me your friend." She yawned, pressing her fist to her lips. "Thank you for coming to my rescue."

Nova left the room, an image seared into his mind of Molly lying in the big bed, covered in bruises, with a smile on her face.

His chest tightened. She had to know how lucky she was the fall hadn't killed her. And yet she'd been more concerned about her guests than herself, worrying who would take care of them, when *she* was the one injured.

Molly was one of those rare creatures who gave and expected nothing in return. The kindhearted individual who would always take care of others and be loved in return. She couldn't imagine anyone pushing her down the stairs and, after considering the possibilities, had convinced herself that she'd tripped.

Nova walked along the landing slowly, inspecting the carpet along the way. The ghost hunters had installed their cameras on tripods, extension cords running from the equipment to the wall sockets, neatly fixed to the floor with duct tape. Despite the addition of the cords and equipment, Nova could see that there was nothing wrong with the carpet on the landing. Nothing protruded that could trip a person.

Molly had specifically said she'd seen something in her peripheral vision before she'd felt a hand on her back. A ghost, she'd said.

Nova didn't believe in ghosts, unless he counted the memories that refused to fade. Any way Nova looked at it, he could see no other possibility. A ghost hadn't pushed Molly. A person had.

As he descended the stairs, he could imagine the pain of hitting the sharp edge of every step as she'd fallen, and his anger grew.

"Nova." Tazer waited at the bottom of the stairs. "I just got off the phone with Royce and gave him a heads-up about the situation."

"I'm staying," Nova said, his words cryptic.

Nicole nodded. "That's what Royce said."

"Are you headed out in the morning?" he asked.

"I am. I'm off to an assignment that won't wait."

"The one the boss was going to assign to me?"

She snorted. "You got that right."

"Be sure to come back in one piece."

"I plan on it. I have an appointment to get highlights

at the end of the month and you know how difficult it is to get on Etienne's schedule."

"You crack me up." He hugged her.

"Hey." She stiffened. "Don't be thinking I'm going to hop in the sack with you."

"Not going there." He rubbed his jaw. "I can still feel the burn of the gym mat on my cheek from the last time I even thought about it."

"Damn right. And don't you forget it." She gave him a quick hug, unusual for Tazer, who kept a distance between herself and fellow agents. Tough on the outside, the woman had a heart buried beneath her kickass attitude. What made her keep her distance was a mystery to the entire team.

Nova meant to find out why, but she never let anyone close enough to get answers. "Take care of yourself."

"I will. I'm the only one who can." She nodded toward the stairs. "Molly's a nice girl."

"Is that approval I hear?" Nova chuckled. "I didn't think you liked other women. Or men, for that matter."

Tazer shrugged. "Some of them are okay."

"Is your steely veneer cracking?"

"Not even."

"Good. Can't have you falling apart when you have a mission to perform."

"Have you ever known me to fall apart on a mission?"

Nova rubbed his chin, thinking back over the jobs she'd been assigned that he knew of. "No."

"Damn right." She glanced around. "Before I get some shut-eye, do you need help checking for ghosts?"

"Only the live ones."

"I'll take the south side of the house."

"I'll get the outside and kitchen area."

"Don't go falling off the cliff," Tazer called out.

Nova grinned. "Watch out for Rose and Ian."

"Maybe *you* should, since you'll be out there by yourself. That fog can hide a lot of sin."

Tazer headed up the stairs for a quick check of the hallway and common areas.

Nova grabbed one of the flashlights from the charger on the wall next to the front door and headed out. He circled the house slowly, careful to keep close enough not to lose sight. If possible, the fog had grown even thicker. He wouldn't have to go far from the house to get lost in it.

At the end of the porch where the swing hung still, he noted the flowers appeared slightly trampled on the ground below. When he had almost kissed Molly, Molly had laughingly attributed the swing's movement as having been caused by a ghost. Nova had assumed a breeze. But there hadn't been a breeze since before the fog descended to claim the coastline.

Had someone been watching them on the porch and stomped on the flowers trying to get away before being seen? The grass beyond the flowers was spongy and didn't retain footprints but for only seconds after Nova tread on it.

He continued around the house, checking the locked rear entrance secured from the inside and the heavy storm-cellar door with a padlock securing it on the outside. There was also a small cellar window at ground level. He tested it, glad to see it was locked from the inside. He continued around the house. When his inspection was complete, he entered the front door and frowned. Something smelled funny. He sniffed the air.

A faint sulfuric scent reached him about the time Tazer hurried out of the downstairs hallway, the collar of her shirt pulled up over her nose. "You smell that?"

He nodded, his adrenaline spiking, pushing him forward and through the dining area to the swinging door into the kitchen. "Be careful. Don't set off a spark."

Nova knew before he took another step what was wrong. "Gas leak."

"Yeah." Tazer nodded toward the stove. "Want me to evacuate the house?"

"Be ready." He headed for the huge, old gas stove and reached for the knobs, turning them hard to the off position. One knob was missing.

He tried to turn the switch without it, but it wouldn't budge. With his pocketknife, he popped the knob off one of the other switches, fit it over the empty one and twisted it to the left. Immediately, the strong gas scent began to fade.

Tazer hurried to the door, unlocked it and flung it open, letting in the cool, damp air.

Nova pushed the window open over the sink and turned on the ceiling fan. Together they opened the windows in the dining room and great room, switching on the ceiling fans until the air cleared of all the gas fumes and they felt comfortable the place wouldn't explode.

Nova stepped out onto the porch and inhaled the fresh, sea-salted air. "That was close."

"Too close." Tazer joined him. "I've half a mind to call Royce and tell him my services are needed here."

"Creed's on vacation in town. I'm sure I can call him if I need help."

"Still. Something's not right. A lot has happened

in one night. And don't tell me it was all coincidence. I might have fallen for the I-tripped-down-the-stairs scenario, but brake failure and a missing knob on the stove?" She shook her head. "Uh-uh."

Adding the porch swing and crumpled flowers brought the odd occurrences up to four. Nova didn't believe in coincidence. Someone was trying to sabotage Molly or the guests of the B&B. And the stakes were getting higher.

Molly must have drifted off. A noise pulled her out of a troubled sleep filled with malevolent ghosts determined to scare her out of her family home. She hadn't had bad dreams about the mansion since the deaths of her mother and father. The fall must have shaken her more than she'd first thought.

She lay huddled in the comforter, the ice bag lying on the bed beside her ankle, making her entire foot cold. For a long moment, she lay still, listening for the noise that had awakened her.

A soft moaning sound came from outside her window. Molly wasn't certain, but she could swear the voice was crying out, *"Help me."*

Molly threw back her comforter, swung her legs over the side of her bed and stood before she remembered her injured ankle.

The moment she put pressure on it, pain zipped up her leg and she dropped to the ground, crying out.

"Molly?" Nova's voice called out through the paneling of the wooden door.

Before she could respond, the door burst open, Nova rushed in, scooped her off the floor and held her in his arms. "Are you okay?"

"I'm fine. Really. I just forgot I sprained my ankle, that is, until I tried to stand. Stupid of me." She pushed the hair out of her face and tried to catch her breath.

Nova held her so tightly against his chest, she couldn't inhale. "I'm okay, except I can't breathe."

"An injury from your fall?"

"No, you're holding me too tight."

"Oh." Immediately, he released his grip and she slipped out of his arms, almost crashing to the floor yet again. "Sorry." When his arms came around her this time, he lifted her and laid her on the bed, as gently as he would a kitten.

"It's one o'clock in the morning. Why aren't you asleep?" she said, her voice gravelly.

"I've been busy."

Molly scooted over in the bed. "Get some sleep."

"I will."

"Here." She patted the bed beside her.

"No. There's only one place that will go, and you're too messed up for that trip."

"Try me." She smiled, tugging on his shirtsleeve, her body warming, waking up to him.

He shook his head. "I'll sleep in the chair."

The stern set of his jaw warned Molly she wouldn't get far convincing him. Her next course of action was to beg, and she just wasn't up to it. "Fine. Suit yourself. But if you get too uncomfortable, you're welcome to sleep here. I'll leave room." She eased over onto her bruised ribs and pretended to go to sleep.

Nova switched off the light on the nightstand, plunging the room into darkness.

A night-light Molly kept in the bathroom provided just enough of a glow to illuminate Nova's movements.

Molly lay back, her eyes adjusting to the darkness.

Nova entered the bathroom, closed the door and turned on the light.

As tired as Molly was, she couldn't sleep when Nova was so close, yet so far. He made brushing his teeth sound sexy.

Or could it be that the self-imposed sabbatical on dating had taken its toll on Molly and her libido was hypersensitive to any male presence?

She rationalized that couldn't be all true. She'd had many male guests at the B&B and not one had made her burn with desire. Until Nova. Sure, she played at flirting, but when things got serious, she backed off, afraid to give her heart away only to have it broken again. Nova had *heartbreak* written all over him. *If* one was to give her heart to him.

Molly had no intention of giving her heart to any man ever again.

The water shut off and the light beneath the door was extinguished. A moment later, Nova entered her bedroom, kicked off his boots and settled in the chair.

Her eyes semi-closed, Molly watched as Nova pulled his shirt over his head and tossed it on the back of the chair, then settled back, extending his long, muscular legs out in front of him.

Oh, yeah, it wasn't just that he was male. It was oh, so much more. He was more male than any other man she'd ever met, the testosterone practically oozing from him. And the dark eyes and jet-black hair gave him a devilish look that she had been helpless to resist.

He sat in the chair…shirtless…all those lovely muscles barely visible in the shadows. Her heartbeat raced, her body heating in all the most inconvenient places.

She bit down on her tongue more than once to keep from begging him to join her.

"Go to sleep, Molly."

She started, unsure how he knew she was still awake. Was the man part cat? Could he see clearly in the dark?

"Sweet dreams," he whispered and she almost believed he cared.

Closing her eyes for real, she lay still, the comforter pulled up beneath her chin. After a while, she succumbed to sleep and the nightmares of reliving her fall down the stairs. A hand being pressed against her back, giving her the initial shove. She moaned as she bumped, hit and tumbled endlessly, her body aching, her mind playing tricks on her. The soft sound of laughter echoed in her ears as she tumbled.

Out of the darkness, strong arms gathered her close, pulling her out of the fall, saving her from plummeting to the bottom of the endless stairs.

Molly nestled against a warm, solid surface, grasping the arms holding on to her. Soon, the tumbling ceased and she could settle back and let go of the terror that had gripped her when she'd pitched forward.

A familiar scent of male cologne filled her senses, the strong embrace reassuring and calming her. Nova. Deep in her subconscious, she knew he wouldn't be there forever, but he felt good holding her for now. Soon she slipped into a deep, dreamless sleep where her home was a happy place filled with people who loved her, including one tall, dark and handsome man with a sexy accent and eyes the color of dark chocolate.

Morning would come too soon and she'd have to

enter reality again. But for now, she was content to remain in the protective arms of her rescuer.

The chair had been so uncomfortable Nova had been unable to sleep. If he'd been honest with himself, he'd have admitted it wasn't so much the chair as the woman lying in the bed beside him.

When Molly started showing signs of distress in her sleep, Nova told himself he would only cuddle her until the bad dreams disappeared. He ended up holding her the rest of the night.

Once he had her in his arms, the smell of her hair, the fit of her soft body against him, made him want to keep her and never let her go.

No matter how dangerous that path was, he couldn't leave.

She nestled against his chest, her hand resting on his stomach.

He lay awake the rest of the night, memories of Sophia clashing with the reality of Molly lying so peacefully in the bed beside him. The warmth and sense of home the B&B created was a far cry from the heat, humidity and danger of the jungle he'd been assigned to.

Molly was all light and happiness compared to the sultry, dark beauty Sophia had been. They were like day and night, yet both in danger. One in a desperate situation she could never hope to escape, with the constant threat of being killed by one of her father's rivals.

In Molly's case, the threat wasn't as apparent. Who would have it in for the pretty B&B owner? He couldn't imagine Molly involved in drugs or committing a crime that would come back to bite her. And she'd probably lived in the same town all her life. Could it be a disgruntled former guest? She had said it was the beginning of the summer season. How many people would have come through already?

Why now? Why would someone decide this day that they were going to kill Molly McGregor?

The only variables he could come up with were the ghost-hunting group and the Stealth Operations Specialists. Was someone targeting Molly, the B&B or someone staying at or visiting the B&B? Would it be worth the documentary film footage to have a mystery to solve along with the ghost-hunting story? But then why the gas? If the house had exploded, wouldn't everyone go up with it? Including the film equipment and crew?

The more he thought about it, the more worried he became. Sleep never happened. A few minutes before five, he slid his arm out from under Molly, rose and dressed. He slipped out of the room, leaving Molly to wake on her own. Tazer was due to leave at five in order to catch the plane on time.

Tazer was up, sitting at the table in the large kitchen, drinking a cup of coffee as if she had all day.

"Miss me already?" she asked.

"Couldn't sleep."

"I don't blame you." Tazer tipped her head toward the coffeepot. "Join me. I have about five minutes before I leave."

"How are you getting to the airport?"

"Gabe McGregor had some business in Portland and promised to take me. He should be here soon."

Nova poured a cup of coffee and sat across the table from Tazer. "Make sure he tests his brakes before he hits that long stretch headed down into Cape Churn."

"He promised he would on his way out here." Tazer leaned her elbows on the table. "Look, Nova, I can stay. All I have to do is call Royce."

"No. There's enough backup here between me, Creed, Gabe and the chief of police. We can handle it."

"Don't trust anyone. If your gut tells you they're bad, assume your gut is right. Don't take any chances."

"Worried about me?"

"Worried I'll have to take all your cases. I have vacation scheduled for later this year."

"Thanks for caring."

Tazer shrugged. "Just one big happy family. Or so Royce thinks."

Wiping all kidding from his face and tone, he touched Tazer's arm. "I'd take a bullet for any one of you."

"Ditto."

Tazer tilted her head. "I think I hear a car engine. That's my ride."

Nova stood on the porch as Tazer climbed into Gabe's SUV and they pulled out of the driveway and onto the highway. The residual fog wasn't as thick but still clung to the land, obscuring the departing vehicle before it had gone the length of a football field.

Nova had a strange feeling of being cut off from the rest of the world, stranded on an island with a potential killer loose among them. Yeah, this vacation was starting to suck.

Molly woke to the sound of her alarm clock buzzing. Had she only dreamed that Nova had held her through the night? She pressed her face into the pillow beside hers and the distinct freshly showered, musky male scent of Nova filled her senses. Warmth washed over her, and she smiled. The smile quickly faded when she realized what she was doing. She was happy Nova had slept in her bed, spooning her, making her feel safe.

Never, never, never get involved with a man who isn't sticking around.

This particular man was leaving soon. She couldn't let herself get used to having him by her side, in her bed or not. She had to stand on her own. She was the only one running the show at the McGregor B&B—with a little help from her brother, who was otherwise employed with the local police department.

Her independence firmly in mind, Molly sat up and groaned. Every muscle she'd ever used ached along with some she didn't know she had. Bruises had darkened on her arms and legs, making her look diseased.

The crutches the hospital had given her stood beside the bed within easy reach. Despite how much she wanted to be independent, she was thankful Nova had been considerate enough to put them there. Perhaps he was already tired of playing nursemaid to her. Well, she'd have to show him she didn't need him.

Throwing back the comforter, she eased out of the bed onto the crutches and headed for the bathroom. If she could manage a shower, she'd feel a lot more capable of facing the day. And warm water on her sore muscles would help loosen the stiffness. She'd be back to normal. Almost.

Molly balanced on one crutch and leaned into the bathtub to adjust the faucet to hot enough to help but not scald. She stripped her nightgown over her head and sat on the edge of the tub to remove her panties, then swung her legs over the rim. So far, so good.

Once inside the shower, she stood up on her good leg and held on to the wall, keeping the weight off her sprained ankle. Having slept with it up all night seemed to have helped. The swelling had gone down, but she didn't want to aggravate the injury by putting pressure on it before it had time to heal.

The hot water did the trick, the spray powering against her skin and muscles, soothing the ache. When she'd finished, she bent and shut off the water, pulled the shower curtain aside and leaned out on the crutches. When Molly reached for the towel, she glanced in the mirror for the first time, almost afraid of how awful she looked. The bathroom was steamy and condensation clung to the mirror, except where three large letters stood out.

DIE!

Chapter 6

Nova was halfway up the stairs when he heard Molly's muffled scream and a thump. He took the remaining stairs two at a time and raced to the end of the hallway. When he burst through the door, his gaze went to the bed, where he'd last seen her. She wasn't there. His pulse leaped and his senses heightened. Something about the room wasn't right, wasn't the same since he'd left it earlier. The bed looked no different, other than the fact that Molly was no longer sleeping in it.

Then it hit him. The room smelled different. The light and tangy citrus scent he associated with Molly was overpowered by a heavier, sultry aroma, one that threw him back in time, into a Bolivian jungle.

His heartbeat stuttered and then raced, banging against his chest like a snare drum. His hands shook and he couldn't seem to get enough air. The same way he'd felt when he'd held Sophia in his arms as she slid down his body, blood soaking through her shirt.

Caught in a memory he couldn't escape, Nova stood with his feet cemented to the floor, his chest aching.

A groan and a string of curses came from the bathroom, breaking through his nightmare. He shook his head to clear away the memories.

Another groan made him throw himself through the bathroom door. Molly lay sprawled on the tiles, the shower curtain partially wrapped around her, the rod lying on the floor beside her and a towel clutched in her hand, her naked body dripping wet.

She glanced up at him, her cheeks flaming. "Damned shower curtain. I can't get it off."

Nova dropped to his knees and dragged her against his chest. For a long moment he held her, fighting off the rush of emotions that came with the memories of Sophia dying in his arms.

When Molly pushed against him, he loosened his hold enough so that he could examine her, his gaze raking over her body, searching for broken bones or gunshot wounds.

"I'm okay." She pushed to a sitting position, pressing the towel to her breasts, her injured ankle out front. "Sore, but okay and angry." Her gaze captured his, her brows descending. "Question is, are *you* okay?"

He closed his eyes for a moment and pushed the jungle out of his mind, then opened his eyes and focused on Molly. "I'm fine. What happened?"

She hesitated a moment, as if she wanted to say something, but decided against it. Then she pointed at the mirror.

Nova had to look twice to see the message scrawled

in block letters. With the door open, the steam had escaped, and the word was barely visible.

DIE!

A hard knot formed in his belly and he balled his fists. If it wasn't clear before, it was now. Someone was targeting Molly. "You need to send your guests home," he said.

"I can't afford to." She reached for the crutches. "I have too much invested in this weekend."

"Someone is trying to hurt you."

"Maybe it's the ghost of Ian McGregor."

"Last night the gas stove was left on. Ghosts can't turn switches and they don't push people down the stairs."

"Wait. What did you say?" She tried to stand without the crutches and winced.

"For whatever reason, someone has it in for you. Let me help you." He gripped her arms and drew her to her feet. When she was balanced on one foot, he tried to take the towel from her.

She held on to it tightly. "I can manage this part myself."

"I know you can, but I'd rather you didn't slip again on the wet floor." He forced a smile at her stubborn expression, hoping to lighten the mood after he'd almost lost it in front of her. "In case you don't remember, I've seen you naked."

"Don't think it's going to become a habit," she grumbled, reluctantly letting go of the towel.

Trying to remain as impersonal as possible, Nova made quick work of toweling her dry, then wrapped the damp towel around her, breathing a sigh when she was fully covered in all the right places. The towel covering her private parts did little to disguise her natural beauty and the sexy curve of her arms and legs, but it helped put something between them besides Nova's imagination. The towel and the lingering memories of Sophia's death kept him from reaching out to stroke Molly's pretty, pale skin. "Better?" he asked, stepping away from temptation.

She nodded, drawing the terry cloth tightly around her and tucking the end in at her breast.

Nova held his hand up. "Stay right here." He checked the closet in the bathroom and then hurried into the bedroom. Molly heard the doors open and close and a moment later, Nova returned to the bathroom shaking his head.

He smiled. "Your rooms are clear. No one is hiding in the closet or under the bed."

Balancing on one foot, her hand on the counter, Molly glanced at the mess on the floor. "Could you hand me my crutches?"

"I can do better than that." Before Molly could protest, Nova lifted her into his arms.

She squirmed to get down. "I don't need you to carry me everywhere. That's what the crutches are for." The more she wiggled, the more he wanted to carry her straight to her bed and make love to her again. To drive deep inside her. She was alive, breathing and angry. His groin tightened and made it difficult for him to walk, but he did, carrying her into the bedroom, setting her down beside her closet.

"I can take it from here," she insisted.

"And I'll let you. If you'll hurry it up. I'm sure your guests will be anxious to discover why you screamed."

He crossed his arms over his chest. "And why they should go home."

"I know you're right. I'll tell them what happened and offer to refund their money. Although some of it will have to wait until I can save up." She bit her lip. "I just hope I can generate more business. Who will want to stay at a B&B that's unsafe?" Her shoulders drooped.

"It's only unsafe until we find out who's making it that way."

"You're right. I know you are. But this big, old, sprawling mansion has always been my home. My parents inherited it from my grandparents, my brother and I inherited it from our parents, and neither one of us can afford to maintain it. Not on my teacher's and my brother's cop's salary."

She glanced around the room as if memorizing the contents. "This was my parents' room. This house has been in our family for over a century." Her gaze returned to him, so sad it made his insides melt.

He raised a hand to cup her cheek, thankful for its warmth. It meant she was alive and still had her life in front of her. "You can't run a place like this if you're dead," he pointed out.

She leaned her cheek into his palm. "I know." Then she straightened. "And I'm not going to figure out who's trying to sabotage me by feeling sorry for myself." She hobbled away from him. "Shoo. I need to get dressed and get my guests fed for their trip home."

Nova smiled, liking Molly even more as she shrugged off her troubles and dug into the task at hand. Molly had more gumption than Sophia, who'd been the apple of her daddy's eye and given everything she desired. Looking back, Nova realized Sophia probably wouldn't have run away with him had she lived. She'd have insisted on staying with her father…the only life she'd ever known or wanted. He had been no more than a human plaything. Oh, she'd probably loved him, but she didn't have the drive and determination needed to sustain a long-term relationship.

After retrieving Molly's crutches and leaning them against the wall near her, Nova strode to the bedroom door and paused with his hand on the knob. "You sure you don't need me to help you get dressed?" He raised his brows, pasting a wicked smile on his face, keeping up appearances as a flirt.

Her ready smile matched his. "You have been a big help, but I can do this on my own."

"Your loss," he replied teasingly to dispel the disturbing thoughts the cloying scent of jasmine had inspired.

"I know," she muttered so low he almost didn't hear. He turned and winked at her, then left her bedroom, closing the door behind him and taking a deep breath of unscented air.

"What was the scream all about?" Josh Steiner demanded. He stood in the hallway, wearing jeans and a polo shirt hanging free of his waistband, his feet bare. He wasn't the only one. Half the ghost-hunting group stood around him in their bathrobes or pajamas, eyes wide and questioning.

"I'll let Molly tell you."

"Is she okay?" Josh asked.

"As okay as she can be, considering she fell down a set of stairs last night." He nodded toward the group. "If you want to go back to bed for an hour, Molly and

I will be preparing breakfast soon. We'll let you know when it's ready."

Josh wasn't convinced, if his frown was any indication. "If you're sure she's okay."

"She is," Nova stated with a confidence he didn't feel. She was in a lot more trouble than she wanted to admit. And he wasn't leaving until he discovered the source.

"Glad to hear it," the woman called Talia said. "Wouldn't want to miss the day's activities. I've never been inside a lighthouse or been to a séance. It should be interesting."

Nova stood guard in the hallway while everyone returned to their rooms. The group would be disappointed when they had to leave. He gave Molly a few minutes, then knocked softly. "Ready?"

She called out, "Yes."

He opened the door and found Molly leaning on her crutches, wearing a sundress in soft blues and yellows. Her damp hair was brushed back from her face, falling down her back in long tresses, curls springing up as it dried.

"I think I can manage the stairs," she said not too convincingly.

"No."

Her lips twisted in a wry smile. "You aren't going to let me try, are you?"

"No." He wrapped an arm around her waist and scooped her up. "How often do you get the royal treatment by your own personal servant?"

She laughed, settling her arm around his neck. "Never. And it's kind of hard to get used to. I've never had a servant."

"Just let me help." He strode toward the stairs.

"I don't want to sound ungrateful."

Nova paused before starting down. "But…"

"But I don't want to get used to it. I've been running this business by myself for the past few years. I'm used to doing things on my own." She glanced at the steps leading downward and her arm tightened around his neck.

"So what you're telling me is that I'm cramping your style," he said, his tone light as he took the first step.

She blushed and her fingers dug into his shoulder. "I don't know that I have a style, but I don't want to get used to having someone do for me what I'm used to doing myself." Her words came out in a jumble. Molly's gaze remained focused on his face, but Nova could tell she was very aware of the stairs.

"Duly noted. I won't be your servant. I'm a volunteer, not a servant." He reached the bottom of the stairs and set her on her feet. "Not so bad, was it?"

"Not as bad as taking the short, bumpy way down on my head, back, side, knees, belly…" She gave him a sheepish grin. "Well, you get the picture."

"I do." He shifted her hand to the banister. "And you have the bruises to prove it. Stay here while I get your crutches."

Nova sprinted to the top of the stairs, grabbed her crutches and returned, a little happier that she was going to call the whole weekend off. Removing the group of ghost hunters from the house should narrow down the list of suspects, if not eliminate them altogether. If all went well, he'd catch the culprit and be on his way back to D.C. in less than twenty-four hours.

The thought of moving on wasn't as appealing as it

had been before he'd first kissed Molly. But once he was on his way, he'd get over her. Since Sophia, he always got over the women he slept with.

Funny, but this time, he wasn't as confident.

Molly sat on a stool, first chopping nuts and then whipping the cream, while directing Nova on the fine art of mixing the perfect batter for maple-pecan scones. She laughed out loud when he wrapped a frilly apron around his middle. Instead of looking less of a man, he was even sexier, making her mouth water, and not for a taste of the croquettes or even the strawberries and whipped cream. No, she was lusting after Nova.

Nova helped her make the waffles, scones and croquettes, asking a few questions but otherwise quietly working by her side. He seemed lost in his own thoughts.

"About earlier…" Molly began.

"Earlier when?" he asked, pulling the oven door open to check the scones, then closing it.

"When you found me on the bathroom floor." Heat rose in her cheeks. "You looked kind of pale, almost like you'd seen one of the McGregor ghosts."

He grabbed the empty bowl they'd mixed the scone batter in and headed for the sink. "I was worried about you."

"Then why did you hug me so hard?"

"Maybe I like you."

"No. It was a different kind of hug. Not a gee-you're-kinda-cute hug."

"Is that whipped cream finished? I could take it out to the table, if you'd like."

Molly bit her tongue to keep from asking another

question. "And by that, you mean, mind your own business."

He pointed a finger at her. "You got that right."

Respecting his wishes, she kept any conversation about his reaction to finding her on the floor to a minimum. But that didn't keep her from thinking about it. He'd held her like someone he didn't expect to survive. The more she learned about the self-proclaimed flirt, the more she didn't know about him. Not that it would do her any good to get to know him better when he'd be out of her life soon.

By the time the scones were almost done, the ghost hunters had filtered into the dining room and kitchen.

Reed Schotzman poked his head through the swinging door. "Anything we can do?"

"Here." Molly handed him the fresh whipped cream and a bowl of sliced strawberries. "Take these out to the table. And I'd appreciate it if someone could lay out the silverware found in the buffet in the dining room. The scones are almost ready and the salmon croquettes and waffles are in the warmer."

"Smells great. We'll get the table laid out." Schotzman disappeared and Talia entered.

"Nice kitchen." She wandered around, touching a pot hanging from a rack fixed to the ceiling and sliding her finger across the granite countertop. "My family's kitchen is a little bigger than this one."

"Must be nice. I always thought this kitchen was big enough until I had more than one cook in it." Now Molly thought it was just the right size and cozy. But when Nova left, it'd feel too big. His presence filled the room in a pleasant, homey way. He'd said he couldn't cook, but had taken direction without any problem.

"I understand you and your brother, Officer McGregor, own the B&B," Talia stated.

Molly smiled. "We do, but I run it. Whatever profits I make, I share with him."

"Must be nice to have a sibling to share with."

"What about you? Do you have brothers or sisters?"

Talia shook her head. "I had a sister."

"Had?"

"She died." Her voice was flat, emotionless.

"I'm sorry for your loss. That must have been very difficult for you."

She shrugged. "I didn't know her well. She lived with my father and I lived with my mother. She was my half sister."

"Still, when it's your only sibling, it had to be hard losing her."

"Harder for my father." Talia lifted the heavy knife Molly had used earlier to chop nuts. "She was his favorite. Sometimes I feel like she's here with me. Kind of like your ghosts here in the manor."

A thread of unease trickled down Molly's back. What did she expect from a ghost hunter? They had to believe in ghosts or else they wouldn't be there.

Reed stuck his head in the door, smiling when he saw Talia. "Oh, there you are. Talia, do you know which fork goes where?"

Talia laid the knife down, smiled at Molly and followed Reed out of the kitchen.

"That's sad." Molly watched as the other woman left. "I don't know what I'd do without my brother. I don't have any other relatives. My parents were only children, and they're both gone, as are both sets of grandparents. It's just me and Gabe's family."

"That's not all." Nova flicked on the light switch on the oven and peered through the glass. "From what I've seen, you have close friends. Sometimes friends can be more like family than blood."

Molly's gaze captured his. "You're right. I love my friends and can't imagine life without them, either." She peered around him at the window into the oven. "I believe those scones are done."

"Hopefully, they won't have to imagine life without you." Nova pulled the trays out of the oven and plucked the scones off one by one, dropping them into a cloth-lined basket.

Molly tucked one crutch beneath her arm and lifted the basket full of scones. "If you could get the croquettes and waffles out of the warmer, we can eat."

In the dining room, the guests had pushed some of the tables together into one long one. They'd gathered around standing behind chairs, waiting for Molly to say the word.

She laid the basket of scones on the table and waited for Nova to set the platter of Belgian waffles and salmon croquettes down, too. "Let's eat."

Chairs scraped away and the guests seated themselves, passing platters and baskets until everyone had been served. Conversation was excited as the group discussed what they would see that day and where they were going, as well as discussing the film footage captured in the night.

Molly waited until they'd eaten most of the food on their plates and Nova had filled coffee mugs full of steaming brew before she began.

With a deep breath, she started off, "I wanted to thank you all for choosing the McGregor B&B ghost hunt for your annual event. However, I want to be open and up-front about what's happened in the past twenty-four hours and give you the option of backing out of your commitment."

"What are you talking about?" Josh Steiner frowned furiously.

"I believe someone pushed me down the stairs last night. Not a ghost. And someone also wrote *a sinister message* on the mirror in my bathroom. And I'm not sure but I think I turned off all the gas burners on the stove last night, but one was left on. Thankfully, Nova and Nicole discovered the problem before anyone was hurt. That's three incidents in less than twenty-four hours."

Josh opened his mouth to say something, but Molly held up her hand. "Let me finish first, thank you. Anyway, given the problems we've seen, I'm giving you the option to leave with a full refund."

The group sat in silence for a few seconds. Then the majority of them turned to Josh as one. Josh's gaze narrowed and he studied Molly as if she were under a microscope. "You're telling me it's too dangerous for us to be here?"

She nodded. "And I'll give anyone who wants to leave a full refund."

Josh stared at the others.

"What do you think?" Reed asked him.

Josh's eyes widened. "What do I think? I'll tell you what I think." He stood so fast his chair tipped over and landed with a crash behind him. "I think we need to be filming everything. Holy smokes, this place is haunted!"

Chapter 7

Nova shook his head. So much for narrowing down the list of suspects.

Josh and his group sat at the table long after breakfast concluded and Molly and Nova had cleared the table. They huddled together, talking excitedly about how to set up the equipment, where to locate it and even asked if they could film inside her bathroom, steaming it so that they could capture the message on a digital video camera.

Josh had been appalled that she would want them to leave, claiming this was one of the best "manifestations" they'd ever encountered and that they'd be crazy to pass it up.

Every man and woman in the group voted to stay and continue on with their paranormal investigation.

"I don't think it's a good idea." Molly glanced from Nova to Josh.

"We're ghost hunters," Josh argued. "We've been places most people won't go. In prisons, old mental asylums and buildings on the verge of collapse. We know the risks and we're willing to take them."

Nova ground his teeth, knowing before Molly said anything that she would give in to group consensus.

"Okay, then." She shot an apologetic glance at Nova. "If you're all set on staying, at your own risk, we'll continue as planned. Meet in the great room in one hour for the scheduled tour of the lighthouse, which is supposedly haunted by a man who plunged to his death from the top of the tower on October 29, 1929, Black Tuesday. I'll tell you more when we get there."

Back in the kitchen, Nova faced Molly.

She held up her hand. "I know, you wanted me to send them home."

"It's too dangerous."

"I could get them to sign liability release statements if you think that would help."

"It might cover your backside for insurance purposes, but a piece of paper won't help if someone starts attacking your guests." He raked a hand through his hair and paced. "I'd get everyone to sign releases. That way your bases are covered if a guest gets hurt. The fact is that someone *is* causing trouble."

Molly chewed on her bottom lip. "Yeah, but who?"

"Someone who wants to hurt you."

"Or you," she pointed out. "Don't forget your brakes weren't working."

Nova grinned, happy she was putting the pieces together. "I'd wondered if you'd picked up on that."

"I did. And I didn't like that *you* were the target."

"You and me both. But that could have been a system malfunction."

"A coincidence?" She raised her brows. "You mean to tell me you're the kind of guy who believes in coincidence?" She poked a finger into his chest.

His lips twisted. "No."

"That's what I thought." She crossed her arms. "And since the car is still at the bottom of the cliff, it'll be a day or two before it's retrieved and the brake situation is resolved. In the meantime, you and I have been targeted specifically and the entire group in general with the gas-stove incident. I think I'll have the ghost hunters set up video cameras in the kitchen just so we can have it covered."

"Good idea."

"Now, since we're done in here, I have a tour to lead to the lighthouse and the library, both of which have been reported as haunted."

"You can't take a tour group up into a lighthouse."

"I can share the ghost story with them from the base of the old lighthouse."

"And you trust them to get up to the top on their own?"

"I told them they shouldn't. But every one of them insisted they'd take their chances and I have it on their release forms that they go willingly. The stairs have been maintained. Short of jumping, they're welcome to climb to the top."

"Is there a railing?"

"Around the old light fixture, but there are large window openings."

"Large enough for someone to fall out?"

"If given a hefty push. They're about hip high." She motioned to her hip. A very curvy, sexy hip.

Nova looked away from her, remembering how his hand had trailed over that hip and how soft her skin had been. "Even if you could, it wouldn't be a good idea for you to go up the stairs. If someone in the group is our saboteur, it would be too dangerous."

"Do I hear you volunteering to make that climb with them?" Her eyes narrowed. "You don't have to."

"I told you I'd help," he said. "If helping means climbing a tower, I'll do it."

"You only volunteered to help out at the B&B."

"I've always wanted to see the inside of a lighthouse. And it will give me an opportunity to study the different members of the group a little more closely."

"Thanks." She grabbed the front of his shirt and pulled him close. "Really. Thanks."

"You don't have to kiss me." His gaze landed on her plump, tempting lips. "I'd do it without a kiss." He wanted one. The smarter move would be to step back and give himself space. She was entirely too intoxicating.

"I wasn't planning on kissing you." Her gaze dropped from his eyes to his lips, making it even harder for him to back away. "But now that you mention it…" She leaned up on her good foot and brushed her lips across his in a brief, less-than-satisfying attempt.

"That's not a kiss," he growled.

Molly tipped her head, her eyes twinkling in challenge. "You think you can do better?"

"Damn right I can." He wrapped his arm around her and pulled her against his chest, his mouth claiming hers in a tough but tender kiss, his lips moving over hers, his tongue thrusting between her teeth to stroke the length of her. When he finally came up for air, Molly's eyes were glazed and her hand rested on his chest, her fingers curled into the fabric of his shirt.

"You win." She licked her lips and settled back on her good foot, tucking the crutch beneath her arm. "I think I'll go call Kayla and warn her we're on our way." She limped away, a small smile curling the corners of her lips, the hem of her dress swaying with her movements, giving him teasing glimpses of her sexy legs.

Hell, he should have left with Tazer early that morning. The longer he stayed with Molly, the longer he wanted to stay. Now he couldn't leave. With what had happened, he couldn't just walk away. She was in no condition to lead a group of ghost hunters around town and up lighthouse towers. And if one of them was setting her up to get hurt, she'd be defenseless, unable to run and barely able to get around.

No, he couldn't walk away. But he could get Royce to run some background checks on members of the ghost-hunting group. Starting with their leader, Josh Steiner, who'd seemed inordinately pleased that a ghost had pushed Molly down the stairs and had been in her private bathroom writing messages on the mirror with what appeared to be lip balm.

What more was there to know about Josh? Nova would have to get a full list of the names from Molly when they got back from the lighthouse tour. For now, he could get Royce and his crew back at headquarters started on the names he remembered.

Nova stepped out onto the porch and was greeted by a soft breeze. The fog of the night before had lifted, leaving a gray, cloudy day, nothing like the summer promised on the vacation pictures posted all over Cape Churn. Storm clouds churned over the Pacific, moving slowly toward them. By late that afternoon, if not sooner, they'd have rain.

Nova hoped the rain would hold off until they completed the tour of the lighthouse. Being at the top of the tallest structure on the highest ground around in a thunderstorm was not his idea of a good time.

He checked for reception. Two bars. He hoped it was enough to get a call through. He hit the number for his boss and waited, watching for the others. To keep from being overheard, he descended the steps and walked toward the cliffs where Ian and Rose McGregor had fallen to their deaths.

Royce answered on the second ring. "Hey, Valdez, what's happening on the West Coast? Tazer get off okay?"

"She left at five our time, nine yours."

"Good. I have a hot one for her," Royce said. "What can I do to help you in your investigation?"

"I need you to put the team's computers to use and run a background check on the following people—Josh Steiner, Reed Schotzman and Talia Dane."

"Think they're the ones who cut your brake lines, left the gas on and pushed your B&B owner down the stairs?"

"I don't know if they're the ones, but we have to start somewhere. We won't get the car up from the base of the cliffs anytime soon to investigate the brakes. I'll see what I can do to get someone out to retrieve it soon. In the meantime, we've had more incidents."

"Oh, yeah? Tell me." Royce's voice was clear and crisp.

Nova told him of the message on the mirror and the voices Molly claimed to have heard in the fog.

"You said the guests at the B&B are a ghost-hunting group from Seattle."

"Yes, sir."

"Are you sure the B&B owner isn't putting on a show for them?"

"Molly wouldn't do that, nor would she injure herself or sabotage the brakes on my rental."

"Sounds like whoever is doing this is getting more serious. The message in the McGregor woman's bathroom was pretty specific to her. Who else would be in her bathroom?"

Nova didn't tell his boss that he'd been in her bathroom. He didn't need to know just how deeply involved he'd gotten with Molly McGregor.

"I'll have Geek run them through the system and see if something comes up."

"I'll get the rest of the names to you later today. Those were the only ones I've been introduced to thus far. They're a strange bunch of ghost hunters and very passionate about what they do. Sometimes too passionate."

"How so?"

"They seemed excited that Molly might have been pushed down the stairs by a ghost."

Royce snorted. "Nice."

"The one called Josh does documentaries on ghost hunting for a local Seattle station."

"I'll check out his ratings and bank situation, as well."

"Good. If he's struggling, he could be setting this whole thing up for a ratings comeback."

"With all the reality shows on television, you'd think one more about ghosts would be lost among the static."

Nova had thought of that. "Unless a ghost manages to kill someone on film."

Molly sat behind her father's desk in the study, going through the notes she'd made when she'd visited the local library. She'd scanned historical reports from newspapers printed all the way back to the late eighteen hundreds, researching the inhabitants of McGregor Manor and other buildings in Cape Churn.

The library had an entire section of historical documents that chronicled the establishment of Cape Churn, mentioning some of the prominent figures from its past, including Ian McGregor, who'd been instrumental in its planned growth. Letters and news articles donated by family members gave her good tales to build on when she'd first dreamed up the ghost-hunting weekend.

The lighthouse, a well-known landmark in the area, had many stories and legends associated with its graceful tower jutting above the coastline.

She'd always thought the lighthouse romantic, a welcoming beacon to those returning home after long and often dangerous voyages at sea. For months after Bill's sailboat had disappeared off the coast, Molly had climbed the tower at least twice a week, carrying her binoculars, searching the water, hoping he'd miraculously return and she wouldn't be alone.

Gabe had been living in Seattle when Bill disappeared. Her parents had been dead for a couple years and the only person she'd had to lean on was Bill, the man who'd been her sweetheart since high school.

When he disappeared, she'd been devastated. She hadn't realized how much she'd come to rely on him to be there for her. When he was gone, she had no one to share her evenings with. No one to talk to about her crumbling financial situation. She hadn't wanted to burden Gabe. His life as a cop in Seattle was dangerous enough without being distracted by a sister who was struggling to keep from having to sell the family home.

She had friends who lived in Cape Churn she met with on a regular basis, but she didn't have anyone to call her own. The transition from engaged to single again had hit hard. Instead of getting out into the dating world, she'd quit her teaching job and thrown herself into restoring the mansion and converting it into a B&B, using the last of their inheritance.

And once the B&B was operating, cash flow was always an issue. In order to make money at the tourism business, she had to spend money. She'd invested in supplies to refurbish the old house, putting in more sweat equity than she ever dreamed she could. Keeping up with her family home was a full-time job and sometimes she wondered if it was worth it.

"Miss Molly?" Reed Schotzman stuck his head inside the door.

"Yes, Reed?" She sat forward, smiling.

"I had a request from one of the group that we have wine with dinner."

"I have it on the menu. Any particular kind or year? Our wine cellar is quite extensive." Her parents had collected bottles through the years, visiting wineries and vineyards up and down the West Coast.

"Something from Concha y Toro would be nice. Perhaps Melchor Cabernet Sauvignon?"

Molly's brows rose. "Are you a wine enthusiast?"

Reed smiled, his pale face suffusing with color. "I'm learning."

"I'll check out what we have." She jotted down a note with the name of the wine he'd specified.

"Thank you. I'll see you in a little while." Reed disappeared.

Molly pushed to her feet, slipped the crutch beneath her arm and hobbled out of the library and to the kitchen, her thoughts on dinner and the wine requested.

The wine-cellar door opened off the kitchen, leading down into the basement that had been carved out of the rocky ground. It remained cool and somewhat humid throughout the year, a perfect place to store the hundreds of bottles of wine her parents had accrued. The old lock on the door was the only one she hadn't replaced with a new lock and key. The skeleton key protruding from the lock was probably the one used when the house had been built. She hadn't wanted to change everything. She could imagine the hands of her ancestors using that key and it brought her closer to them.

Molly propped her crutch against the wall, flipped the switch for the lights in the cellar and gripped the handrail attached to the wall that ran parallel to the steps.

Nova had insisted she call on him for any help she might need. She shrugged off his advice. The least she could do was locate the wine, if they had that brand. If she couldn't manage bringing it up, she could send Nova after it before dinner.

Leaning heavily on the handrail, she managed to take one step at a time, careful not to put too much weight on the injured ankle. Though the swelling had decreased substantially, the dull pain when she put pressure on it reminded her not to aggravate the injury more than she had to.

When she reached the bottom of the stairs, she hopped on one foot to the first row of wine-bottle racks. Her parents had organized different bottles by type of wine, then had gone alphabetically by winery. Sauvignons were near the back of the cellar. She was able to reach the back row by hopping, holding on to the racks and hopping again. After a quick perusal, she discovered just the wine Reed had requested and there were three bottles. Enough for everyone to have some that night, if they wanted.

Satisfied with her find, she turned to hop her way back to the stairs when the lights blinked out, followed by the solid click of a door closing. Molly landed on her good foot and wobbled, her equilibrium challenged by the darkness surrounding her.

She reached out, hoping to find a rack near her to lean on. Unfortunately, there wasn't one within arm's reach. Teetering dangerously, she would have fallen if she hadn't braced her injured foot on the floor.

Pain shot up her leg, and she cried out, forcing herself to endure it until she could shuffle her way to the nearest wine rack she could lean on to relieve her tender ankle.

Many times as a child, she'd played hide-and-seek with Gabe in this cellar, but not with the lights out and not after having been attacked. A cold feeling flittered across the back of her neck, slithering down her spine.

Was she alone?

"Hello?" she said into the dark, her voice shaking. She moved forward carefully, straining to see any light.

When she passed a tall wine rack, she caught a glimpse of a small wedge of gray filtering in from a window at the opposite end of the huge cellar. It was enough to give her hope, but not enough to illuminate her path to the staircase. Molly had to rely on her memory to find her way out of the cellar.

One rack at a time, she moved forward, half hopping and putting some weight on the injured ankle. By the time she reached what she hoped was the last row, her ankle throbbed, she was close to tears, and she still had to find the stairs and climb them.

Letting go of the rack, she inched forward, hopping, shuffling and scooting her feet forward, her hands out in front of her, debating whether or not to scream for help.

Surely someone would hear her, except they were all supposed to be gathering on the front porch by now. With the sound of the waves crashing against the cliffs and the solid walls of the manor between them, what were the chances they'd hear her?

Molly clamped her jaw tight and groped for the handrail, finally finding it after bumping her foot on the riser, sending another shot of agony up her leg. The pain only made her more determined to get herself out of the cellar by herself.

One step at a time, she climbed to the top, mentally kicking herself for going down into the basement in the first place. The wine could have waited for Nova to find.

When she reached the top of the stairs, Molly breathed a sigh of relief and twisted the knob.

The door didn't open.

She twisted again and pulled hard, realization dawning.

It was locked.

"Hey!" She shouted and banged on the door. "Someone let me out!"

Molly pressed her ear against the door and listened. Nothing. No voices, no sounds.

With a deep breath, she raised her fist and banged on the door again, yelling, "Let me out! I'm locked in the cellar!"

A waft of cool air stirred the hairs touching the sides of her cheek, causing a chill to slither down her spine. Molly's hand stilled and she grew silent. Though she'd thought herself alone in the basement, for that brief instant, she felt as if someone else was there with her.

She spun on the steps and reached out. "Who's there?"

Her hands met with cool air. Cooler than it had been a moment before.

Her heart beating faster, Molly turned back to the door, her hand poised to bang.

The muffled sound of footsteps sounded on the other side.

Molly banged again. "Help! Let me out of here!"

The footsteps paused, then continued, fading away.

What the heck? She knew whoever had been on the other side of the door had to have heard her yelling. Then why did that person leave?

Unless the footsteps belonged to the person who'd shut and locked the door.

Chapter 8

By the time Nova ended the call to Royce, it was past time for the group to meet out on the porch. Already, three of the eight people were leaning against the railing, talking to each other and staring out at the cape.

Two more ghost hunters emerged, joining the others, followed by Josh.

Nova returned to the house. "Where's Ms. McGregor?"

Josh shrugged. "Don't know. Last I saw her was at breakfast."

Nova pushed past the man and entered the house. "Molly!" He listened, but the whirring sound of a ceiling fan in the great room was all he could hear. He yelled again, "Molly?"

A muffled knocking sound came from the kitchen. His pulse kicking up a notch, Nova ran through the dining room and into the cavernous kitchen.

"Help!" a voice called out, the sound barely audible through the thickness of a heavy wooden door.

"Molly?" Nova called out.

"I'm okay, just stuck in here. Turn the key and unlock the door."

He peered at the old-fashioned lock that required an equally old-fashioned skeleton key. "No key. Do you have a spare?"

"Check the drawer beside the back door," she answered.

Nova yanked open the drawer and rifled through everything from a hammer, batteries and boxes of matches to thumbtacks. Everything but a skeleton key. When he located a heavy-duty screwdriver, he returned to the door, jammed the screwdriver between the door frame and the door, and whacked it hard with the hammer. The wooden doorframe split. On the second whack, the wood splintered away. "Step back. I'm going to force it open."

"Okay."

He gave her a moment, then threw his shoulder into the wooden paneled door.

It sprang open faster than he expected and he almost went flying down the stairs. He caught himself at the last moment on the doorframe, driving a splinter into his hand with his effort.

"Oh, thank God." Molly limped up the steps and threw herself into his arms, hugging him around the middle. "I thought perhaps you'd all left without me."

His pulse slowly returning to normal, Nova stroked her back with his uninjured hand. "How could we leave without you? You're the star of this crazy show."

She chuckled, the sound a cross between laughter

and a sob. "I shouldn't have let it get to me, but it was dark and I felt like someone was down there."

He frowned at the light switch on the wall. "You don't have a switch inside the cellar?"

"No."

Her answer made his chest tighten and his gut knot. Someone had locked her in the cellar and turned off the light, leaving her to fumble around in complete darkness. "What happened? How long have you been in the cellar?" He tilted her chin up. "Are you sure you're okay?"

She nodded, biting her lip. "I am now."

Her response warmed his heart. Before he was tempted to pull her into his arms again, he stepped away and descended into the cellar. Within the span of a few minutes, he'd searched all of it, checking behind stacks of boxes, behind wine racks and old bicycles. No one else was in the basement and no one could have gotten past him and Molly. He climbed the stairs, looking up into Molly's eyes. "No one's here."

She sucked in a deep breath, nodding at the same time, as if she'd expected him to come up empty. "I know it sounds strange, but I think it was Rose."

"The ghost?"

"Yeah. I felt her presence as a chill against my skin about the time I heard footsteps in the kitchen. It was as if she was warning me."

"You heard footsteps?" Footsteps meant someone had been in the kitchen.

"I yelled, but whoever it was didn't unlock the door."

"Who knew you were going into the cellar?"

"No one." Her brow furrowed. "No, wait. Reed might have known I'd go into the cellar. He asked for a certain type of wine for dinner. I went down to see if I had it."

Nova's hands turned to fists. "Let's find the man." He spun toward the front of the house.

"Wait." Molly grasped his elbow. "Anyone could have followed me."

Nova couldn't believe she'd stick up for the man who could be responsible for her captivity. "Not everyone asked you about wine, which you obviously keep in the cellar."

"Yes, but it doesn't mean he locked me in."

"Let's ask."

She shoved her crutch beneath her arm and followed him out of the kitchen.

Reed and Talia descended the stairs. Talia's hair was tangled, her face flushed.

Reed's pale skin suffused with bright red. "I'm sorry. Are we late?"

"Where have you been for the past twenty minutes?"

If possible, Reed's face burned even brighter red. "Well, uh…"

Talia grinned. "He was with me in my bedroom."

The pale-skinned man tugged at his shirt collar. "We were…talking."

"Before that, where were you?" Nova asked, determined to get to the bottom of the situation.

"I was getting dressed. Brushing my teeth." Talia frowned. "Why?"

Nova studied her for any indication that she was lying. So far, by all indications, either she was good at lying, or she was telling the truth. "Someone locked Molly in the cellar."

"Oh, my." Talia leaned against Reed. "How awful."

Reed pulled her close. "Do you think I did it?"

"Of course not," Molly assured him, touching his arm.

Talia shook her head. "Reed's been in my room. He waited while I brushed my hair and teeth. He couldn't have made it down to the kitchen and back in that short of a time."

Molly smiled at them. "I'm sorry, it's just that Reed was the only one who knew I would go looking for wine in the cellar. I jumped to a conclusion."

"You knew?" Talia stared up at Reed, her forehead wrinkling.

He nodded. "When you mentioned you'd like wine for dinner, I took it upon myself to request my favorite."

Talia cupped his cheek. "You're so sweet."

Nova's gut told him they weren't telling the whole truth, but he had no evidence to refute their story. Perhaps someone else did follow Molly into the kitchen and took advantage of the opportunity that presented itself.

"Are you two ready?" Molly asked brightly.

"I don't know." Talia touched a finger to her chin. "Now I'm concerned you don't trust us."

Molly shook her head. "Of course we do. Come on, let me make it up to you with a trip to see one of the most beautiful historical lighthouses on the West Coast."

Leaning on her crutch, Molly led the way to the door and out onto the porch, where the rest of the group waited. Within minutes, they'd all loaded into four different vehicles and headed toward town.

Nova drove Molly's SUV, Molly sitting quietly in the front seat beside him for the first couple minutes.

"I don't get it," she finally said, worrying that plump lower lip again.

"Get what?" Nova glanced her way.

"If someone is trying to hurt me, why lock me in the cellar?" She glanced across at him. "It wasn't as if I wouldn't be found sooner or later. And most likely sooner, considering everyone was waiting on me. It doesn't make sense."

"Unless someone is messing with your mind."

She stared out the side window. "Why?"

"I don't know." And he hated not knowing, especially when the occurrences were piling up.

"Do you think there really is a ghost in the house?" she asked softly. "I swear I felt a presence. I've heard sobbing on a couple occasions now. Do you think Rose is trying to communicate with me?"

"You're asking the wrong person. I don't believe in ghosts. I believe there is someone playing with your mind."

"How does that explain the sensation that someone was with me in the cellar? It was a cold waft of air that touched the back of my neck."

"A draft," he rationalized.

"The cellar doesn't have any vents or open windows. It's pretty airtight and the door was locked."

"I stick with the facts."

"You make all your decisions based on fact?"

"Yes."

"I know you, Creed and Nicole are some sort of agents. Are you telling me you have never made a decision based on gut instinct? I thought the best agents rely on instinct or more of them would be dead. What is so different between a feeling someone is with you and gut instinct?"

She had him on that one. He'd ignored his gut instinct to get out of Bolivia when he should have and it had cost him everything. His undercover operation, Sophia and nearly his life.

"We're here and the ghost hunters are anxious to see the tower." Two of the three vehicles full of Molly's guests had arrived and unloaded.

"Convenient timing," she muttered and pasted a smile on her face as she climbed out of the car before Nova could get out to help her.

He pulled her crutches from the backseat and handed them over.

Gabe's wife, Kayla, stepped out of the lighthouse cottage, a baby on her hip. "Right on time." She held out a key. "This is to open the door."

Nova took it.

"Mind if we come along?" Kayla asked. The baby giggled and held out her arms to Molly.

"Oh, sweetie, I'd hold you, but I can't with these old crutches." She bent forward and kissed the baby.

The child grabbed her hair and held on.

"Sorry." Kayla chuckled and peeled the baby's fingers out of Molly's hair. "She's used to Auntie Molly holding her."

Molly's smile drooped. "And I love it. Maybe after the lighthouse tour and before we head to lunch at the Seaside Café."

"You'll have to tell Nora hello for me. It's been a while since Gabe and I had a chance to eat there. He likes to stay home when he's off work." Kayla leaned close. "I suspect he eats there for lunch every day."

Something tugged at Nova's insides as Molly played briefly with the baby. With her sunny, optimistic disposition, she'd make a good mother. Now, why that thought came to mind at that exact moment, he didn't know. But that kind of thinking would only get him in trouble. He'd be better off settling back into his love-'em-and-leave-'em style of relationships. He liked it better when he didn't care enough to stick around. Seeing Molly with a baby only reminded him of something he could never have.

An image of Emma and Creed pushed into his thoughts. Creed was a Stealth Operations Specialist like him and he'd taken the plunge into a long-term relationship with Emma. They were so well suited to one another, Nova couldn't imagine Creed with anyone else. And Emma had accepted that he was an agent dedicated to serving, his missions taking him all over the world and placing him in dangerous situations.

Creed had been a confirmed bachelor, married to the organization and happy with his single life. He'd never experienced the loss of someone he loved like Nova had. Would he be as willing to commit to love again if something happened to Emma?

Seeing them together the night before was yet another reminder of the things Nova had sacrificed to be free of heartache.

Though the image of Sophia's smiling face had faded from his memory, the vivid memory of her dying in his arms was not something he'd ever forget.

The baby, frustrated that Molly wouldn't hold her, reached her chubby little arms toward Nova.

For a moment he stared at the child.

Molly laughed, the sound warming Nova inside. "She wants you to hold her."

He took the baby in his hands and held her up. She batted at his face and giggled, the sound making his heart squeeze hard. His hands completely engulfed her little body. She was so tiny, so needy and yet trusting of him.

"Hold her against you." Molly eased her toward him. "She won't bite…much."

He rested her against his chest, her face level with his.

Tonya stared at him, then grabbed his cheeks in the palms of her hands and bussed his face with an open-mouthed, sloppy kiss.

He'd never had a baby kiss him. Despite the slobber and the sticky hands, it was the most amazing thing he'd ever experienced.

Kayla smiled and took her from him. "Congratulations, I think she likes you. She doesn't usually go so willingly to strange men."

"We should go," Nova choked out. "Your guests are getting impatient." He nodded toward the ghost hunters, who'd moved past the lighthouse to climb on the jumble of giant rocks at the edge of the cliff.

"I see that." Molly laughed. "What is it about giant rocks that people feel compelled to climb them?"

Nova glanced once more at Kayla and Tonya and grinned. "You have a beautiful child."

Kayla hugged her baby. "I know, and I count my blessings every day."

Molly's smile disappeared as she faced Kayla again. "Speaking of blessings, although I'd love for you and

Tonya to join us, you might not want to hang with me today. I've been having a string of bad luck."

Kayla's eyes widened. "Don't tell me you sprained your other ankle."

"No, but there have been other things happening at the B&B. And I wouldn't want you or Tonya to be collateral damage if my luck continues to be as lousy."

Kayla's brows dipped. "Anything I can do? You want to stay here for a couple days? I'm sure Gabe wouldn't mind."

Molly touched Tonya's cheek. "Can't. I have a B&B full of obligations."

"Given your *luck,* I'm surprised you're not sending them home."

"They wouldn't go." Nova's gaze followed the ghost hunters as they clambered over the rocks at the base of the lighthouse perched on the cliff overlooking Cape Churn. "They're convinced it's all ghost manifestations."

Kayla's brows rose. "Are they ghostly manifestations?"

Nova's glance shifted to Kayla and then to Molly. "Another believer?"

Molly grinned. "Maybe."

"In ghosts?" Kayla kissed her baby's cheek. "Sometimes I think Tonya's biological father is looking out for us both. He would have loved her as much as Gabe and I do."

Nova fought to keep from rolling his eyes. If Kayla was blissfully happy to believe in ghosts, who was he to attempt to burst her bubble? "We should go. Your fans are waiting."

"Thanks, Kayla."

"Be careful. Can't have anything happening to Tonya's favorite aunt."

Molly snorted. "I'm her *only* aunt."

"Exactly." Kayla kissed Molly's cheek. "*I* love you, too, so don't take any risks."

"Trust me, I won't." Molly took off on her crutches.

When Nova turned to follow, Kayla's hand snagged his arm. "Casanova?"

"Ma'am." He faced the woman and baby.

"Molly tends to only see the good in people. She's a very special, trusting woman."

His gaze shifted to the woman determinedly continuing on with her ghost weekend, despite a sprained ankle, a frightening message and being locked in her cellar. "And she's very stubborn."

"She's had to be. Her parents saddled her with that mansion she can't afford and she refuses to take any of our money for its upkeep."

"Why doesn't she sell it?"

Kayla smiled. "It's the only home she's ever known. She and Gabe grew up in McGregor Manor. She wanted her children to grow up in it, as well." Kayla sighed. "From what I understand, her fiancé died before that could happen. Gabe said she's never been the same since. She's been fiercely determined to stand on her own two feet. Without any help whatsoever."

His lips twitched at the way Molly's dress fluttered in the breeze as she moved along on her crutches. "And how's that going for her?"

"Better than you'd think. She's made that old albatross of a house pay for itself. Mostly."

"So what do you want from me?"

"I got the feeling you stuck around because you kind of like her."

He frowned. "I'm staying until we find out who pushed her down the stairs." And who sabotaged his brakes, almost getting him and Nicole killed on their way to the airport.

"Yeah." Kayla gave him one of those I-can-see-right-through-you looks. "You couldn't take your eyes off her at dinner last night."

"I admire beautiful women. So sue me."

"Just do one favor for me."

He hedged at the intensity of her voice. "If I can."

"Make sure she doesn't get hurt." Kayla's gaze was as fierce as her words.

Nova wasn't a complete idiot. He read into those words and the inflection of her tone. The double meaning was clear. Kayla didn't want her friend physically hurt or emotionally damaged.

He didn't want to see Molly hurt any more than her friend did. If he could, he'd be with her twenty-four-seven just to keep whoever was terrorizing her from doing permanent damage. But he couldn't guarantee anything beyond neutralizing the threat. He had a job that took him all over the world. "I'll do my best."

Kayla's lips pressed into a thin line. "Do better."

The more people he met indigenous to Cape Churn, the more he realized how much Molly was loved. Not only did she have a home worth fighting for, she had family and friends all around her, providing the loving support she deserved.

Why she wouldn't accept help from her brother was a mystery. From what he'd seen of Molly, he guessed she didn't want to burden her brother's young family with the financial responsibility of keeping the manor running.

Nova hurried to join the woman who'd maintained a position front and center in his thoughts for the past twenty-four hours, studying her face as if for the first time. The sunny smile he'd noticed first had a hint of sadness, and the fine lines across her forehead indicated a propensity to worry. And she'd had plenty to worry about, taking on the restoration and operation of a place as big as McGregor Manor.

Molly stood in front of the lighthouse's large, solid-oak door, her face animated, her eyes twinkling as she spun the yarn of a man from Los Angeles who'd come to Oregon, following the woman he loved.

"James Carter came to Cape Churn to ask Penelope McGregor to marry him. As was the tradition at the time, he asked her father if he could marry Penelope."

Nova found himself caught up in the story as much as the group of ghost hunters. They were listening intently to Molly's words, waiting for what happened next.

"Penelope's father asked James how he intended to support his daughter. James told Penelope's father of the success he was at investing, that people trusted him to make the right decisions in regard to their fortunes.

"Her father wasn't impressed, asking if he'd made investments of his own with money he'd earned. He assured her father he had and that his investments were gaining nicely and that he hoped to build a home in the near future.

"In the two weeks he was in Cape Churn wooing Penelope and her father, the market tanked, investors began selling stocks at alarming rates and everything

James had traded became worthless, practically over-
night.

"Penelope's father refused to let her marry James.

"When James asked her to run away with him and
start over, she declared she couldn't live the life of a
poor person and refused to go with him.

"It was the final straw. James had lost all his money,
his clients, their respect and Penelope. He had nothing
left and he felt horrible about all the money his clients
lost in the stock-market crash, on top of which, he received death threats for the part he'd played investing
their money and not pulling out before it was too late.

"With no place to go, no home, no wife, he fell into
despair. The hotel where he'd been staying kicked him
out.

"He wandered out of town, aimlessly driving with
no place to go until he spied the lighthouse. The Devil's Shroud was creeping into shore, and the lighthouse
blinked, the only beacon to warn ships to stay clear
of the rocky shoals, the only light in the encroaching
darkness and fog.

"James aimed for it, climbed the tower and stared
out into the nothingness. Some say the fog pushed him
over the edge. Whatever it was, they found his body
the next morning at the base of the rocky cliff below
this very lighthouse. The newspapers claimed it was
suicide.

"I think he died of a broken heart." Molly stopped,
her eyes glazed, her gaze sweeping up the tower.

The crowd applauded her story and waited eagerly
while she unlocked the door to the tower. "Please be
careful on the steps. They can sometimes be slippery,
and at the top, don't stray too close to the windows. The

view is to die for. But let's not test that theory today. Mr. Valdez will accompany you to the top."

Half of the group dived through the door, impatient to reach the top, hurrying up the steps despite her warning.

The rest of the group took their time, studying the architecture and commenting along the way.

Nova waited until the last one entered the tower, then he turned to Molly. "Don't go anywhere. I'll be down as soon as possible."

Her lips twisted and she glanced down at her crutches. "I promise not to wander down the side of the cliff today."

"Seriously." He touched the side of her face, wanting to say more, but not sure what. He said nothing. With one last glance around the exterior of the lighthouse, he hurried after the ghost hunters to make sure no one fell out a window or was pushed.

He didn't like leaving Molly alone, but then everyone was in front of him; he'd been sure to conduct a head count as they entered. Molly would be alone and on firm ground. What could happen to her with no one around?

As he climbed the stairs in the tower, he paused at each long, narrow window along the way to catch a glimpse of the ocean or the lighthouse cottage, depending on which side of the tower he was on. The breeze had pushed the clouds aside and the sun shone down on the ocean and the craggy cliffs, giving what Nova considered a false sense of everything being just fine. He knew better, but when the sun shone like it did, he, too, could get caught up in the optimism.

The breeze at the bottom of the tower took on a different feel on the way up, finding cracks and crevices in the old bricks or windows, creating a soft wailing sound. The voices of the tour group echoed up the tower until they must have emerged at the top, leaving silence and the soft wailing sound. He could imagine words in the moaning wail.

Halfway to the top, Nova stopped, a chill slipping up his spine to the base of his skull. He listened to the variations of the wind.

In the midst of the whistling moan, he imagined the whispered words *"Mi cielo."*

Nova stiffened, his thoughts reeling back in time. Sophia had whispered that term of endearment in his ear whenever they made love.

He strained to hear the sound again.

"Mi cielo."

Someone had to be playing with his mind. Nova launched himself up the stairs, searching for whoever was whispering those words.

He'd only gone ten steps when he sniffed, the air smelling different there. Sweeter, more cloying...almost like...the perfume Sophia had worn.

His heart beat faster and his hands grew clammy on the handrail. A flood of memories spilled over him, making him breathe harder, his knees shaking.

What was happening? Why were memories of Sophia threatening to overwhelm him?

A window up ahead shone light into the tower. He headed for it, hoping to open it and let in fresh air to clear his head.

When he reached it, he looked for a way to open the glass. The panels were firmly fixed with no way to open it short of smashing it. To break the chain of memories bombarding him, he glanced out at the sea, the rocks, the cliff below, and his breath lodged in his lungs.

"Molly."

For the first couple of minutes, Molly leaned against the brick wall of the lighthouse, resting her arms from the crutches. When the sun came out, she glanced across the jumble of rocks to the sea, admiring the way the light caught the ripples, making them shine. Something in the boulders blinked at her as the sun glanced off it.

Molly remembered her promise to Nova and stood still. But when the sun's rays continued to bounce off the object, her curiosity won out. She could get to the boulders and back before Nova and the tour group descended the tower steps.

Tucking the crutches beneath her arms, she pushed away from the tower and worked her way across the smooth surface to where the boulders rose up out of the ground. The shiny object was perched on a rock not far from where she stood. If she left her crutches behind, she could balance against the rocks easily.

Propping the crutches carefully, Molly reached for the first big stone, used it as a brace and hopped toward the next, performing this motion until she arrived at the location where the object rested on top of a smooth, flat boulder.

Upon further inspection, Molly recognized it as a rhinestone-encrusted hair comb. And it looked practically new. With no pockets in her dress, she shoved the comb into her hair. She'd ask if any of the folks had accidentally left it when they had been climbing among the boulders.

A quick glance up at the tower confirmed her guess. The tour group was still milling around the top where the old light fixture had been when the lighthouse was still operational. This particular lighthouse had been decommissioned when they'd built an all-electric, unmanned one across the cape.

Molly was working her way back to the crutches when Nova burst through the door at the base of the tower and ran toward her.

She hurried forward, afraid something had happened to one of her guests. When she reached for the crutches, in her hurry, she knocked one over and it clattered against the rocks, lodging between two of them.

Balancing on one leg, she bent to grab the crutch, frustrated by her lack of mobility and feeling a bit guilty that she had broken her promise to Nova and had been caught.

"What the hell are you doing out here?" he demanded.

Just when Molly had the crutch at the tips of her fingers, Nova grabbed her around the waist and swung her around, crushing her against his chest.

"I was trying to figure out what was in the rocks," she answered.

"To hell with the rocks. You could have gotten yourself killed."

"I was doing just fine on my own until you came along." Crushed as she was against him, she pushed for space. That was when she realized he was breathing hard and his jaw was so tight, a muscle twitched. "It's no big deal. You don't have to be so upset."

"I'm not upset, damn it." He held her at arm's length for a moment, then pulled her close again, burying his face in her hair. "I saw you from the tower and thought…"

"That I would throw myself over the edge?" She laughed. "Hardly. And everyone was up in the tower with you. I would have been fine if you hadn't scared the life out of me by grabbing me from behind." The warmth of his breath stirred the hairs around her neck.

With his arms around her, she felt safe and cared for. She basked in that feeling, knowing it wouldn't last and that he only cared because of his pride. He wouldn't let anything happen to her on his watch.

When he finally leaned back and stared down into her face, he let out a long, shaky sigh. "I'm sorry."

"For charging at me like a crazed bull?" She cupped his cheek. "Don't worry about it."

Nova's brows drew together. "Why did you come out to the rocks?"

"I saw something sparkling in the sun and thought maybe one of the members of the tour left something out here."

"And it couldn't wait for me to come down out of the tower?"

She shrugged, her cheeks growing warm. "You have to understand, I'm not used to someone doing things for me."

"You've been on your own. I get that." He shook his head. "Did you find what you were looking for?"

His gaze locked on her and she swallowed hard, butterflies flitting against the insides of her belly. He looked as if he might lean down and kiss her and she wanted him to, really badly. "As a matter of fact—" Molly raised her hand to her hair "—I found this."

Nova dragged his glance from her eyes to where her hand rested against her hair. The warm, soft look in his eyes changed in an instant to a hard, cold stare.

"Where the hell did you get that?"

Chapter 9

Nova shoved Molly to arm's length, then reached out and plucked the rhinestone comb from her hair. "Where did you get it?" he demanded again.

Molly wobbled, trying to get her balance back, leaning on the crutches. "I found it on the rocks."

"You just *found* it?" He glanced around, searching for her. For Sophia…which was insane, considering she'd died in his arms years ago. The voices in the tower, the smell of her perfume, first at the B&B and then in the tower, were adding up. Now the comb he'd given her for her birthday. That damned rhinestone bling she'd wanted. It had shone brightly like diamonds against her jet-black hair. She'd worn it with a royal-blue cocktail dress at one of her father's lavish parties.

Nova thought he'd never seen a more beautiful woman in his life. Hers was a timeless beauty, her skin perfect, no blemishes or scars. She'd made him want to quit the spy business, to run as far away as he could get from drug cartels and arms smugglers so that he could start a real life with her. Maybe have children and live the life of a farmer or something blissfully mundane.

The party had been thrown to celebrate success at suppressing a rival drug lord. Cardeña had invited the leaders of other cartels and men whose people still straddled the fence on their allegiance. Sophia had played the beautiful hostess to her father's guests, wearing the comb Nova had given her. He'd been torn between his role as an undercover informant and wanting to take Sophia away from her father's corruption. The rival cartel had been gunned down, every one of the members murdered, along with their women and children. Nothing remained of them, and Cardeña wanted the other cartel leaders to know exactly what he'd done.

Sophia's smile shone as brightly as the rhinestones. Since her death, Nova wondered if she'd known how violent her father was. She had to have known, as close as they were. As far as Alfonzo Cardeña was concerned, he had only one child—Sophia. The man had many affairs, but he'd only married Sophia's mother and she had died in childbirth. Sophia had one cousin in the United States, but she rarely saw her. Sophia was Alfonzo's only family and he was hers.

"What's wrong?" A hand on his arm brought him back to the present.

He glanced at the hand and then at Molly. "I know this comb."

"Does it belong to one of the guests?" she asked.

"No."

"I was going to see if someone had dropped it or set it down and forgotten where she'd put it."

"Don't." He slid the comb into his pocket. "I'll take care of it."

Her forehead wrinkled. "Are you sure?"

"Absolutely." He checked his watch, anxious to leave, to get the hell away from the tower, to hear back from Royce on the background checks of the names he'd given and to give him more to find out about. Standing around only made him antsy. Who the hell would know about Sophia? Bolivia and all that had happened down there had long been buried with Sophia's death and his extraction. "Aren't we due to arrive at the Seaside Café in fifteen minutes?"

Molly continued to stare at him for a moment and then glanced at her watch. "Yes. It's that time. We should round them up and head for town."

Nova walked back toward the lighthouse, set on gathering the tourists and moving on as soon as possible.

Molly propelled herself along beside him. "Did you run into any ghosts up in the lighthouse?"

He stumbled, his gaze shooting to her. "No. Why would you ask that?"

She raised her brows. "Sorry, I wouldn't have if I'd known you'd bite my head off. I was only asking to be polite."

"Nothing. I saw nothing." Nothing tangible, anyway. He'd felt Sophia's presence, heard the name she used to call him in the moaning of the wind through the windows and smelled her perfume. Or thought he had. None of what he'd experienced had any evidence of its existence, other than the hair comb Molly had discovered on the rocks.

If all the so-called manifestations were factual occurrences, someone knew about him and Sophia and was playing with him now. First Molly, now him. Why the two of them? What did they have in common? Other than sleeping together one night.

One by one the tour group emerged from the lighthouse. Talia and Reed, followed by Josh, the last man out.

Talia grinned, her arm hooked through Reed's. "That's a first for me."

Josh asked, "How so?"

"My first kiss in a lighthouse. It was amazing. I felt like I was on top of the world." She glanced at Nova. "I didn't see you at the top. Don't tell me you're afraid of heights?"

"No." Nova turned the comb over in his pocket, the prongs digging into his palm. He pressed into them, the pain keeping him grounded. "I had business to discuss with Ms. McGregor."

"We need to head to town," Molly said. "The Seaside Café is expecting the group there at noon and it's getting close."

"Great, I'm hungry." Six-foot-four Reed rubbed his belly. "All that climbing burned off breakfast."

"Then let's go." Molly balanced on her crutches. "We still have the library to visit after lunch and then a séance tonight."

"This is great." Josh gave one last glance up at the tower. "Think I could get in here at night with my cameras?"

"I'm glad you liked the lighthouse. It does make for

good photos and I'm sure it will be lovely in your documentary. But let's wait until tomorrow." Molly smiled at Josh's enthusiasm. "I have a special guest coming to conduct the séance."

Josh's brows furrowed. "We've been to too many séances to count. I have enough footage of those."

"But you haven't been to a séance in McGregor Manor with Siobhan."

"Siobhan?" Tamara Bigsby, one of Josh's groupies, asked. "As in Seattle's famous ghost whisperer?"

Josh grinned. "You went all-out, didn't you? We've been trying to get her to visit our group for months."

"She comes to Cape Churn to vacation and she agreed to do the séance as a special favor to me."

"Will she be staying at the B&B?" Talia asked.

"I offered, but she'll only be there for the séance. She has a cottage along the shore."

"Wow. We've got to make sure we have enough time to set up before she arrives. I want to get it all on camera." Josh headed for his van and climbed in, his gaze on the road in front of him, probably already thinking of where to conduct the séance, the lighting and the placement of his equipment.

Nova studied the leader of the ghost hunters. He seemed intelligent, as if he could find out things if he dug hard enough. He'd learned about McGregor Manor, a place off the more frequented tourist paths. But was he the kind of man who'd make things appear to be worse than they were for the sake of thrill seekers?

Molly headed straight for the car, while Nova dropped off the key with Kayla. He caught up with her before she reached the door handle, pulling it open for her.

Once they were settled in her car, Molly didn't hesitate. "Now, will you tell me why you went ballistic on me when you saw the hair comb? And while you're at it, tell me why you didn't mention it to everyone."

He shifted into gear and pulled out onto the highway before answering, "I gave this comb as a gift to a woman two years ago."

Molly sat silent, staring out the window.

When she didn't say anything, Nova felt compelled to continue. "I was undercover. She was my front. The reason I was able to get into where I needed to be. I pursued her until she fell in love with me."

"And you fell in love with her."

He didn't refute it. He couldn't. "It's been two years."

Molly nodded. "And you gave her gifts. I get that. So you think she followed you and left it for one of us to find it?"

He shook his head, his hands tightening on the steering wheel until his knuckles turned white. "She couldn't." The scent of blood filled his senses, as it always did when he relived holding her body in his arms as she bled out. "She's dead."

Molly gasped, her eyes wide, flooding with unshed tears. "I'm sorry."

"She was wearing the comb shortly before she died." She'd taken it off and put it in her pocket to keep from losing it. When they'd taken her body away, the comb was lost. I haven't seen it since that time."

"She must have meant a lot to you."

He nodded. "I should have gotten her out."

"Out?"

"Away from her family. Out of Bolivia."

"Bolivia?" She stared at him across the console. "Was she transported to the States for burial?"

"No. She was buried there."

"Then how did the comb make it back here?"

"My question precisely."

"I see why you were so shocked to see it." Molly turned around, peering out the back window. "Who would have known you back then? Do you recognize anyone from the group of ghost hunters?"

He shook his head. "No."

Molly pulled out her cell phone and checked service, then paged through her contacts and selected one. "Kayla. No, we didn't forget anything. I was just wondering if anyone came out to the lighthouse before us." Molly listened. "No one, huh? No, just wondering. Thanks for letting us in. Give Tonya a kiss for me. I'll talk to you soon."

Molly clicked the off button and let the phone rest in her lap. "No one came out earlier this morning than us. Kayla had her easel set up outside as early as seven when Gabe left for work. She put it up right before we arrived. She'd have noticed someone by the lighthouse since she was painting it."

"It could have been left earlier." But that didn't explain the voice he'd heard whispering Sophia's pet name for him or the perfume. "I'd like to talk to my boss."

"When we get to the café, we can split off from the group."

"I'd like you to keep an eye on them while I check in."

"You're right."

"Promise me, if you see anything…no heroics."

She glanced down at her ankle. "In case you hadn't noticed, I'm in no condition to be heroic."

He glanced at her legs. "I don't know. The way you were climbing around those rocks was pretty gutsy with a sprained ankle."

She blushed, a twinkle returning to her eyes. "I've never been one to stand around when there's something sparkly shining close by."

"You don't strike me as a woman who wears a lot of bling."

"I'm not, but I do notice when something is out of place."

The town of Cape Churn came into view. "Do you know everyone in town?" Nova asked.

"Everyone who lives here on a permanent basis and many of the seasonal transplants."

"Must be nice."

"It is. I've never wanted to live anywhere else."

"What about traveling?"

"I've done some. I backpacked around Europe one summer during college." She smiled. "It was magical. But I wanted to come home by the end of the summer." She stared across at him. "What about you? Where's home?"

He shook his head. "I don't have one." Saying the words made it sound pathetic. "Oh, I have an apartment I pay rent on in D.C., but it's not really home. It's a place to park my clothes."

"Don't you get tired of traveling all the time?"

"Sometimes."

"Are your parents still around?"

He shook his head.

"Siblings?"

"I'm an only child."

"So you have no place to call home?" When she looked at him that way, as if he was to be pitied, he straightened.

"You don't miss what you never had."

She nodded. "In my case, I don't want to lose what I had. McGregor Manor is the only home I've known. It holds all the memories of my childhood and my parents. I was one of those fortunate people who grew up in a loving family. I want that for whatever family I have."

Nova could see that about her. She was kind, generous and determined. She'd have it all someday because she was that persistent about going after what she wanted.

For a moment he envied the guy she'd eventually marry and the two or three kids they'd have. He'd dreamed of marrying Sophia, if he could have gotten her out of Bolivia, but he'd never dreamed past the two of them as a couple.

Sitting in the front seat of Molly's SUV, he could picture sitting in a rocking chair on the sprawling porch of McGregor Manor with Molly by his side, a couple grandkids running up and down the steps.

"You need to turn here," Molly said.

The image of the two of them growing old together shocked him so much he almost drove right past the street. He hit the brakes and made the turn a little faster than he'd intended, pulling into the parking lot of the Seaside Café.

The other three vehicles parked and the group entered the café, all talking at once.

Nova helped Molly out of the SUV and handed her

the crutches. "I'll be back in a few minutes." He nodded toward the café. "Stay close and keep an eye on them."

"Will do." She touched his arm. "Don't be long."

He glanced down at her hand on his arm. That simple touch went a long way toward warming the parts of him that had gone cold when he'd discovered the hair comb in her hair. He held open the café door for her and waited as she entered, then he walked away, sat on a bench across the street and dialed Royce. Someone in the group of ghost hunters had to be the one causing all the trouble. The questions were, who and why? And by damn, he'd find out before that person did something that couldn't be undone.

Molly sat at the end of the table filled with her guests, feeling like a chaperone on a school trip. With a bum ankle and a troublemaker among the ghost hunters, she didn't feel all too congenial. But she put on a game face and pretended everything was all right while searching every face of the eight people before her. How hard would it be to figure out who was causing so much trouble?

It had to be someone among the group. The fastest way to end it would be to send everyone home. Then she wouldn't have to worry about who was terrorizing them, Nova would be gone and she'd be alone in McGregor Manor, out on a lone stretch of road.

The home she'd clung to and all its memories didn't seem quite as appealing as it had. Perhaps it was time to adopt a dog. A really big dog with sufficient training to attack anyone who posed a threat to her.

So much for running a B&B by herself. If she didn't feel safe, it wasn't worth it. Which ultimately meant giving up the manor. Her salary as an elementary-school teacher wasn't enough to sustain the place.

That afternoon she'd ask Gabe about a dog. Maybe he knew of a good training facility in Seattle that could supply one that would provide the kind of protection a single woman needed. Then she could continue on, business as usual, hoping she didn't scare her customers away with a big, vicious dog.

"Ms. Molly, are you feeling okay?" Nora Taggert swung by her table, carrying a pot of coffee. "I heard about your accident."

Molly smiled at the café owner and the wife of Cape Churn's police chief. "I'm fine, just a sprained ankle."

"Never did like the idea of you runnin' that bed and breakfast out there so far from town. You sure you don't want to sell that old place and move closer in?"

She shook her head. "It's my home."

"Honey, home is where the heart is."

"Yeah, and my heart is in McGregor Manor. There are decades of memories etched into the woodwork there, and I don't want to lose them."

"You don't lose memories in your heart—you make more to add to them. Different places, different homes, you learn to love where you are."

"Says the woman who's lived here half her life."

Nora's face lit up. "There was a time Mr. Taggert and I traveled the world, moving from place to place, earning enough to travel to the next town or city. Guess you could say we were like gypsies. It wasn't until we landed dead broke here in Cape Churn that we found our little slice of heaven."

"You see, Mrs. Taggert, I didn't have to travel all around the world to learn what I already knew. This is where I want to live. If I have children, I want them to grow up here and fall in love with the place just like I did."

"I just don't like to think of you out there all by yourself."

"I'm a big girl. I can handle almost anything. I have protection and I'm thinking of getting a dog."

"Well, as long as it's a big dog and it knows what's what about protecting you, I guess you might be okay."

"I have to be okay. I'm the only one looking out for me."

"You have your brother. Why don't you have him and his pretty little artist wife move in with you?"

"He's getting to know his wife. He doesn't need to have too many others in his house, especially with a new baby and teenager to deal with."

"Well, can I at least pour you some coffee, since you don't need a meddlin' old woman's advice?"

Molly chuckled. "I'd love coffee." She held her cup out and Nora filled it full of the steaming brew.

Once she'd been around the table, taking orders and pouring water and coffee, Nora headed for the kitchen to place their selections with the cook.

When Nora left, the ghost-hunting group bombarded Molly.

"Ms. Molly, tell us about the ghost at the library," a tall, leggy young man named Preston Todd asked.

Anita White, a slightly chunky woman with dark, curly hair, glanced around the aged but cheerful interior of the café and asked, "Are there any ghosts associated with the Seaside Café?"

Josh leaned his elbows on the table, his gaze intent. "Who will we be trying to contact at the séance tonight?"

Molly fielded all their questions, promising to tell them all the legends she knew of after they got their food. "As for the séance, I've asked to connect with Rose and Ian. Maybe we can find out what really happened to them that night they died."

"I'm all for skipping the library visit so that we can set up the cameras for the séance." Josh glanced around the table for approval.

"Before you make a decision, you should know the library is the old courthouse and they had the jail in the basement. It dates all the way back to the late eighteen hundreds."

Anita smacked the table with her palm. "We're going to the library. All those in favor?"

Everyone raised their hand except Josh, who eventually added his vote to the rest. "Might as well. I can set up the equipment when we get back. And an old jail sounds interesting. I have some of my equipment in the car. I could shoot some video while we're touring the building."

Nora arrived bearing trays of everything from fish fried in beer batter to her own special recipe for seafood chowder with chunks of halibut, salmon, scallops and prawns mixed in the creamy sauce.

The group dug in.

While pushing her food around her bowl, Molly wondered what was keeping Nova from joining them. Had he decided he'd had enough fun with her little group of ghost hunters?

* * *

"Anything on the names I gave you?" Nova asked as soon as Royce picked up in D.C.

"Valdez. I take it things are heating up?"

"Damn right they are." He explained what occurred at the lighthouse.

"Bolivia," Royce repeated. "That was a nasty affair. We almost didn't get you out of there. Hang on, let me check with Geek and see if he's come up with anything."

The pause on the phone gave Nova too much time to think, his thoughts going back to the jungles of Bolivia. Too many questions had remained unanswered.

He hadn't gotten Sophia out before she'd been killed. Would she have come, had she lived? And who had shot her? No one confessed to the killing or took credit for murdering the most notorious cartel boss's daughter.

Sophia's father blamed him for his daughter's death, because he was the only one with her at the time. Not that he blamed Nova for the actual shooting, since the bullet had gone all the way through Sophia and nicked Nova in the shoulder. Otherwise Alfonzo would have killed him on the spot. However, the drug lord accused him of being responsible for his daughter and he'd taken her outside the compound, which was strictly forbidden without an armed escort. He'd placed Nova under house arrest until he decided what he would do with him.

Alfonzo had raged around the compound demanding answers and getting none. He'd executed more than one of his bodyguards when they'd been unable to provide answers. The weapon was found in the pool Nova and Sophia had been swimming in minutes before she'd been shot. No footprints, besides their own. And no fingerprints were found on the gun. Nothing that would give them any idea who was responsible.

Leaders of the rival cartels who'd attended the party the night before pleaded innocence and each had alibis. That didn't stop Cardeña from taking out his anger and grief on all those around him. He drank himself into a stupor and staggered around the compound with a loaded gun, shooting at anything that moved, including his guests and servants.

The cartel leaders left while they could, and in the midst of everything happening, Nova made his escape, crossing into Peru and catching a plane to the United States from there. The DEA had their information, and Nova had his life to get on with and grief to deal with. Like Alfonzo, Nova blamed himself for Sophia's death. He should have done more.

"You still there?" Royce's voice cut into his musings.

"I'm here."

"Got a hit on Josh Steiner. Apparently, he's declared bankruptcy once and the Seattle film industry has rumored that his ghost reality show will be cut from the local networks. It's enough of a motivation for him to come back from this trip with a winner on film."

"That doesn't explain how he would know about me, Sophia and the cartel in Bolivia."

"No, it doesn't, but it gives him motivation to make the trip worth his time," Royce said. "Reed Schotzman has been booked before. His last girlfriend had a restraining order put out against him for stalking her."

"Apparently he has a new girl in Talia Dane. Again, nothing that says either one of them would have a problem with me or know me from my past. What about Talia?"

"Nothing on Talia Dane. No criminal record or record of bankruptcy."

Nova stared across the street at the diner. Nothing Royce had passed along set off any bells inside. But that didn't mean one of them wasn't the culprit. He returned his attention to his boss. I have more names for you." Careful to talk slowly and enunciate, he listed the other names of the group. "It has to be someone from this ghost-hunting trip. I've smelled Sophia's perfume twice. Once in the B&B and once in the lighthouse. The first time I thought my mind was playing tricks on me. When Molly found the hair comb, I knew better. Only the ghost-hunting group was in that tower with me."

"Someone couldn't have gone up prior to your arrival?"

"Molly checked with the woman who lives beside the lighthouse. We were the only ones there and that perfume couldn't have been that strong if sprayed before daylight."

"I'll get Geek right on these names. Anything going on with you and the McGregor woman?"

Nova hesitated.

"I take your silence as a yes." Royce chuckled. "Just remember, if someone has it in for you because of what happened in Bolivia, they might use Molly to get to you. Stick with her. As already proven, she's in as much danger as you are."

"I'm on it." Nova disconnected the call and crossed the street to the café, not feeling any better than when he'd started the conversation with Royce. It only made him more certain than ever that whoever was giving them hell had something to do with him and knew what had happened in Bolivia.

Chapter 10

"The city planners built this building to last. Knowing how rugged the coastline was and how violent the weather could be so close to the shore, they used granite for the foundation and specially forged bricks for the exterior walls. It was said no prisoner could escape once incarcerated in the basement." Molly led the way through the Cape Churn Library, explaining the history of the building, starting in the basement. "Some of the cells have been preserved as they'd been over a hundred years ago. Others have been used to store holiday decorations and other items." She paused in front of a particular cell.

Josh wore a small video camera attached to his head with a Velcro strap, and he carried another video camera attached to a lightweight tripod, asking questions as they went. "Did anyone die in this prison?"

A chill trickled across her skin, raising gooseflesh. "As a matter of fact, someone did. This cell contained the notorious Daniel Olsen, who had been arrested for the murders of five of Cape Churn's ladies' maids. He claimed he didn't kill them, that the Devil's Shroud had been responsible."

"I read about the Devil's Shroud," Anita said. "It's legendary for this area. The stories say the Devil's Shroud causes ships to run aground on the rocky point, for people to disappear in the fog and for others to do things they normally wouldn't."

"As was the case with Olsen?" Reed asked.

"And the failed brakes in Mr. Valdez's vehicle last night?" Talia queried.

Molly bit down on her tongue to keep from snapping back. Instead, she replied, her voice tight, "Although the fog plays havoc with ships close to shore, I find it to be a convenient excuse for troublemakers."

Anita laughed. "Touché."

Molly continued, "The morning of his trial, Daniel Olsen was found hung from the light fixture. The jailers reported it as suicide, that he'd used the sheets on his bunk to tie off."

"I'd hate to have been the one to find him," Mel Wilkins whispered. "This place is creepy enough without finding a body hanging from the light fixture."

"Do you mind if we turn out the lights?" Josh suggested. "I'd like to turn on my infrared camera and see if we pick up any thermographic images in the cells."

Molly's gaze shot to Nova. The thought of turning off the lights in as unsettling a place as the old Cape Churn jail was bad enough without a potential killer lurking among the current occupants.

"Oh, yes, please, Ms. McGregor. We always show something different on the infrared camera," Anita added.

Molly bit her lip and gave in. This was a ghost-hunting tour, after all. "Is there anyone who doesn't want to be down here when the lights are off?" Molly moved toward the light switch on the wall near the exit.

"I'm out of here." Mel pushed past her and climbed the stairs to the first floor. "I'll wait up here."

"I'll wait with Mel. I can see the video later." Preston moved past Molly as well, climbed the steps and closed the door at the top.

"Let me get set up in front of Olsen's cell before you flip the switch."

Nova stood beside Molly, his brows pulled low. "You sure you want to do this?"

"It's a ghost-hunting tour. The lights have to be out at some point. What could happen?" She faked non-chalance although her hand shook on the light switch. After all that had happened, lights out was the last place she wanted to go. And the door closed at the top of the stairs reminded her too much of being locked in her cellar.

"Okay, I'm ready," Josh called out. "Hit the switch."

Molly studied the rest of the group for a second. All gazes were on Josh's camera.

You have nothing to fear, she told herself, then flipped the switch, her gut telling her instantly it was a mistake.

The jail fell into pitch-black.

"And now the infrared." Josh's disembodied voice echoed against the bricks. A soft click and the video display on the back of the camera lit up with red, orange, yellow and blue blotches, the glow lighting Josh's face.

"Look," he said. "There in the middle." He pointed at the middle of the screen, depicting the center of the cell. Darker red squiggles faded outward into yellow and green.

"Is it a ghost?" Anita asked, her voice shaking with excitement.

"Could be." He turned the camera to the corners, and the lights faded more to blue and green. As he pivoted the camera back to the center, the colors grew warmer. "Wow. That's amazing."

"You're recording this, aren't you?" Anita asked.

"Damn right."

"Ooooh, you could be getting the ghost of Daniel Olsen on video."

"Shh," Josh said. "Listen."

The hint of a soft whisper filtered through the darkness.

Molly strained to hear; it sounded almost like a song. Beside her, Nova stiffened and his hand covered hers, pushing the light switch to the on position.

"What the hell?" Josh blinked and shot an angry glance toward Molly. "We weren't done recording."

"Sorry, folks, show is over." Nova jerked his head toward the door. "We still have to make it through the rest of the library and there's a storm coming in. We should be back at the B&B well before dark."

"I was getting some great footage," Josh grumbled, gathering his camera and folding the tripod. "I might want to come back here tomorrow to do some more recordings."

"I'll see what I can arrange," Molly responded noncommittally. She wanted to know what had spooked Nova into flipping the switch back on.

Molly led the way out of the basement and up into the main portion of the old courthouse that had been converted into the library. The courtroom still had one column of seating, now used by patrons to sit and read. Shelves of books lined either side of the benches and the checkout desk was the old judge's bench.

"This is so cute," Anita said, her eyes wide, taking it all in.

"The historical society decided to leave the courtroom as close to intact as they could and still add shelves for reference materials," Molly offered. "The antechambers are split into fiction, nonfiction, self-help and other categories. In 1958, Miss Fenton, the librarian, was found dead in the romance antechamber. She was lying among the *A*'s, a copy of *Pride and Prejudice* beside her."

Mel sighed and leaned against Preston. "How sad. But what a great book to die with."

"Since then, the librarians and volunteers say that every once in a while, Miss Fenton will push a book off a shelf."

"That's amazing." Anita turned around. "Which way is the romance chamber?"

Molly pointed toward the antechamber in question.

Half of the group headed that way; the other half split up and wandered around the old courtroom.

Molly grabbed Nova's hand and drew him out the front door. "What was that all about?"

"What?" His expression was blank, the muscle twitching in his jaw the only evidence of his earlier mood swing.

"The light switch," Molly persisted.

"I thought they'd had sufficient time."

She rolled her eyes. "Oh, please. When the lights came on, your face was pale. Did you see a ghost?"

"No." His hand tightened around hers. "I heard one."

"Heard one?"

"The whispering sound we were trying to hear."

"It could have been a draft."

"No, it was a song. One Sophia sang when she was happy."

Molly's heart tightened. It was back to Sophia. "Two of the group members were up the stairs. They couldn't have hummed or played the song loud enough to be heard in the basement. That narrows it down to the other six."

"Right. But which one?" His gaze followed the others as they disappeared into the antechambers.

"Hopefully, we figure it out sooner than later. You know, Gabe's been after me to purchase security cameras for the manor. I'm beginning to think he's right. Not that I have the money for it right now. But I do have a webcam on my laptop. Perhaps tonight at the séance, we can have a camera of our own set up."

"I can do even better." Nova grinned. "We'll have the computer guru back at home office record and monitor the webcam. If he finds anything interesting, he'll notify us."

Molly grinned. "I like that. I wasn't sure when we'd have time to review the video if we were involved in the séance. And for that matter, I could have the webcam recording through the night. If anyone is up roaming around, we could catch them on video."

Nova pushed the hair back out of her face, tucking it

behind her ear. "Thank you for understanding. Sophia was one of the darkest points in my life."

Molly's heart dipped into her belly. "She must have been very special to you."

"I thought I was in love, and I thought she loved me. I'm not even sure she did. But I never got to find out. What bothers me most is that, based on the trajectory of the bullet, I was the original target. I spun her around in front of me to kiss her when the shot was fired."

Molly's fingers tightened around his. "You couldn't have known."

"I should have been the one to die that day."

Molly's heart hurt for him at the same time she felt a stab of longing. For the first time in her life, she was envious of a dead woman. The thought made her turn and walk toward the front door. Anything to get away from a man who felt so strongly about a woman he once loved. She'd always wanted to be loved as much. Never had she felt as loved by her fiancé. Maybe that was why she hadn't been willing to give up everything to follow him. She hadn't loved him as much as she wanted to be loved.

Nova followed her through the door and out onto the front stone steps.

"I should cancel the rest of the weekend and send them all home," Molly said.

"It's a little late for that."

"Why?"

He nodded toward the western horizon, out across the cape. "Weatherman predicted strong storms for tonight. If you send them home now, they'll be caught driving in a downpour."

The afternoon sun had been completely engulfed in clouds so heavy they made daytime into an early dusk.

"Fog last night. Storms tonight." Molly shook her head. "You get the feeling someone is trying to tell us something? Either that or my luck is really lousy."

"I don't believe in luck."

"I believe in making my own luck. It's called hard work." Molly snorted. "Perhaps it's time to start believing in luck."

"Come on. Let's get back to the manor before the storm beats us there."

Molly went back inside the library to gather the group. She found all but three of them.

"Where's Josh, Talia and Reed?"

"Help! Someone come help!" Reed yelled from the stairs leading into the basement. "Talia's hurt!"

Adrenaline spiked inside Molly, sending her hurrying forward on her crutches. "Where is she?"

"In the basement. I told her not to go back down there. I had a bad feeling." Reed ran down the steps ahead.

Nova stopped Molly before she could limp her way down the steps. "Stay up here with the rest of them. I'll take care of her."

"I need to help her."

"Help by calling 9-1-1," he said. "You'll lose cell-phone reception in the basement."

Molly couldn't argue that point. She pulled her cell phone out of her pocket and started to dial.

"I'm okay," a shaky voice called out from the bottom of the steps. Talia, leaning on Reed's arm, worked her way up the steps, a cut and a bruise on her forehead, her hair a tangled mess.

Nova hurried down to help Reed by slipping Talia's arm over his shoulder. Together, they half lifted, half guided her the rest of the way up the stairs.

"What happened?" Molly asked.

"I came back down because I wanted to see if I could connect with the ghost if I came alone. I'm not sure what happened, whether I tripped or if someone pushed me down the stairs. I must have hit a step on the way down. That's where I got the bump." Talia touched her forehead gingerly.

"I heard her scream and found her lying at the bottom of the stairs." Reed's brows were knit in concern. "Who would push her?"

"I don't know, but we should take you to the hospital and have you checked out for concussion," Molly said.

Talia shook her head. "No, really. I'm fine. I don't want to ruin the evening."

"It's on the way." Molly waved aside her protests. "I can send the rest of the crew back to the manor."

"Okay, then. Maybe it won't take too long."

Josh appeared with his headband camera, carrying the infrared camera on the tripod. "What's going on?"

"Talia had a fall."

"Are you okay?" Josh asked.

"I will be when I get back to the manor."

When Anita filled him in on what had happened, his eyes widened. "Was it the ghost? Did he do that?"

"I don't know."

Josh looked past Talia to the stairs leading down into the old jailhouse. "I should stay and set up a camera to record any activity."

"We've had just as much activity at the manor and it

has a nice soft bed to sleep in," Anita argued. "I'm for heading back to the manor for our scheduled séance."

The rest of the group agreed and loaded up in the vehicles and headed out of town, while Nova and Reed helped Talia into Reed's car. They followed Nova and Molly to the hospital where Emma Jenkins was on duty.

"This is getting too weird. First Molly and now Talia. We'll let the on-call doc have a look at you. Come on back." She led her to a room.

Nova, Molly and Reed waited in the lobby of the emergency room.

"Who would have pushed her down the stairs?" Reed paced the length of the emergency room and back. "I was looking through the courtroom one minute, the next she'd disappeared and I heard her scream. I tell you it took ten years off my life."

"Did you see anyone come out of the basement when you heard her scream?" Nova asked.

Reed shook his head. "No. That's what was so weird. Do you think it could have been Daniel Olsen?"

"The ghost?" Nova asked.

"Yeah. I saw the infrared video. There was something in that cell."

"I seriously doubt it," Nova said. "Maybe she tripped."

"Maybe." Reed stopped pacing and balled his fists. "If I find out someone, not a ghost, pushed her down those steps, I'll kill him."

Half an hour later, Emma led Talia out. "She's free to go."

"The doctor said I didn't show signs of a concussion. Other than bruising, I'm good to go." She smiled up at Reed. "Let's get back to the B&B. We don't want to miss the séance."

Reed's brow wrinkled. "I think we should see about getting a room in town."

"No way," Talia said. "I came for the ghosts. I'm staying."

"It's completely up to you two," Molly said. "I'll refund your money and everything."

"You advertised the best orange-marmalade salmon in Oregon. I wouldn't miss that for anything. I'll just be careful around stairs from now on." She nodded toward Molly. "At least I didn't end up on crutches."

Molly gave her a brief smile. "There is that. But I don't like the idea that someone might have pushed us. I really should call this whole thing off."

"Oh, please don't. I very well could have tripped. I've been known to be clumsy." She hooked her arm through Reed's elbow. "Come on. We should get back. The doctor said there was a storm coming and that it's already starting to sprinkle."

Just what they needed. Molly would have groaned if she didn't have to pretend that everything would be fine. Hell, everything wasn't fine. Her world was coming apart and even the weather was scheming against her.

As they exited the emergency room, the sky opened up, splattering rain on them. Reed ran for his vehicle and drove around to collect Talia. Once she was loaded and on her way, Nova turned to Molly.

"Stay here. I'll get the car."

"No. I don't mind a little rain."

Unable to run, Molly propelled herself forward on her

crutches. Halfway to the vehicle, she was drenched and wondering why she hadn't just let Nova get the SUV.

A step ahead of her, Nova reached the vehicle first, opened the door and held it while she leaned the crutches against the back door and slid into the seat.

Nova stowed the crutches and rounded the SUV, climbing in, rain dripping from his hair and chin. Once out of the rain, he switched on the engine and turned the heater to warm. Though it was summer, the rain blowing in off the Pacific was cool; the air temperature had dropped fifteen degrees.

Molly sat in her seat, shivering. "Would I be a cop-out if I said drive until you run out of gas?"

"No, you'd be justified." His lips twisted. "Just say the word and we'll hit the road to somewhere else."

"You'd do that for me?" Her heart warmed along with her face as the heater took the chill out of the air.

"You bet."

She leaned her head back on her seat and pretended the sheets of rain blocked out the rest of the world. That if she wanted, she could disappear and forget about someone trying to terrorize her and Nova. After several moments, she sat up, eyes wide open. "I don't know how agents do it. How do you live with so much uncertainty?"

"It's part of the job. Sometimes we know who the bad guys are. Other times, we have to figure it out."

"This is one of those times you have to figure it out."

"Right." He reached out to take her hand, weaving his fingers through hers. "Preferably before someone else gets hurt."

"Or dies," she whispered, knowing that was on his mind, with all the reminders of his lost love. "We should get going. This rain is only going to get worse, and I have supper to prepare for my hungry guests."

"One of which is a problem."

"Yeah, but we don't know which one."

"Maybe we should ask Rose and Ian to point him out." Nova chuckled. "If they did that, I might start believing in ghosts."

"Be careful what you wish for. Ian and Rose just might surprise both of us."

As Nova drove the road along the cliffs toward the B&B, Molly clung to the armrest, wishing for the first time she didn't live so far out of town on such a dangerous road.

Then again, the road might be the least dangerous thing she had to worry about.

Chapter 11

A strange vehicle was parked beside the others at the B&B when Nova pulled up with Molly. Through the blurred, rain-drenched windshield, he counted the lights shining from the downstairs windows and some of the rooms upstairs. Darkness was settling in early with the storm hovering along the coast, soaking the roads, forests and land.

Lightning illuminated the clouds from within, the answering rumble of thunder warning Nova to get inside before the electrical storm caught up with the rain over Cape Churn.

He leaped from the vehicle and ran around the other side as Molly threw open her door. Before she could get out, he scooped her up and ran for the porch.

"Thanks," she said as he deposited her near a porch column. "You don't have to carry me everywhere, you know."

"I know." He grinned, turned and ran back to the SUV for her crutches. When he made it back to the porch, his shirt was soaked.

"Let's get some dry clothes on, then I have to get supper on the stove. I think Siobhan is here and I promised her dinner in return for our séance."

Nova handed the crutches to Molly and shook the water out of his hair before entering the manor.

A woman with jet-black hair and ice-blue eyes rose from a wing-back chair. "Ah, Molly, I'm glad you made it in safely. I was worried about you."

"Siobhan, I hope you beat the storm out here."

"I did. It had started sprinkling about the time I pulled into the drive." Siobhan wore the kind of outfit Nova would expect of someone who was to conduct a séance.

A russet corset was cinched tightly over a tiny waist. A matching russet skirt, overlaid with black lace, draped in handkerchief style around her knees. She wore some kind of separate sleeves of black lace that hung down like those on a wizard's robe. Nova couldn't help thinking that she could hide a machine gun in all that fabric.

She turned a warm, black-lipsticked smile on Nova. "I'm sorry, we haven't had the pleasure." She held out a pale hand tipped with black lacquer polish that matched her lips.

"Casanova Valdez." He took her hand, surprised at the strength of her grip. Her pale skin and diminutive body disguised the inner command of the woman.

Her light blue eyes twinkled. "I'm going to bet you don't believe in ghosts and séances. Am I right?"

"Let's just say I'm not a big fan of the practice."

"Perhaps after tonight you will be more open-minded?" Her black eyebrows winged upward.

"We'll see," he said.

"He'll take a lot of convincing." Molly grinned. "If you'll excuse us, we need to dry off and get to work on supper before my guests declare mutiny."

"Take your time." Siobhan waved her hand, her flowing sleeve adding drama to the movement. "I had a late lunch."

When Nova bent to scoop Molly into his arms, she held up her hand.

"I'll manage the stairs on my own, thank you."

Nova experienced a twinge of disappointment, but he nodded. "I'll change in the bathroom on this level. Yell if you need help getting down the staircase."

Siobhan's gaze darted from Molly to Nova, her lips curling as if she knew a secret.

Nova grabbed the duffel bag he'd stashed behind the couch and headed for the bathroom. He wasn't sure what to think about Siobhan. He wanted to think she was a bit of a flake, but his gut told him not to underestimate the woman. Behind the dramatic makeup and black lipstick was an astute woman who saw more than she let on.

The séance might prove more interesting than he'd originally anticipated. At the very least, it would be entertaining with Siobhan at the helm.

Inside the bathroom, he pulled his shirt over his head, tossing it over the towel rack to dry. Then he unzipped his jeans and started to drag them down his legs when he felt the prongs of the hair comb digging into his leg.

Fishing the rhinestone comb from his pocket, he

laid it on the counter, staring at it as he stripped off the rest of his clothing.

He climbed into the shower, rinsed under hot water, thinking the entire time, going over all the participants in the ghost-hunting weekend. Who were they? What connection did they have to him and to Cardeña or Bolivia?

Not one of them had an accent and he wasn't sure if any of them spoke Spanish. Could one of them be a drug runner who received shipments from Cardeña? So many questions remained up in the air with only one thing clear.

He was the target and his association with Molly made her a target, as well. If he'd left last night, perhaps she wouldn't have been hurt. But because he'd stayed and made love to her, whoever was out to make his life hell would now use Molly to increase the intensity of his hell.

It was too late to leave now. He'd already sealed Molly's involvement. If he left, he'd leave her exposed and temporarily crippled. His only course of action was to find out who was behind the attacks and neutralize the threat.

His determination solidified, he dressed quickly, stashed the comb in his duffel and exited the bathroom as Molly was inching her way down the stairs, working with one crutch and holding on to the railing.

Her bright gold hair was still wet, combed back and tucked into a neat French braid. She'd changed out of her sundress into a seafoam green dress that floated in layers around her hips, complementing her hair and changing the green of her eyes to a softer, bluer color.

The difference between Molly and Sophia struck

him again. Molly was all light and sunshine, even on a cloudy, stormy day. Sophia was sultry, dark and secretive.

He found it strange that Molly lightened his heart simply with her presence. Her warmth and goodness helped to dispel the darkness he'd carried around for years.

Nova found himself wanting to stay with this woman, to be included in her life, even to live in the old manor that she fought so hard to preserve.

Molly limped over to him. "Should I change?"

He shook his head. "No. Why?"

"You frowned at me the entire time I was coming down the stairs." Her lips curled upward. "I thought I had something on my dress."

"You look beautiful." He swallowed hard at the sudden lump forming in his throat.

"And that's a reason for you to frown?" Molly laughed. "Next time, I'll come down in my sweats and a ragged T-shirt."

"You'd be just as beautiful. And that's the problem." He hooked her arm and steered her toward the dining room. "Come on, we have dinner to cook."

The dining room was a hive of activity. Josh was setting up a camera at one end of the room, while Anita adjusted the lens on one at the other end.

"I assumed we'd have the séance in the dining room around the table." Josh glanced up from twisting the clamps on the tripod legs of his camera. "Siobhan said that was her preference."

Molly glanced at Siobhan.

She stood in the corner of the room, a smile tugging at the corners of her lips. "I prefer to do the sé-ance around a table, if that's okay by you?"

"Absolutely," Molly agreed. "As soon as dinner's over and the plates are cleared, we can begin. We'll be in the kitchen if anyone needs anything."

Lightning lit up the windows and a clap of thunder sounded so close it made the crystals on the chandelier over the dining table rattle.

Molly hurried into the kitchen and started unloading the salmon from the refrigerator, balancing on her one foot while carrying a large tray of fillets.

"I'll get that. You tell me what to do and I'll do it." Nova took the tray from her hands and set it on the worktable in the center of the kitchen.

"For someone who's a disaster in the kitchen, I could get used to having you around." Molly reached into the pantry for orange marmalade, soy sauce and the canister of a long-grain-and-wild-rice mix.

Within minutes they had rice steaming, the salmon seasoned and in the large oven, and raw spinach leaves, romaine lettuce and apples on the cutting board.

They worked in relative silence, Nova thinking about all that had happened, wanting to be out among the guests, watching for any moves that would pinpoint one of them as the person responsible for the troubles they'd experienced from the moment they'd arrived.

A chunk of apple rolled off the counter and dropped to the floor. When Nova bent to pick it up, his head nearly collided with Molly's, who'd reached for it at the same time.

"I got it." He rose slowly, inhaling Molly's perfume, or rather lack of perfume.

Molly smelled clean, like citrus-scented shampoo

and sunshine. Her bare feet dangled above the floor, having kicked off her sandals while she sat on the stool beside the worktable.

He wanted to touch her, to trace his fingers along the curve of her calves to the tender skin on the insides of her thighs.

When he straightened, he stood close enough he could easily claim a kiss. And he wanted to. Badly. Still, he hesitated.

Her tongue darted out to wet her lips, making them shine and all the more tempting. "Why don't you just kiss me?" she whispered. "You know you want to."

"I can't."

"Can't or won't?" She set the knife she'd been using down on the cutting board and reached out, curling her fingers into the collar of his shirt. "Would it help if said I wanted it, too?"

"No." He groaned, knowing it was useless to fight the inevitable, when he'd end up kissing her, anyway. Nova tossed the piece of apple into the trash and gathered Molly in his arms. "This is why you're being targeted."

"I get that."

"By making love to you, I put you in harm's way." His lips hovered over hers.

"I didn't want to be attracted to you. I'm not into one-night stands, but—"

"One kiss wasn't enough," he finished for her.

"I know, right?" She trailed a finger along the side of his cheek. So soft and intimate.

"I want more." He spoke his thoughts aloud.

"Who's stopping you?" Molly leaned closer, her breath warm on his lips.

"Me."

"Then get out of the way." She laced her fingers behind his neck and pulled him nearer, sealing her lips over his, her tongue darting, pushing between his teeth, sliding the length of his.

She tasted like heaven. Sweet like the fruit-filled pastries she'd rolled out on the pastry sheet. Salty like the soy sauce she'd added to the rice. Better than anything he'd ever known.

A sharp *thunk* jerked Nova out of heaven into reality. The sound had come from behind him. He spun to see who it was.

There was no one there. Just the wall with pots, pans and utensils hanging from hooks.

"What was that?" Molly asked, peering around him.

"I don't know." He checked to ensure the door leading outside from the kitchen was secure and locked. The cellar door stood open from when he'd had to force the lock to get Molly out earlier that day. He descended into the cellar and made a quick pass. No one was down there and nothing looked out of place.

"Nova?" Molly's voice sounded from up in the kitchen. "You should come up here."

Something in her voice made him take the steps two at a time.

Molly stood in front of the wall with the pots, pans and utensils on the far side of the kitchen, staring at something protruding out of the Sheetrock that he hadn't noticed before.

Molly turned toward him. "That's one of my steak knives."

He glanced at the knife and then back at the direction it must have come from. The swinging door into the dining room rocked gently on its hinges.

Had he or Molly been even an inch over from where they'd been kissing, one of them would have been hit by the flying knife. And it had been thrown hard enough to bury a couple inches in the drywall.

Nova ran for the dining room and flung the door open.

Lightning flashed through the windows and thunder clapped hard, shaking the chandelier again. The dining room was empty. He followed the sound of gasps and voices to the front of the manor and the open entry door, where all eight of the guests and Siobhan stood on the porch, just out of reach of the rain.

"Mr. Valdez, you have to see this." Anita grasped his arm and pulled him out onto the porch. "It's beautiful."

Lightning feathered the sky, spreading across the clouds in thin, jagged bolts. The answering thunder rumbled on and on as if it would never end. Before the thunder tapered off, another bolt shot out like a spiderweb of electricity.

Nova could see it in his peripheral vision, but he wasn't concerned with the deadly lightning. He scanned the faces of the group, looking for the one guilty of throwing a knife that could have seriously injured Molly.

All gazes were turned toward the sky. No one looked back at him.

He waited patiently for one of them to turn. The first one to look back at him was Anita, her eyes alight, a smile spread across her face. "Isn't this perfect weather for a séance?"

"The electric energy in the air should have the spirits stirred," Siobhan agreed. "It is a good night for a séance."

Another bolt of lightning was followed immediately by a loud clap of thunder. The lights in the house flickered off and on.

With no indication as to who had thrown the knife, Nova wasn't taking any more chances by leaving Molly alone. He hurried back into the house.

She leaned on one crutch with an oven mitt over one hand, about to pull the salmon out of the oven.

The aroma of soy sauce, oranges and salmon filled the air.

"It's done. As soon as we can fill the plates, we can eat."

"Doesn't anything bother you?" he asked her.

She nodded. "Hell, yes." She turned toward the oven, muttering, "You do. Far too much for my own good."

"I heard that." He took the oven mitt from her and removed the salmon from the oven, placing it on a trivet.

"A lot of what's happened bothers me. But I can't let it stop me." Molly adjusted the temperature on the oven and Nova slid the tray of pastries in.

"Could you serve the salads while I make a bed of rice on the plates?" Molly asked.

"First tell me where you keep your laptop with the webcam."

She nodded toward a counter on the far side of the kitchen. "Over there."

He crossed the room and found the device, booted it, and carried it and the electrical cord into the still-empty dining room. Within minutes, he had the laptop positioned on a shelf in the buffet, half-hidden by a large serving platter, giving the camera a clear view of the room. He'd tucked the power cord behind the porcelain cups and bowls and down to an electrical outlet on the wall.

When he'd finished he headed back to the kitchen, the guests filtering into the dining room behind him.

Molly handed him a tray loaded with the small bowls filled with spinach salad with apple chunks, sprinkled with a balsamic-raisin vinaigrette. He took the tray into the dining room and set a salad bowl in front of each seat at the long table.

Molly had busily been laying out plates, placing a scoop of long-grain-and-wild-rice mix in the middle of each of them.

"Okay, it's your turn." She showed him how to lift a portion of salmon off the pan and lay it over the bed of rice. Then she handed him the spatula.

He'd never been much use in the kitchen, but working with Molly he found he liked preparing food and making it look as good as it tasted. One by one he transferred the mouthwatering orange salmon to their beds of rice. Molly came along behind him and added a smear of orange marmalade across the fillets and a dash of soy sauce to the rice.

"I'll get these out there while they're hot," Nova said.

"All I have left to do is wait on the pastries and then we can join them."

Nova loaded the plates onto two trays and ducked into the dining room.

When he returned to the kitchen with the tray full of

empty salad bowls, he traded the empties for the second tray of dinner plates and left the kitchen.

Back again, he caught Molly trying to remove the hot tray of pastries from the oven. "Let me." He grabbed a spare oven mitt and slid the pan of desserts out onto a rack to cool.

All the food made his stomach rumble. How could he be so hungry when someone was trying to hurt Molly?

"Too worried to eat?" she asked.

"I should be. But I can always eat. Especially when it looks this good." He helped Molly remove her apron by untying the back, surreptitiously admiring the curve of her backside beneath the frothy layers of her pretty dress. He grabbed her around the middle and hauled her back against him. "You are entirely too beautiful."

"Sure. I bet you say that to all the girls you leave behind." Though Molly's words were flippant, Nova suspected there was a harder edge to their meaning.

He'd left his share of women behind, careful never to fall in love or risk staying long enough for the women to fall in love with him. Thus his reputation as a ladies' man. Since Sophia had died in his arms, he'd been very cautious about putting another woman in danger because of his job.

When he'd first eyed Molly, he'd only thought of a little flirtation. He'd have been well on his way back to D.C. by now if his brakes hadn't failed and if he'd restrained himself from taking advantage of the beautiful B&B owner by kissing her. And she wouldn't have been in the danger she was now.

"I need to get into the rooms of your guests and see

if there's anything that indicates one of them is responsible for all that's happened."

"I'm sorry. I can't let you do that." Molly shook her head. "That would be violating their privacy."

"Pretend I'm the cleaning lady—whatever you need to tell yourself to get over that. Someone is trying to kill us. I want to know who."

"I can't."

"Molly, what if something happens to one of your guests?"

She chewed on her lip for a few moments. "I can't give you the master key, but if you were to find it in the top drawer of my dresser, I wouldn't be the wiser."

He grinned and pressed a kiss to the tip of her nose. "You're an amazing woman."

Her cheeks pinkened. "Not so much with a sprained ankle."

"Come on. You need to get off your feet."

"Foot," she corrected. With the help of one crutch and his arm, she entered the dining room and took her seat at the end of the table.

Nova sat beside her and they ate their meal.

The conversation around the table centered on the upcoming séance and the chance of connecting with Rose and Ian McGregor.

"Do you think Ian pushed Rose?" Anita asked, then took a bite of salmon.

"Was Ian the ghost who pushed you, Molly?" Preston asked. "He wouldn't have, had he known how good this salmon was."

"The meal is lovely," Siobhan added. "Well worth one little séance, if you ask me." She smiled. "I don't suppose you want to make the séance or palm reading a regular event here at the B&B, while I'm here during the summer?"

Molly smiled at Siobhan. "I think we could work out a trade. Have you tried my clam chowder?"

"Last year." She pressed a hand to her chest. "It was to die for."

"Please." Molly trembled. "Nothing's that good."

"I don't know. Some people are willing to die for love. Do you suppose Rose and Ian died for love?" Talia nodded at the basket of bread rolls. "Reed, could you pass the rolls, *por favor?*"

Reed handed her the basket, his gaze practically worshiping Talia. "Love of a person is a little higher in importance than love of food."

"Not to some." Anita laughed. "I swear my brother would just as soon stab you as let you have the last slice of barbecue brisket on a tray."

A slash of lightning brightened the room, thunder making the silverware on the plates rattle. And then the electricity went off.

Nova held his breath in the pitch-black and listened for movement, wondering if their attacker would make a move. If so, he'd be ready. Fists tightened, he waited for anything that sounded like trouble.

When the lights blinked out, Molly's breath caught and she waited for something horrible to happen. When it didn't, she forced starch into her backbone and continued on, business as usual. *No use borrowing trouble,* her mother would have said. It would find her soon enough.

"Looks like we'll be finishing our meal in the dark."

One woman, who sounded like Mel Wilkins, laughed, her voice shaking.

Given all the uncertainty of the last night and the day at the library, Molly empathized with Mel. She felt the same, but she couldn't show it. Not with someone playing her to get a reaction or worse.

"No, we'll finish it as we should have started...by candlelight." Molly pushed her chair back and rose to her feet. The soft bump of the rubber stopper on her crutch sounded across the floor. She walked with a hand held out, feeling for the antique buffet set against the wall. When her fingers encountered wood, she ran them across the front, slid open a drawer and felt around for the box of matches she kept there for lighting candles. Taking out one wooden match, she ran it across the coarse side of the box, the sound loud in the expectant silence. The little glow from a match head added to the lightning show outside, as Molly lit several candles in the candelabras on the table.

Soon the room was filled with the warm yellow light of burning, scented candles, chasing away the boogeyman in the dark. At least for the most part.

Anita clapped her hands. "Beautiful."

Nova rose, took one of the long candles and lit the other candelabra at the opposite end of the long table. When both had been safely lit, Molly returned to her seat and pretended to finish her meal. The loss of power plus the fear of what might happen next killed her appetite. She pushed food around on her plate, disappointed that she couldn't enjoy the wonderful meal she'd planned and had Nova's help preparing.

Nova finished before her, picked up the empty plates and carried them into the kitchen without Molly prompting him. She was grateful for all his help. She bet he hadn't known how hard it was to prepare meals for a group this large, but he'd been a good sport and followed all her instructions to a T.

Anita and Preston rose and gathered more plates from the table, as well.

When Molly attempted to stand, Anita raised her hand. "Let us. You've been on your feet enough today."

Nova, Preston and Anita made multiple trips in and out of the kitchen until the table was cleared of dinner plates, wineglasses and the remaining salad bowls.

"Dessert first or séance?" Molly asked.

"I don't know. The pastries in the kitchen looked amazing," Anita said. "But I'm still full from dinner. Let's do the séance."

The rest of the group nodded in agreement.

"Siobhan?" Molly glanced at the woman.

She sat straight in her chair, her face serene. "I'm ready whenever you are. I just need to get my bag and set up a few things. I'll need a picture of the person or people you want to summon."

"We're summoning Ian and Rose McGregor. You can find their picture in the gilded frame on the mantel in the great room." Molly glanced at Nova.

He nodded. "I'll get it."

Josh leaped from his chair. "Could you give me a few minutes to get the positioning right on the video recorders?"

"Why don't we all take a fifteen-minute break?" Molly said. "That will give Josh time with his equipment, our medium to get set up, and it will give me time to straighten up the kitchen."

The group, sans Josh, adjourned to the great room,

where Nova got a fire going in the fireplace. With the electricity still off, Molly carried one of the candles with her into the kitchen, balancing on her crutch. She kept a collection of candles in the pantry for just such an occasion. As secluded as the mansion was, it wasn't unusual for a storm to knock out the electricity and for the county electric cooperative to take their time restoring it. Lighting several candles, she placed them around the room and went to work on cleaning the dishes.

Nova had scraped and stacked the plates in a sink full of soapy water. The man was entirely too helpful. She really should consider hiring an assistant when he was gone. Not that anyone could possibly replace Nova.

The thought of Nova leaving made her chest hurt. She'd known him only a few days and yet she felt as if she'd known him a lot longer. Heck, they'd already been through so much: the man had carried her up and down the stairs, they'd made love and they'd nearly been stabbed with a knife.

For the first time in two years, she hadn't compared the man she was seeing with Bill. Not that she'd seen anyone since Bill, though she'd considered a couple of the local men but ultimately dismissed them. With the B&B to run, she'd been too busy. And she wouldn't be seeing much more of Nova. He'd be gone when the trouble went away.

She took less than ten minutes to wash the plates. She'd leave the glasses for later. After drying her hands on a hand towel, she stepped back out into the dining room.

The guests had taken seats around the table. Talia stood near the middle of the table, arguing quietly with

Reed. "No, I want to sit closer to Siobhan, where I sat earlier."

"Can't you take one of the empty seats?" Reed was urging.

"No. I can't hear well enough. I have to sit closer to the medium."

Anita glanced over her shoulder. "I'm sorry, Talia, did I take your seat?" She rose and offered the seat to Talia. "I'll sit in the middle. It doesn't matter to me."

Talia took the seat and smiled at Anita. "Thank you. I think the fall down the stairs must have affected my hearing."

Anita shrugged. "I don't mind at all."

Molly took the seat beside Anita and crossed her fingers in preparation of telling her half-truth. "Mr. Valdez said to start without him. He wanted to add wood to the fireplace and then make a call to the electric company."

"Okay, then," Siobhan said. "Let's get started by blowing out the candles in the candelabra."

Molly took a breath and blew out the candles closest to her, the lightning choosing that moment to illuminate the room. Her stomach seized. In that moment, even the storm seemed to be warning her that trouble was brewing.

Siobhan raised her hands and slowly lowered them to the table. She'd set out three candles and an incense holder, burning sandalwood incense. The miniature portrait of Ian and Rose McGregor lay on the table beside the candles, their faces ghostly in the limited lighting. "Join hands, please."

"This is so cool," Anita tittered. "A Siobhan séance.

Wait until I tell the folks who couldn't come. They'll all be so jealous. I'm so glad I got the time off."

"Shh." Josh frowned across the table at Anita. "Let her start. We're on video."

Molly held out her hands, taking Anita's on one side and Preston's on the other.

"When all hands are joined, we form a circle. No matter what happens, don't break the circle or we could lose contact. Do you understand?" Siobhan glanced around the room, her gaze connecting with those of the participants until she received a nod from each of them.

Seemingly satisfied, she closed her eyes. "Let us have a moment of silence to gather our thoughts and focus on those confined to the spirit world."

The participants grew still and silent. Some closed their eyes. Molly kept hers open, watching the faces of the others, trying to discern who was the liar, the fake, the one who'd come to McGregor B&B not for the ghost hunters' weekend but to get to Nova.

It had to be someone who'd joined the party late. Someone who'd been following him, perhaps heard he was in town and having dinner at the B&B. Molly mentally ticked off the names of the people who'd registered at the last minute. Anita and Preston had joined the group, taking the place of the two people who'd had to drop out.

Molly held their hands, wishing she could tell by someone's grip if they were a threat to Nova, her or others of the group.

Most of the guests were from a Seattle ghost-hunting group. Only Talia had called the day the event was to start, asking if there were any spaces left. She'd said she'd always wanted to spend the night in a haunted house.

Molly glanced down the table where Talia held Siobhan's hand, her eyes closed, eyelids twitching. She'd been the recipient of one of the attacks, which ruled her out of the list of suspects.

It didn't make sense for any of the group to be there specifically to terrorize Nova; he hadn't been in the area more than a week following the operation he, Nicole and Creed Thomas had conducted to stop a terrorist. Who would have known he was even there?

After a long pause, the medium spoke softly, barely above a whisper. "We must chant together to call the spirits of Ian and Rose McGregor. Please repeat the chant with me. *Spirits of those who walked before us, come toward the light of this world. We call upon Ian and Rose. Come among us.*"

She started again, the room full of people joining in this time, making the chant fuller, richer, more intense with the combination of voices, low and high.

"Spirits of those who walked before us, come toward the light of this world. We call upon Ian and Rose. Come among us."

Molly chanted with the rest, clearing her mind of all the thoughts of conspiracy and terror. She focused on the words of the chant and the image of Ian and Rose in the miniature portrait in front of Siobhan.

The storm continued to rage outside, lightning acting like a strobe light, adding to the soft glow of the candles with the harsh flash of electricity shooting through the clouds. Thunder shook the ceiling, the crystals on the chandelier above them clinking together.

A cold sensation swept across Molly's skin, raising gooseflesh on her arms.

"Keep chanting," Siobhan encouraged. "I feel something."

"Spirits of those who walked before us, come toward the light of this world. We call upon Ian and Rose. Come among us."

Molly felt it, too, her skin getting colder, her breath warming the air in front of her, condensing into tiny clouds with each puff, as if she stood in a walk-in freezer. Her mind didn't tag it as unusual; something inside her head told her it was okay, to stay put and listen and all would be revealed.

Molly's heart raced, but she remained in place, trusting the voices in her head.

Chapter 12

Nova used the excuse of refilling the logs in the fireplace and making a phone call to the electric company to get out of the séance. Surely with everyone in the room, whoever was causing problems would be busy and watched.

Not only would all be accounted for, but he'd have time to go through all the rooms and check for any evidence that would identify who might be after him. He didn't know what he was looking for. He hoped he'd know once he found it.

Using the master key he'd gotten from Molly's dresser, he started in the first room at the top of the stairs. If the séance ended early, he would have more time to exit unseen from the rooms at the end of the hallway.

He'd memorized the guest-register names and assigned room numbers. The first one he came to belonged to Anita White from Seattle. Printouts of the advertisement for the B&B ghost-hunting event lay on top of the dresser, with a printed date of the day before she'd arrived.

Anita had emptied her suitcase, placing her clothes in the drawers and closet, and stashed her suitcase beneath the bed. After a quick perusal of the drawers and pockets in her jackets and jeans, Nova checked her suitcase. It was clean except for an old luggage-handling tag from a trip to Cabo San Lucas, Mexico.

A trip to Cabo didn't necessarily mean she'd met up with Cardeña. Nova stored that bit of information in the back of his mind and moved on to the next door.

One after the other, he searched through the rooms, coming up empty. Near the end of the hallway, he entered Preston Todd's room and quickly went through the drawers and closet. The man had hung what he could and left the rest of his things in his suitcase on the floor, pushed up against the wall. When Nova opened the top, his blood froze. Inside was a small case. The kind used to transport a handgun.

The case had a lock on it. Nova lifted it. It felt heavy enough to have a gun inside. He set it aside and went through the rest of the suitcase. Besides the man's itinerary for the ghost-hunting weekend, dated a week prior, he found nothing else that could lead him to believe the man was one of Cardeña's hit men. Still, a man carrying a gun was one to be watched. The question was whether to leave the gun with Preston and risk it being used against himself or Molly, or take it and let the man come asking.

The last rooms at the end of the hallway were Reed's

and Talia's. He entered Talia's room first, going through her suitcase, finding nothing of interest. Her purse lay on the dresser.

Nova rifled through her wallet, pulling out her driver's license. The license had been issued three years ago and the picture didn't look much like the Talia downstairs. The one in the picture was heavier, which could account for a lot. Weight loss changed the shape of the face. In the picture, her hair was spiked, dyed dark brown with fuchsia tips. The woman downstairs had long, dark brown hair, no pink tips. Again, the picture was three years old. She could have grown out of that phase of odd-colored hair. He snapped a photograph of the driver's license using his smartphone camera.

The address on the license indicated she was from Portland, unlike Anita and most of the event-goers, who'd driven down from Seattle as part of an organized ghost-hunting group.

Also in the purse, he found a phone. He turned it on and waited for the device to boot, then for it to find enough reception. When it did, briefly, it chirped, indicating a missed call and a text message.

Nova snapped a photo of the phone numbers and the recent calls. He also snapped a picture of her most recent text messages. Then he turned off the phone and stowed it where he'd found it in the purse and replaced the purse exactly as he'd found it.

On the dresser, Talia had a printout of an email acknowledging her reservations for the ghost-hunting event. The printer time stamp read early the day before, but the emails dated over a week ago. Hers hadn't been a completely last-minute decision. She'd considered it a week ago.

The last room at the end of the hallway was assigned to Reed Schotzman.

Before he entered, Nova retraced his steps back down the hallway to the top of the stairs. The glow of the fireplace was the only light coming from the great room. He could hear chanting in the dining room but then it stopped and a soft voice barely carried to him. The séance was in full swing. He could easily finish the search and still get back in time to be there at the conclusion.

He headed back to Schotzman's room and switched on his flashlight as he went through the drawers. The man had put away his clothes, his socks and underwear neatly lining the drawers. Almost too neatly. OCD neat. His suitcase was zipped and stored in the closet. On the nightstand was a bottle of pills. Nova shone the light on the label. Lithium carbonate. He recognized the drug as one used to treat bipolar disorder.

Beside the bottle lay a skeleton key.

His heartbeat kicked up a notch and he fought to keep from running down the stairs to confront Reed about the key. After several deep, calming breaths, Nova walked to the bathroom and came back with a tissue. Using the tissue, Nova lifted the key from the nightstand, wrapped it gently and slid it into his pocket. If it was the key to the cellar, Reed had some explaining to do.

He searched the rest of the room and found a pair of binoculars and a cell phone. He turned on the cell phone and the display lit up. Nothing in the text messages connected him to Cardeña, but the pictures

proved interesting. There were a couple pictures of
the group and one of Molly and Nova standing together
outside the lighthouse. The last twenty or more were of
Talia, taken at odd angles, as if he didn't want her to
know he was taking pictures of her. One was a picture
of her taken through the open door of her bathroom.
Talia wore only her underwear and bra and appeared
to be unaware of anyone snapping her photo.

Nova set the phone back on the dresser exactly
where he'd found it and left the room, not liking what
he'd seen. One thing was certain: Reed needed to be
watched. When he had a chance to get him alone, he
planned to ask the man about the key. He wasn't sure
how he'd mention the photos. Based on what Royce had
reported, the man was known for stalking.

Molly held hands with Anita and Preston, but she
felt as if she weren't really a part of the circle, as if she
was floating above them, staring down at the people
gathered around the table in the dining room.

"Rose?" Siobhan spoke the name, her monotone
voice hypnotic. "If you are with us, give us a sign."

Lightning flashed and the thunder rumbled closer.
Only the center candle flickered as if someone blew
hard enough to extinguish it, but it came back burning brightly.

Anita gasped beside Molly.

Molly couldn't move. She felt as if her body were
held in stasis, as if it wasn't hers to command. Yet she
wasn't afraid. Whatever was holding her wasn't there
to harm her. She could sense a benevolent spirit moving through, around, beside and above her.

"Rose, is Ian with you?" Siobhan asked.

The center candle flickered again and burned brighter.

"We would like to know about your deaths," Siobhan said. "Did Ian push you over the edge of the cliff? Shake the candle's flame if yes."

Molly held her breath and waited for the candle flame to flicker. It didn't.

Ian hadn't pushed Rose to her death. Deep inside, Molly had known. How, she couldn't tell.

"Did someone else?" Siobhan asked.

The center candle's flame stood still for a moment. Molly could feel the spirit's hesitancy.

Then the middle flame flickered.

"She was murdered by someone else," Anita exclaimed. "Who?"

"Was it someone you knew?" Siobhan asked, ignoring Anita's excited words.

The middle candle's flame flickered.

Molly's heart beat faster, her skin cool but clammy. She felt as if she had been running through the fog, tiny droplets of mist clinging to her skin. When she closed her eyes, she could see the cliffs in front of her. McGregor Manor was behind her, completely hidden in the Devil's Shroud. And someone was out there between her and the house. She couldn't get around that person.

"Ian!" she called.

"I'm here," Ian whispered.

"Be careful," Molly warned. Ian's face shimmered in the fog, changing from the handsome gentleman in the portrait to the dark-skinned, dark-eyed Nova who'd made love to her the night before.

"Are you in the house, Rose?" Siobhan asked.

As if her voice didn't belong to her at all, Molly answered, "No." She didn't even sound like herself. Her normally clear, smooth voice was softer and higher pitched.

"Are you by the cliffs?"

"Yes." Molly's body shook, the cold seeping into her bones, the night getting darker, the fog thicker.

Ian called out, *"Rose!"*

He was too distant to help. The person following her emerged from the fog, dressed in a long cape, with a hood pulled up over his head.

"What do you want?" Molly whispered. "Leave me alone."

The cloaked individual pushed back the hood. A woman with deep russet hair and cold blue eyes glared at her. *"I want you to die."*

"Why?" Molly asked.

"Because you know my secret." The woman reached out and pushed her, shoving her over the edge of the cliff.

Molly could feel nothing but air all around her as she tumbled through space.

"You aren't going to die," a voice whispered to her.

"Rose?" Molly reached out, her hand tingling with the cold, still air. "Wait. What are you talking about?"

"You will live."

"Rose," she whispered, wanting her to stay, to tell her what she meant.

Her fall to the rocky base of the cliffs slowed and she floated in the air, unable to land, unable to move.

"Beware of people who aren't all that they seem."

"I don't understand." Molly's feet touched the ground and she could feel Rose slipping away, Ian following her.

As her world came back into view, Molly blinked.

Everyone was staring at her, their eyes wide.

Then the candles in front of Siobhan snuffed out.

Lightning lit up the dining room, thunder rattling the chandelier above her. Then a loud snap sounded; the crystals shook violently.

Molly's gut told her to move. She tried to stand, pushing to her feet so fast her chair tipped and fell backward, taking her with it. She slammed against her back, her head bouncing off the Persian rug, her vision blurring.

Another snap above and in the flash of lightning Molly caught a glimpse of the huge, old chandelier falling toward her.

"Get back!" she yelled.

Before anyone could move, the chandelier crashed down on the table, crushing the candelabras and scattering broken crystals over the tabletop, floors and the stunned group of people. Those at the far ends of the table remained out of harm's way, but those in the center were showered with glass.

Ironically, the lights in other parts of the house blinked back on.

"Don't move!" Molly pushed her hands against the floor, shards of razor-sharp broken crystal lodged in her palm, and she cried out.

"You should follow your own advice." Nova appeared at her side and bent to lift her away from the table and broken crystal. He carried her into the great room and sat her on the couch, then went back for the others.

Nova helped the men assist the women out of the dining room.

Reed held Talia's elbow, helping her step over the crystals.

"Rose took possession of her body." Talia pointed at Molly. "I'm right, aren't I? And Ian tried to kill her again."

Molly blinked, her head clearing from the strange and disastrous séance. Had Rose been inside her, trying to tell her story?

Josh came rushing out of the dining room, carrying his camera, his face alight. "I got it all on infrared video. Everything."

Anita, led by Preston, carried the other video camera. "From what I could tell, we got it all on full spectrum, as well." She was scratched and bleeding on her arms, but smiling. "This is going to be great. We made contact!"

Nova escorted the last person out of the dining room and went to Molly. "What happened in there?" he asked.

Siobhan brushed fine shards of glass off her long sleeves. "I'll tell you what happened. Rose and Ian were with us."

Nova only gave her a brief glance, then gripped Molly's arms. "Are you okay?"

She rubbed the back of her head with her unhurt hand, feeling better than she should have. "I guess. It was all so strange."

"You don't know the half of it," Nova grumbled. "Is your first-aid kit still in the bathroom?"

"It should be." She let him pull her to her feet, holding on to her arms, then leaned on him as she hopped toward the bathroom. Once inside, she pointed to the cabinet where she kept it. "In there."

Nova pulled out the plastic box and went to work with tweezers, plucking glass from her palm, cleaning and bandaging her hand.

Molly was amazed at his cool efficiency and troubled by something he'd said. "What did you mean I don't know the half of it?"

"I checked the chain that held the chandelier. A ghost didn't drop that chandelier on the table. The chain holding it was deliberately cut. It was hanging on by a single electrical wire until the thunder rattled the building and shook it loose."

Her blood chilled in her veins. "Who had access and was capable of cutting it?"

"We were gone all day." Nova's eyes narrowed. "Except when you, me and Reed were at the hospital with Talia."

"Six of the participants came back early." Molly tried to think, her head still muzzy from what she suspected was a visit from prior inhabitants of McGregor Manor. "Could it have been one of them?"

"Josh and Anita aren't all that upset by the chandelier's fall."

"I'm calling my brother." Molly tried to go around him, forgetting that her ankle was still sore. She gasped when she put pressure on it.

"Not so fast." Nova's arm crept around her waist. "I agree to having your brother out here, but make it seem like he's come to help with the chandelier as your brother and co-owner of the B&B." Nova checked his phone for a signal. It barely had two bars, but it might be enough to place the call. He handed her his smartphone.

Molly made the call to Gabe, quietly explaining what had happened and her need for discretion.

"Got it. I'll be there in eight minutes," he said.

When Molly handed the phone back to Nova, their hands touched and that same electric current rippled through her that had the first night.

It must have struck him, too. He pocketed his phone with one hand while grasping her outstretched hand with his free one. "I wish I was here under different circumstances."

Her lips twisting into a wry grin, Molly squeezed his fingers. "If nothing had gone amiss, you wouldn't be here at all."

He nodded. "You're right."

"And we have a potential killer lurking within the walls of this B&B. He's already made three attempts on others. You, me and Talia. I can't sit around and wait for him to make good on the next attempt."

"I agree." Nova sighed. "When else could someone have cut that chain?"

Molly thought back to the beginning of the day, which seemed like such a long time ago. "You know, I remember someone arriving after us at the lighthouse tour. Was it Reed and Talia?"

Nova closed his eyes. "Could have been. Didn't they park after the rest of the crew?"

"Yes. But Talia was pushed in the old jailhouse. She's just as much a victim as you and I. It doesn't make sense."

"None of this makes sense. I found Talia's cell phone in her suitcase." Nova pulled out his smartphone and scrolled to his saved pictures, displaying Talia's driver's license, missed calls and the text message. "She had five text messages from a T. Pullman. He or she said, 'It'll be tomorrow before I can join you.'"

"I thought she was with Reed."

"Maybe T. Pullman is one of her friends."

"Could be. She didn't mention a plus-one in her reservation." Molly thought back to the first day Reed and Talia arrived. She had to admit they didn't seem to know each other. Perhaps Reed had felt sorry for her, since she was the only one not from the Seattle ghost-hunting group.

"I found this." He pulled the key out of his pocket.

"My cellar-door key." She grabbed for it. "Where did you find it?"

"In Reed's room."

Molly fought the urge to march into the kitchen and demand to know why the hell he'd locked her in the cellar and pocketed the key.

Nova's lips twitched on the corners. "I wouldn't confront him."

"But he locked me in the cellar."

"You might casually pull out the key and see what his reaction is. Body language tells a lot more than words sometimes."

She nodded. "Agreed. But I'd still like to tell him what I think about a man who locks a woman in the basement."

"Perhaps there's something even more disconcerting."

"What could be more disconcerting than finding the key to the cellar in a guest's room?"

"I found a gun in Preston's room."

Just when Molly thought things couldn't get worse. "A gun?"

"Yes, but don't worry. I confiscated it and put it in your room beneath your bed."

"What if he asks where it is?"

"Tell him to talk to me."

"Oh, I don't like this." Molly wrung her hands. "I'm not cut out for spy business or lying."

"Would you rather he kept a loaded gun in your home? What if your assailant got ahold of it? Or worse, what if Preston *is* the assailant?"

"Wouldn't he have used the gun by now if he was going to?" God forbid someone should start shooting in the manor. She'd thought being pushed down the stairs was bad enough.

"Not necessarily. I have a feeling whoever it is likes playing with us and is trying to scare us."

"He's succeeding." A chill rippled down Molly's back. "But why?"

"Because of me and what happened in Bolivia."

"Why now? It's been two years."

"I don't know."

"Well, when you find out, let me know. In the meantime, I have a dining room to clean up before I go to bed." Not that she'd sleep under these conditions. And despite how tired she was, the dining room wasn't going to clean itself. She entered the great room, leaning on her crutch and carrying the first-aid kit. "Anyone need this?"

Anita held out her hand. "I could use a disinfectant wipe and a bandage."

When all the guests had been taken care of, Molly pasted a smile on her face. "If you all would like a pastry, you can gather in the kitchen. I have coffee brewing. Thank goodness no one was badly hurt."

"I'm all for pastries," Josh said. "With the video footage I got, I feel the need to celebrate. The network *has* to air this. It's amazing."

"I know, right?" Anita and Josh took one of the candles Nova had lit from the mantel and eased around the mess in the dining room to reach the other side and the swinging door into the kitchen.

The storm's intensity had shifted to a steady rain, the lightning and thunder diminishing, moving farther inland, taking the lightning and noise with it.

"Molly, I have to head back to Cape Churn before it gets too much later." Siobhan gathered the bag she'd carried in.

"What about your candles and incense?"

"If they are salvageable, you can keep them for the next time I come."

"You'd come back? After all that drama?"

Siobhan stared hard at Molly. "I know you felt Rose and Ian. I felt them, too. I'd like to visit with them again, if you don't mind my coming out."

"You're always welcome," Molly said. "And thank you."

Leaning on one crutch, Molly saw Siobhan to the door, and Nova held an umbrella and walked her the rest of the way out to her car.

Headlights reflected in Molly's eyes as Gabe's SUV pulled into the driveway. He got out and spoke briefly to Siobhan and Nova.

Siobhan backed up and drove away.

Gabe, dressed in jeans and cowboy boots, followed Nova up the porch steps.

"Hey, sis." He gathered her in his arms, giving her

a brief hug. "I hear you've had a little excitement here tonight." His gaze bore into hers.

"I'm okay. Things are just a bit nutty around here right now."

"Want me to set up camp?"

"No, I have Nova." Molly glanced at the man beside her brother, realizing how dependent she'd become on his support and protection. "At least until this ordeal is over."

In a quiet voice, Nova explained all that had happened and his theory of why.

When Nova was done, Gabe frowned and focused his attention on Molly. "I really think you need to send all these people home and come stay at the lighthouse cottage for a few days until this dies down."

"Can't." Molly shook her head, her lips pressing into a tight line. "Whoever is doing this can't get away with it."

"And you're willing to risk your life to stop him?" Gabe asked.

She crossed her arms over her chest. "He's pissed me off."

"What if one of your guests gets hurt?" Gabe asked.

A wad of guilt lodged in Molly's chest, and she let her arms fall to her sides. "I'll ask if anyone wants to leave again. Last time I did, they all wanted to stay. Apparently, the ghost vibes are strong and they will risk a little danger to get their paranormal fix." When Gabe opened his mouth to say something else, Molly raised her hand. "I said I'll ask."

They entered the house. Muffled laughter came from the direction of the kitchen.

"I'd like to get a look at that cut chain first," Gabe said.

"I'll go offer to make tea or something to keep the guests in the kitchen a bit longer." Molly limped through the mess on the dining-room floor and eased through the swinging door into the kitchen.

"And when the chandelier fell in the middle of the table, I almost had a heart attack," Anita was saying. "The best part is it's all on film." She pointed at Josh. "You should see your face on the full-spectrum video. It's hilarious."

Reed frowned. "I don't see why it's so funny. That chandelier had to weigh fifty pounds or more. Someone could have gotten seriously hurt."

"Yeah. I almost sat where Molly sat," Mel said, pressing a hand to her chest.

"My brother is here to help with the cleanup. Can I get anyone coffee, tea or hot cocoa?" Molly asked.

"I'd like some tea," Talia said, her hand absently running over the chopping knife Molly had left on the counter. "I hope it calms me. I can't imagine sleeping after all the excitement."

"Molly, you were answering questions Siobhan was asking to Rose." A woman named Barbara approached her. "Was that all part of the show?"

"Show?" Molly laughed. "I wish it was *all part of the show.*" She paused on her way with the teakettle to the sink. "I don't know what happened. One minute I was chanting, the next, the chandelier fell. It was really strange."

Anita raised her camera and hit the record button. "Could you hear Rose in your head?"

"I felt as if I was hovering over the scene. And I sensed Rose warning me about something."

"Maybe she was warning you the chandelier was about to fall," Mel said.

"Or about the ghost who pushed you down the stairs last night," Josh offered.

"I'm not sure." Molly shrugged and continued to the sink, where she filled the kettle with fresh water. "All I know is that it's getting a bit dangerous around here." She set the kettle on the stove and turned the burner up before facing them with her announcement. "I really think we should call the rest of the weekend off and send you all to town to stay the night in a hotel."

As soon as the words were out of her mouth, the ghost hunters started talking all at once.

"You can't stop it now!" Anita cried.

Preston stepped forward. "We're getting some great contact with Rose and Ian. As dangerous as it seems, we have to stay."

"We want to know who pushed Rose off the cliff," Barbara said.

"This has been the best ghost-hunting trip yet." Anita grinned, her eyes bright in the light from the candles.

Josh stood silent, a smile playing at the corners of his lips. "Who wants to stay the night in town? Raise your hand."

Not a single hand rose.

"You see? We're not easily scared." Josh's chest puffed out. "We'd like to stay and continue filming. We still have tonight, another full day and tomorrow night."

Molly let out a long breath. "I don't want anyone else hurt."

"We'll take our chances. Right?" Josh glanced around at the others.

Everyone nodded.

"Okay, then." She lifted the pan of pastries. "Let's finish off the pastries. You can ask questions and I'll see if I can answer them." Molly braced herself for the remainder of the weekend, wondering if she was making the right decision to let the guests stay when their lives could all be in danger.

What if one of them crossed paths with their nemesis? Could she live with the guilt if someone died on her premises?

Chapter 13

"You see here." With a flashlight beam, Nova pointed to the chain where the metal had been neatly cut. No rust or continued rubbing had weakened it. He handed the light to Gabe and went to work on cleaning the broken crystals off the table and chairs.

"He used a bolt cutter or something heavy-duty to snip through that thick chain." Gabe glanced around the room. "We keep tools in the basement. When the guests clear the kitchen, I'll check it out. My father had a place for every tool and every tool in its place. Molly's been good about keeping it that way. She's a lot like our dad." Gabe smiled. "Not that she looks like him. She's the spitting image of our mother."

Nova could imagine an older version of Molly and it made him sad for her loss. "Whoever cut it had to have turned off the power to it or else they would have been electrocuted."

"It had to have been when everyone was gone during the day. Otherwise, the only other time I know of the electricity being off was when everyone was sitting at the dinner table."

"The electric wires appear to have been damaged prior to the fall as well or they would have ripped through the drywall when the chain finally gave way." Gabe snapped pictures of the chain and wires and the position of the chandelier where it landed on the table.

"Who was sitting here?" Gabe asked, indicating the side of the table the chandelier had hit closest to.

"Your sister." Nova's jaw tightened. "I found her in her chair, flat on her back on the floor."

Gabe shoved a hand through his hair. "Damn."

"Yeah." The sick feeling he'd had since he'd found the hair comb in Molly's hair intensified. "If he's trying to make me sweat, he's doing it through Molly."

"Why Molly?"

Nova glanced away. "I made the mistake of kissing her." He'd done a whole lot more than kiss her, but he didn't have to tell her brother.

Gabe's lips turned up in a grin. "And she let you?"

Nova's brows twisted. "If I recall, she started it."

"I'll be damned." Gabe looked at him as if evaluating him for the first time.

Nova frowned. "Why so shocked?"

"She hasn't dated anyone since her fiancé was lost at sea."

"Molly mentioned she'd been engaged."

"Sad thing is that his boat was found, but they never found his body." Gabe reached for a broom. "She never got closure. I was working in Seattle at the time and wasn't here to help her through her grief."

Poor kid. Nova could understand now her reluctance to get involved with anyone else. "She must have loved him." The thought made his chest pinch hard. Not that he had any reason to be jealous or envious. He could never be what Molly needed. Not with his job and being gone all the time.

"I don't know. They dated all through high school and after. They seemed more comfortable with each other than anything. And from what Molly told me, Bill never did like McGregor Manor. He thought it was an albatross Molly had to bear."

"This place?" Nova's brows rose. "It's part of your family. It's part of who she is."

"Bill never saw it that way. He wanted her to be free to travel whenever he went on one of his sailing adventures." Gabe glanced across at Nova. "I'm glad she had her feet firmly on dry ground. He'd asked her to accompany him on the sailboat trip he'd planned that day he disappeared."

Nova could hear Molly's voice through the wood paneling of the kitchen door and his heart swelled. Had she gone with him that day, Nova never would have gotten to know her. "She might have died with him."

"Exactly. He planned to sail out to one of the outer islands and then down the coast to northern California. Because of a delay getting off work for the weekend, he didn't leave until late in the day. The Devil's Shroud crept in before he could navigate past the rocky point of Cape Churn."

"I suppose Molly took it hard." Nova found himself wishing for a moment that he could have been loved enough to be missed that much.

"I thought she would, but I think she missed his

friendship more than anything. When I finally got time off to come down from Seattle to see if she was okay, she seemed fine. She had been in the middle of repurposing the manor into a B&B. I think the renovations kept her too busy to be sad. She really seemed all right."

"Let's get this out of the way." Nova took one side of the heavy chandelier, Gabe grabbed the other and they lifted it off the table.

"We might as well take it to the cellar. My father had one corner set aside as a workshop," Gabe suggested. "Molly will need time to decide what to do with it."

"Seems a shame to dispose of it."

"Knowing Molly, she'll find a way to restore it. She's handy like that. No challenge is too big for her." Gabe laughed as they carried the chandelier toward the kitchen door. "I mean, it was a huge task to convert our old home into a B&B. But she did it, without anyone else's help."

Nova could tell Gabe was proud of his sister.

He'd never had a sibling to be proud of him or to be proud of. As a boy, he'd wished he had a brother. An older brother who could have been there to play with him after school or a younger brother who would have followed him around.

Some kids thought their younger siblings were pests. Not Gabe. He obviously loved his sister.

"Coming through," Gabe called out, backing into the kitchen. They carried the chandelier past the guests, who moved out of their way.

Gabe went first down the steps into the basement. Molly handed a flashlight to Nova, stuffing it into his hand, and she held a flashlight over his shoulder, lighting their way.

Once in the cellar, they moved to the back, where a workbench had been set up in the far corner.

Nova could hear the conversation start up again in the kitchen above. They set the chandelier on the workbench and he shone the light on it.

Gabe glanced toward the stairs and lowered his voice even more. "I'm glad you called me out here. I was going to phone you, anyway, once I had more details, but now is as good a time as any to let you know we discovered a woman's body today behind the fish-packing plant."

Nova's heart slammed into his gut. "What?"

"We found a woman behind the fish-packing plant late this afternoon."

This bit of news didn't bode well for what had been happening around Molly and him. "Any idea who she is? Did she have any identification on her?"

Gabe shook his head. "No." The concern in his eyes was visible in the glow of the flashlight. "I had her fingerprints run through the Integrated Automated Fingerprint Identification System with no hits."

"Which only means she doesn't have a criminal record."

"I did a search on the missing-persons' database and no one meeting her description has been reported in the past twenty-four hours."

Nova didn't like it. With all that had happened so far, having a woman turn up dead in Cape Churn wasn't a good sign. He didn't believe in coincidence. "How'd she get there?"

"Apparently, she was killed there. How she got there is unknown."

"What about her car?"

Gabe shook his head. "We found an abandoned vehicle a couple blocks away, parked on the side of a street. We don't think it's the one she arrived in."

"Why?"

"It belonged to someone else and was reported stolen two days ago in Seattle."

"Do you think this woman stole the car?"

"No. We ran the woman's fingerprints against those found in the car. The fingerprints didn't match the woman. Then we ran the fingerprints found on the car through the IAFIS and didn't get any hits."

"I'll make a trip into town tomorrow," Nova said. "Is the body still at the medical examiner's?"

Gabe nodded.

"Did he find anything unusual about her murder?"

"No. But he confirmed it was death by blunt-force trauma. Someone hit her in the head with something like a tire iron. Long, narrow and heavy."

"Was the tire iron in the car?"

"No."

"I don't like it," Nova said.

"Yeah, and it happened too close to the time yours and Molly's troubles started."

"Exactly. I could have my boss run the fingerprints."

"I don't know what he'd find that we don't have on the IAFIS database."

"You'd be surprised."

"Any help would be appreciated. I'm sure her family would like to know what happened to her."

Nova was sure they wouldn't be happy upon hearing the news. But closure was better than being left wondering.

"While we're down here, let me have that flashlight." Gabe took the flashlight from Nova and shone it on the walls.

Tools hung from a Peg-Board over a counter with outlines of the tools drawn on the Peg-Board indicating where each one was supposed to be hung. In most cases, a tool hung where it was supposed to be. Even the larger tools had hooks drilled and anchored into the concrete blocks of the wall with an outline around the tool. A long length of rope hung in one of the outlines with a seat harness hanging beside it.

"Is Molly a rock climber?" Nova asked.

"Hardly." Gabe laughed. "I used to scale the cliffs when I was younger. I kept all my gear in case I decided I wanted to do it again. But that's not important. What is important is *that*." He focused the beam on a three-foot outline empty of its content.

"Do you know what was supposed to be there?" Nova asked.

"I have a good idea."

"Bolt cutter?"

"Yup. Red handles, if I remember correctly. If they're around, they shouldn't be hard to find." Gabe nodded and shifted the light around the room. He and Nova spent the next few minutes inspecting the rest of the cellar and they didn't find the bolt cutters.

Nova had been away from Molly long enough and found himself anxious to get back to her. "Let's finish cleaning up the dining room."

Gabe followed Nova up the stairs into the kitchen, where a teakettle had just started screaming.

Molly pulled the kettle off the stove. "Can I interest you two in a cup of tea or hot cocoa?"

"No, thanks." Gabe handed Nova the flashlight. "Kayla and I just finished a cup."

"She's got you drinking tea?" Molly laughed. "That's new."

Gabe's cheeks turned a ruddy red. "Says it's calming and better for me at night than coffee."

"She's right, you know."

"Don't you go gangin' up on me, too." Gabe lightly punched his sister's arm.

"What about you, Nova? Want something?" She glanced at him, her pretty green eyes shining, appearing optimistic.

He wanted something, all right. It wasn't tea. "I'll pass." With his mind on Molly and what he really wanted, he decided leaving the room would save him from embarrassment. He grabbed a broom and dustpan from the corner.

Gabe followed with the lined trash can and a stainless-steel mixing bowl.

The crystal drops they could salvage went into the mixing bowl and the rest they scooped into the trash. In less than fifteen minutes, they had the room cleaned and the chairs lined up around the dining table as if nothing had happened, except for the damaged ceiling and lack of overhead lighting in the room. Candles would have to do for the meals until Molly had the chandelier fixed or a replacement brought in.

Gabe peeked into the kitchen. "All clear."

The guests exited the kitchen and headed for the great room or the front porch.

"Hey, look, the rain cleared," Josh called out from the porch. "The moon's shining bright over the ocean."

Anita followed him out the door. "Beautiful."

Molly, on her crutch, walked with her brother to the door and out onto the porch.

Nova lagged behind, watching those who'd settled in the great room.

With eight guests to keep an eye on, he couldn't be everywhere, and the more he was around Molly, the more he wanted to be around the woman. She was smart, pretty and full of pluck, and she made him forget the real reason for staying longer.

Four of the guests remained in the great room with their cups of tea and hot chocolate. Talia sat in a floral wing-back chair, while Reed stood by the fireplace, staring at the tintype photo Gabe had settled in its place after cleaning the dining room. He'd also lit an oil lamp and placed it on the other end of the mantel. The single oil lamp plus the fire in the grate provided sufficient lighting for the entire room.

"Not a bad-looking couple," Reed said. "I can imagine them living here a hundred or so years ago. I bet this place hasn't changed that much." He turned back toward Talia. "Ever wanted to live in a house like this?"

Talia shrugged. "Big houses don't mean a better life."

"You probably grew up in one or you wouldn't be saying that."

"No, as a matter of fact, my mother and I lived in a crappy little two-bedroom apartment in L.A. when I was growing up."

"I thought you said you had a sister."

"I did. Half sister. She lived with my father in a big house."

"If you didn't like your apartment, why didn't you live with your father?" Reed asked.

Talia glanced away. "I didn't know he existed until I was fifteen."

"That's cold."

She shrugged. "It was a long time ago."

Nova leaned on the wall beside the banister leading up the stairs, his gaze on the front door, while he studied Reed and Talia through his peripheral vision.

"When did you decide to move to Oregon?"

"When I got tired of L.A."

"When was that?"

"I don't know, maybe two years ago." Talia set her teacup on the side table and rose from her chair. "I'm going out for some fresh air. Anyone want to join me?"

"I'll be out in a minute," Reed answered. "Just finishing up my cocoa."

The other two occupants of the great room set aside their cups and joined Talia as she went out onto the porch.

Alone with Reed, Nova fingered the key in his pocket and finally pulled it out, rolling it over in his palm.

He crossed the room to the fireplace, close to where Reed stood. Staring into the flames, he asked casually, "You with the group out of Seattle?"

Reed nodded. "I am."

"That's a nice drive down. Not too far."

"I rode with Anita and Josh. They talked the whole way."

Nova chuckled, his gaze going to the door. "Talia's not with the rest of the group, is she?"

Reed's gaze followed Nova's "No. She's from Portland."

"She's nice-looking."

"Yeah." Reed shot a glance at him, his eyes narrowing. "So?"

"Known her long?"

"No. We just met yesterday." Reed turned away from the fireplace. "Why? You interested? I thought you and Molly were...you know."

"Relax, I'm not interested in Talia. But I noticed you were."

"So what if I am? It ain't a crime."

"No, it's not. But your snooping and taking photos without her consent is." Nova sauntered to the fireplace and glanced at the photograph of Rose and Ian. "You don't strike me as someone who falls for all this paranormal mumbo jumbo. Do you believe in ghosts?"

Reed studied him before answering. "Not so much."

"Then why are you here?"

With a shrug, Reed faced the front door. "My shrink told me to join a group. I'd get to travel, meet people and make friends. So far, it's working."

While Reed had his back to Nova, Nova placed the key on the mantel next to the photo.

Nova moved away, hoping Reed would return his attention to the photograph he'd been staring at earlier. "Seems to me it wasn't much easier to meet people back when Rose and Ian were alive, does it?"

Reed cast a glance at the photo and sneered. "Rose was stupid."

"Why?" Nova tried to sound conversational instead of like he was interrogating the man.

"She should have been happy with Ian instead of falling in love with a guy who had no intention of marrying her."

"She didn't know that."

"No, but she should have figured it out sooner. In my opinion, she deserved to die."

"You think Ian killed her?"

"Nah. Not if he was as sick as the story said. He probably didn't have the strength to push a puppy over the edge, much less a grown woman. He was probably easy to push over the edge, as well."

The man had a point. Still, his declaration that Rose deserved to die had Nova's stomach churning, considering a woman had died, probably the day Reed had arrived, and Reed had a restraining order against him for stalking. The man had proved to be unstable.

At this point, the dead woman, Reed and Bolivia had no connection in Nova's mind. "You spoke of travel—have you done much?"

Reed shook his head. "Only stamp I have on my passport is when I crossed the border into Canada."

"You haven't been anywhere else?"

"Only to other parts of the U.S." Reed faced the photo of Rose and Ian. "I never wanted to spend a lot of money on travel. I was saving, thinkin' I'd be getting married soon."

"I take it that didn't pan out."

"I thought she loved me." Again, he shrugged. "Guess she didn't. Women can be such liars."

"Tough break." Nova stepped away from Reed and headed for the door.

When he reached the open door, he paused, keeping a watch on Reed by the fireplace.

Just when Nova thought Reed would never take the bait, the man froze. Slowly, he reached out and picked up the key, slipping it into his pocket.

Then he spun toward Nova and the front door.

Nova stepped through as if he was just about to, anyway.

Why did Reed have the skeleton key in the first place and why did he take it from the fireplace? One thing was certain: he hadn't had it by accident.

What did it prove? That Reed could have been the one to lock Molly in the cellar? It wasn't proof he'd pushed her down the stairs or killed the woman in town. Granted, the man wasn't happy with women. Then again, he was practically stalking Talia. Did that make him a danger to the women…and possibly a killer?

Molly stood out on the porch until the last guest retired, afraid to leave one of them alone in case the attacker struck another random victim. Up until Talia was pushed down the stairs in the jailhouse, Nova had assumed he was the target and Molly by association.

Now it was a free-for-all, and she didn't want to take chances.

Everyone else gave up by eleven. Not Anita and Josh. They sat in rocking chairs until nearly midnight, talking about what they'd discovered that day and playing back the video on their cameras.

Molly was ready to go to bed long before either of them budged. If not for Nova sitting on the porch swing next to her, she'd have been bored out of her mind and sound asleep.

Nova had joined her shortly after Gabe left, taking the seat beside her.

"Rough day, huh?" He pushed with his foot and set the swing into a gentle motion, his arm draped over the back, barely touching her shoulder, but enough to make her feel protected, cared for and appreciated.

She relaxed against his arm and leaned her head back, staring at the moon and stars shining brightly over the ocean, spreading a blanket of sparkles across the rippling waves.

"Your home is beautiful," he said, his voice low, his words meant only for her.

"Thank you. I wish I could take credit for it. Ian built a wonderful house for his bride. It's too bad she didn't realize it until it was too late."

"Too many people don't recognize what they have until they lose it."

"I know."

"Is that how it was with you and your fiancé?"

Molly lifted her head away from his arm and turned to stare up at his face, which was a pale blue in the moonlight. "I didn't realize what I *didn't* have until Bill was gone."

Nova frowned. "What do you mean?"

Leaning back again, she closed her eyes and let the cool night air relax her. "We grew up together as friends. When we were old enough to think about marriage, we assumed we were right for each other without knowing what else was out there. I think we tried to make it fit when we should have explored and made sure we were exactly what the other wanted. He wanted to live in exotic places. I wanted to travel, but I always wanted to come home to where I'd grown up."

"You're lucky to have a place to call home."

"You don't have such a place? No family to go home to?"

"Not since my grandparents died."

She sighed. "That's sad."

"Some would say it sets you free to do whatever you want."

"Not me. I like having roots. No matter where I go or what I do, I know I have a place to come home to. A place filled with memories of the people I love. My parents, my grandparents, my brother and me."

"I remember the house my grandparents had in San Antonio. It was small and had a tiny yard, but it always smelled like home. *Mi abuela,* my grandmother, was an immigrant from Mexico. My grandfather was second generation. They both spoke English and Spanish in the house. *Mi abuela* cooked traditional Mexican food, from homemade corn tortillas to salsa, beans and rice." He closed his eyes and inhaled. "I can still smell it. I miss them."

"What about your parents?"

"We didn't live in the best part of town. My mother was collateral damage of gang warfare. She caught a bullet in a drive-by shooting."

Molly gasped. "I'm so sorry."

"Don't be sorry for me. I was a toddler when she died. I barely knew her, and I never knew my father."

"You must have been lonely." She rested a hand on his leg. "Any brothers or sisters?"

"No." He smiled. "You're fortunate to have a brother like Gabe. He's a good man."

"I know. I'm glad he came back to Cape Churn to live. Kayla, Dakota and the baby make it even better. More family around to love."

"*Familia es todo.* Family is everything."

They sat for a while in silence, listening to Anita and Josh exclaim over video clips.

"Is that why you travel so much doing the job you do? Because you no longer have family to come home to?"

Nova shrugged. "Partly. I love the work I do. I know I'm making a difference and helping make our country a better place to live."

She chuckled. "When you put it like that, it sounds so much more important and gratifying than running a bed and breakfast."

"You provide a great service to people who aren't fortunate enough to live in a place like this."

"The B&B was the only way I could save our family home. I couldn't afford the upkeep on my teaching salary. Gabe couldn't have a life of his own when he was sending money home all the time."

His arm tightened around her shoulders and she snuggled closer, accepting his warmth as the night grew colder, the breeze off the ocean chilling the air. "You've done a great job with it."

"I couldn't give it up. Not even for Bill. This is my home. The marks tracking our growth as kids are still on the doorframe in the kitchen. I refused to paint over them." She glanced up at him. "Sounds foolish, doesn't it? To be so attached to a place."

"Not at all. You hold on to it with both hands. It's a legacy. One you should be proud of. One you've fought for and kept alive."

"Thanks." She had worked hard to make the B&B a success. Now she felt as if she wasn't in constant fear of losing her home. Still, it was missing something. Or rather someone. Having Nova beside her on the swing brought it home to her with a clarity she'd avoided since Bill died.

For years, she'd fought to be financially independent, able to stand on her own. She'd achieved that goal and discovered that while it was rewarding, it wasn't enough.

She wanted someone to share it with. Someone who could appreciate McGregor Manor for all its history and family traditions. Someone like Nova. When that thought passed through her mind, her heart stopped for a second, then skipped into high gear, pounding against her chest. She wanted to share her home with Nova, a man she'd only just met. Someone she knew very little about, but what she knew, she liked and trusted implicitly.

"We're headed to bed," Anita announced.

So wrapped up in how good it felt to be relaxing in Nova's arms, Molly hadn't noticed that Anita and Josh had packed up their equipment and were standing by the front door.

"I'm not sure what you had planned for tomorrow," Josh said, "but we'd like to go back to the library and set up our cameras in the jailhouse and in the romance anteroom. And if we have time, we'd like to get more footage of the lighthouse, inside and out."

Molly nodded. "I think it can be arranged. I'll call the library tomorrow when they open."

"Today was great. Thanks and good night." Josh turned and followed Anita into the house.

"I think that's our cue to hit the sack." Nova stood and stretched, then extended a hand to Molly.

She accepted it and expected to rise beside him.

Instead, he gave a firm tug and pulled her against him. With one arm clamped around her waist, he tipped her chin using his other hand. "I've wanted to do this all evening."

She stared up into his shining eyes kissed by moonlight, her stomach fluttering and her pulse pounding. "Do what?"

"This." His head dipped and his mouth claimed hers.

Molly melted against him, ignoring the fact he'd be gone within days. Allowing herself to live in the moment, she'd take whatever she could get out of the time she had left with him. Why worry about tomorrow? She wrapped her arms around him and leaned up on her good foot, pressing her breasts against his chest. The exhaustion of a moment ago faded away, replaced by a heat and energy that rivaled the electrical storm of earlier that evening.

He broke off the kiss, just when it was getting good, and rested his forehead on hers. "Come on, you need some sleep." He handed her the crutch and took her free elbow in his hand.

Sleep was the last thing on her mind. As she entered the house, she didn't do her usual perusal, looking for things to pick up or straighten. Her gaze and her mind were focused on getting to her bedroom.

The stairs seemed longer than the night before and she couldn't wait to get to the top, counting the seconds until they could close her door and forget everything else but making love.

If that was what Nova had in mind. *If* the stars

aligned and nothing else happened to ruin the ending of an otherwise disastrous day.

By the time she reached her door, Molly expected to find something horrible waiting for her inside. After all that had happened, she wouldn't be surprised to find a snake in her bed or someone waiting with a gun pointed at her chest.

"Wow. I'm afraid to open my bedroom door," she said, staring at the knob as if it had grown tentacles.

"Let me." Nova stood her to the side of the door, out of range should someone jump out upon opening. Then standing to the side as well, he pushed the door open.

Nothing happened.

Molly chuckled, the sound shaky at best. "I don't know what I expected, but I'm glad it was nothing."

"You and me both." He dragged a hand through his hair and grinned. "We're getting punchy."

"Can you blame us?" Inside her room, she stood awkwardly. After snuggling with the man all evening, she found herself suddenly shy. "You don't have to stay."

He graced her with a soft smile. "Do you want me to?"

More than anything. She nodded.

"Then I will." He sat in the chair beside the bed and pulled off his boots. "You get the shower first."

"I'd rather you went," she said. "I want to gather my clothes." And collect her thoughts and nerves and anything else that had gone haywire when he'd agreed to stay.

"Okay." He turned and locked the door, then retrieved his bag from behind the chair. "I'll only be a few minutes.

"Take all the time you need," she said, twisting her fingers, her heart galloping inside her ribs.

Nova's lips curled into that sexy smile that made her toes curl. "Don't worry, *bella dama,* I'll sleep in the chair." With that comment, he entered the bathroom and pulled the door closed behind him.

"I wasn't worrying about where you'd sleep, but now I am." She wanted him in her bed. Now that he'd proclaimed he'd sleep in the chair, how could she convince him to share her bed? Would it be too forward to ask?

Why was she so nervous? They'd made love the night before, no questions asked, no promises made. After a full and nerve-racking day and evening together, she should have had her fill of him.

Not even close. She wanted more. And the only way to convince him was to show him how much more she wanted. With shaking fingers, she shed her clothing.

The sound of water running made her bold. He'd be in the shower. He wouldn't see her right away. The anonymity gave her courage, and she opened the bathroom door.

He stood behind the shower curtain, the shadow of his big, hulking form taking Molly's breath away.

She loved how impressive his body was, from strong, broad shoulders to thick, powerful thighs. He'd carried her up the stairs as if she weighed no more than a pillow.

Careful not to make a sound, she leaned her crutch against the wall, grabbed the towel rack and pushed aside the curtain.

He stood with his back to her, his face beneath the spray, unaware of her presence.

Until she climbed into the tub behind him and curled her arms around his middle, holding on tight.

He unwrapped her arms from him and turned, a grin stretching across his lips, a twinkle in his eyes. Then he was kissing her, holding her against his wet, slick body, his member pressing into her belly.

All the longing she'd felt throughout the evening welled up in her and she kissed him back, deepening the connection, prolonging the warmth and intimacy. When he broke away, she breathed in the scent of soap and Nova.

"What took you so long?" he asked.

Molly laughed. "Do you know how hard it is to climb into a tub with one leg?"

"If there's one thing I've learned about you in the one day I've known you, it's that you don't give up easily. Not on something you want."

"And I want you." Leaning up, she brushed his lips with hers.

"Even when I'll be gone so soon?"

"I'll take what I can get for as long as I can have it."

"And that will be enough?"

"It'll have to be for now." She curled a hand around the back of his neck. "Now shut up and kiss me."

His reminder of the temporary nature of their liaison made a solid lump form in her throat. She wanted the chance to get to know him, to learn all his stories, to find out what he'd been like as a kid. She wanted to walk on a beach at sunset with him, eat at fancy restaurants and picnic in a field with this man. But if one night was all she had left with him, she'd take it and be glad she had at least that much time to get to know him. Every delectable inch of him.

Molly slid her bum leg up the side of his thigh and hooked it around his waist.

Nova cupped her bottom and lifted, wrapping her other leg around him, then turned until she was beneath the warm spray. His shaft pressed against her opening, nudging to enter, yet holding back.

Water sluiced over her shoulders, running off the tips of her breasts and onto his chest. Balancing her with one hand, he ran the bar of soap over her shoulders and down her front, to lather a budded nipple.

Molly moaned and pressed against his hand and the bar of soap. "Do you have any idea what you do to me?"

He chuckled, the vibrations of his chest making her tighten in anticipation of a more intimate connection. "I think so. But it can't be nearly as crazy as you make me."

She nipped the corner of his ear and ran her hands through his thick black hair. "Show me."

He cupped her cheek in his palm and brushed his lips across hers. "Protection?"

"In the top drawer of my nightstand."

With all the patience of a house fire, he rinsed them off and stepped out on the bathmat, dripping wet. He set her on her feet, gently, careful not to aggravate the injured ankle. Then he went to work drying her off, his hands rubbing the towel across her body quickly and efficiently.

She laughed. "In a hurry?"

"Something like that." When he'd finished drying her, he ran the towel over himself.

"Hey, that's my job." Molly grabbed a fresh towel and started to dry him off. When she came to his stiff erection, she started to wrap the towel around it.

Nova groaned, jerked the towel out of her hands and tossed it to the floor. "I can't take anymore."

"Tsk, tsk. The best was yet to come," she murmured, pressing a kiss to his chest and capturing one of his little brown nipples between her teeth.

He scooped her into his arms and marched into the bedroom, laid her across the bed and crawled up between her legs.

She leaned over and rummaged in her nightstand for a condom, digging deep beneath the clutter, praying that they were still there. When her fingers curled around a foil packet, she sighed and pulled it free.

He tore the packet open, rolled it down over himself and leaned over her on his hands. "What's your view on foreplay?" he growled.

"Only when necessary."

"And is it necessary now?" he said through gritted teeth.

She debated teasing him, but the animalistic gleam in his eyes made her too hot to hesitate. "No."

"Good." He slid his fingers into her, testing her channel. "You're so wet." Another finger joined the first at the same time as he stroked between her folds with his thumb.

Molly's back arched off the bed. "Please," she moaned.

"Please what?" he asked.

"Please, I want you." She wrapped her hand around his member and guided him into her. "Now."

He thrust deep, filling her until her channel stretched, accommodating his full girth. Once inside he paused, letting her body adjust to him.

"Don't stop now," she cried, ready for more.

Nova rode her hard, pumping in and out of her.

Molly raised her hips to meet each of his thrusts, the pace increasing until she launched over the edge, sensations exploding inside her, making her entire body quiver with the force of her release.

Nova grasped her hips and drove into her one more time, his body tense, his member throbbing, the spasms slowly fading with each passing minute. Then he collapsed on the bed beside her and gathered her into his arms and whispered, *"Tu me vuelves loca."*

Molly cupped his face. "Meaning?"

"You drive me crazy."

"In a good way or a bad way?" She swept her thumb across his full bottom lip, loving how soft it was.

"In the best way." He crushed her to him and held her tight, burying his face into the side of her neck.

"Good, because you drive me crazy, too." Molly nestled against his chest, loving the feel of his strong arms around her and the added weight of his body in her bed. She could get used to everything about this man. Already, she couldn't imagine how empty her bed would feel when he was gone.

She feared something would come to a head tomorrow. Whoever was after Nova would be done playing games and do something stupid.

Molly vowed to be ready, no matter what. And if it meant solving the mystery and Nova leaving, she had to be prepared for that, as well.

Chapter 14

Nova lay awake for another hour, wishing he could freeze this moment in time and remain with Molly, just like they were. He inhaled the fragrant, citrusy scent of her hair and brushed his lips across the curve of her shoulder.

She was so beautiful and hopeful that she made him believe he could have a life outside of his work. With her. What would it be like to come home every day to her smile, her body and her sweet personality?

Molly McGregor made him feel more alive than he'd felt in years. She had strong beliefs in family, tradition and love. She clung to an old house that could well have spelled her financial ruin. She'd persevered, kept it alive and still a part of the McGregor family despite the naysayers, including her former fiancé.

She worked hard, cared about people and loved fiercely. Everything a man could want in a woman.

Molly deserved a man who would be around to partner with her in her endeavors, to share her triumphs
along with her failures and lift her up when she was
down.

Envious of the person who would fit that bill, Nova
found himself wishing it could be him. What chance
did he have of a real life? His work with the SOS kept
him away so often he wouldn't be there for Molly when
she needed him. She'd be no better off than she was
now. He brought no value to a relationship with her.

As much as he wanted her, he knew he wasn't the
man she deserved. His mind made up and sad about
it, he closed his eyes on her beauty. Though his hands
cradled her still, he slipped into sleep.

He couldn't function without some rest, and as long
as he was with Molly, he felt confident he could protect
her. It was when he wasn't there, he worried.

He woke several times during the night from imagined sounds. Twice he rose to trace the source of the
sound only to come up empty-handed.

By five, he'd slept all he was going to that night. He
rose, dressed and went downstairs in search of coffee.
Thankfully, the electricity was back on. Fifteen minutes later, he'd mastered the coffeemaker and held a
mug of the steaming brew in his hands as he stepped
out on the porch to enjoy the morning.

By seven, the guests trickled down the stairs one
at a time. Josh and Anita carried canvas bags of video
equipment, setting them down by the front door.

"Good morning," Anita greeted him.

"You two are up early."

"We have a lot to do today," Josh said.

"I guess that means starting with breakfast." Nova led the way to the kitchen and rummaged through the refrigerator, trying to figure out what Molly had in mind for breakfast the second morning of the ghost-hunting weekend. He found bacon, eggs, butter, chives, olives and mushrooms. "Omelets it is," he decided.

Anita and Josh entered the kitchen behind him and got to work helping him whip the eggs and flip the bacon. Before long they had several plates of steaming omelets and veggies to carry out to the dining room.

Others had gathered around the table expectantly.

Before the last omelet was flipped from the pan to a plate, Molly entered the kitchen hobbling on one foot, her other taking some of the weight. "I'm going to have to find a new job. My assistant is cooking circles around me."

"I learned from the best." He winked at her and handed her a plate. "Sit. Eat."

"I should be waiting on you."

"Got it covered." With his omelet on the plate, he followed her to the dining room.

"We have all the equipment packed and ready to go to the library," Anita announced.

"What time do they open?" Josh inquired.

Molly laughed. "Eager to chase some ghosts?"

"You bet." Josh shook the pepper shaker over his food and shoved a bite into his mouth.

"They open at eight." Molly glanced at the clock on the wall. "I'll call when we're through here."

Nova hoped that whoever was the troublemaker would choose a different option for the day, thus setting himself apart from the others. At this point, his money was on either Preston or Reed.

Nova wondered with Reed's record of stalking if that automatically made him a candidate for a killer. He'd hitched a ride from Seattle with Anita and Josh. How did that explain the abandoned stolen car found close to Jane Doe in town? Unless Jane Doe had nothing to do with what was happening at the McGregor B&B.

"Is everyone going?" Nova asked.

All the guests nodded an affirmative.

Damn. So much for singling out the culprit. Nova went back to his original plan of stopping by the morgue and paying a visit to the only other SOS agent in town, Creed Thomas. He'd swing by the Cape Churn chief of police to see if they'd come up with anything on Jane Doe. He'd also see if they could forward the fingerprints to his boss. Royce had connections to other fingerprint databases and he got results faster.

Nova hadn't told Molly about the Jane Doe the previous night, choosing to let her get a good night's sleep without worrying more. On the way to Cape Churn that morning, he filled her in on what Gabe had told her.

"And you're just now telling me?" She glared at him.

"After having a chandelier fall in your lap, I didn't think it would benefit you to worry more."

"Do me a favor and let me make that decision. I'm not a china doll that can be broken easily. You don't have to handle me with care."

He grinned. "Point taken. And I know all that. But I didn't see that you could do anything with the information last night. Now that we're on the way to town, you needed to know. I didn't want you to be surprised."

"Thanks." She sat in the passenger seat, looking anything but thankful.

"I'm sorry. I should have told you last night."

For a long moment, she didn't comment. "I get it. But don't do that again. If it has anything to do with what's going on, tell me right away."

"Agreed. Although I'm not completely sure it has anything to do with what's going on."

"It's just a random killing?" Molly snorted. "I thought you of all people wouldn't believe in coincidence."

"I don't. And you are *muy inteligente.* I should always keep that in mind."

"Do that."

He stopped in front of the library where the ghost hunters were unloading their vehicles. "Are you going to be all right while I go check on a few things?"

"I'll stay with the librarian."

"Do that," he said, using her words. "I'd hate anything to happen to you while I'm out running around."

"Just do me a favor. When you get back, fill me in on what you learn."

"I will." He leaned across the console and pressed a kiss to her lips. "You are *inteligente y bonita.*"

She touched his cheek. "That kind of talk will get you places, Casanova."

"My plan *exactamente.*"

Her mouth twisted in a wry grin. "I see why you have the reputation you do."

Nova got out of the vehicle, but by the time he rounded the front, Molly was standing gingerly on both feet.

"My ankle's getting better." She limped a step or two, grimacing slightly. "And I need to quit relying on you so much."

Her words hit him in the gut. Already she was anticipating his departure. "Don't push it too soon or you'll set the healing back." Nova handed the crutch to her.

She accepted it. "You're right. I should give it more time. I can make it inside on my own. Go. Check with Gabe and the chief. I'd like to know what's going on."

"I'll be back shortly."

"I don't have to stay with them all morning. When I have them set up, I can head back to the B&B. I have cleaning and food-preparation duties I need to address."

"Will do."

He stayed a minute more, until Molly disappeared with the others into the library. He debated staying until Molly had completed her duties coordinating with the librarian. She'd clearly stated she wanted to quit relying on him.

She was right. He had no permanent place in her life. Once he figured out who had it in for him and Molly, he'd wrap it up and be gone from Cape Churn.

Nova pulled his cell phone from his pocket and dialed Creed's number.

"Thomas speaking."

"Meet me at the morgue," Nova said.

"Anyone I know?" Creed asked.

"I hope not." He clicked the off button and dialed Gabe McGregor.

"Valdez, everything okay out there with my sister?"

"So far. She's at the library with her ghost hunters. I'm headed for the morgue. Can I get a meeting there with you and the chief of police?"

"I'll see what I can arrange. I gave Chief Taggert the heads-up this morning that you wanted to get involved and also gave him the rundown of what's been going on out at the B&B."

"Good. We need to stop this before someone else gets hurt."

Nova drove to the morgue on the northeast corner of town, arriving at the same time as Creed. Gabe arrived a moment later in his patrol car and the chief seconds afterward.

Nova shook hands with the chief.

"I hear you're having some trouble out at the Mc-Gregor place," Chief Taggert said. He motioned for Nova to lead the way into the morgue. "You thinkin' our Jane Doe is connected?"

"I don't know. So far I haven't had anyone pop out as a solid suspect. I'm concerned about a couple of the men in the group, though." He briefed the chief on what he'd discovered through Royce's investigations and his own foray into the B&B rooms where the men were staying.

"Okay, so one is a stalker with a key that could have belonged to the cellar door Molly was locked in. The other man owns a gun." The chief shook his head. "Not much to go on."

Nova briefed him on what he'd found at the lighthouse the day before and the significance of the rhinestone comb. "If this is someone out for vengeance against me, this person had to know about Bolivia. I have Royce checking the backgrounds on the rest of the ghost hunters. He didn't find anything on Talia Dane. No criminal record, no record of leaving the country. Schotzman claims he's only been to Canada.

Nothing so far as South America. I'm waiting to hear back on the rest."

"How can we help you with that side of the investigation?"

"I'm not sure you can."

"How is Jane Doe part of this mystery?" the chief asked.

"I don't know. Have you had any luck matching fingerprints?"

"We're trying for access to the Oregon DMV fingerprints and those from the surrounding states. So far we've only gotten agreement from Washington State."

Nova handed the chief a business card. "Send an electronic copy of the prints to this email address. My boss has connections and might get to that information quicker."

"Will do."

By then they'd entered the examination room, where two stainless-steel tables sat in the middle of the floor. One empty and spotlessly clean, the other occupied by a female body. The medical examiner straightened. "Ah, Chief Taggert. You brought visitors."

"I did." Taggert introduced Creed and Nova.

"We wanted to get a photo of the victim's face and run it through facial-recognition software."

The M.E. grimaced. "That would be great, except there's a problem." He pulled back the sheet, exposing the woman's head. "Her face was smashed by the same instrument used to crush her skull."

The woman's face was battered so badly, no facial-recognition software would find a match. She had bright, unnaturally orange hair that had been obviously dyed.

"Any distinguishing marks?"

"She has tattoos on her neck, forearms, ankles and thighs of dragons and moons in a variety of colors."

When someone reported her missing, she'd be easily identified. Until then, they still didn't have a clue.

Another dead end.

Nova thanked the M.E. and gave the chief his card to call if he learned anything else. In the meantime, he needed to get back to Molly, the image of the dead woman's damaged face tough to erase from his mind. He balled his fists as he left the morgue.

Creed followed him.

Nova stopped at Molly's vehicle and faced his friend. "Up until they found this woman's body, I wasn't sure this was anything more than foul play and mind games to frustrate me."

"Anything I can do to help?" Creed asked.

"Be there if I need you."

"That goes for me, too." Officer McGregor joined them. "Molly's on her own at that B&B. I'd move back in, but I don't want Kayla, Dakota and the baby placed in danger."

"That would only compound the problem." Nova climbed into the SUV. "Just be there if I call."

"Then don't hesitate to call. I'm also thinking I could stand some of Molly's cooking."

"She makes great clam chowder," Gabe agreed.

Nova drove back to the library, his pulse quickening as he got closer. What else could happen to make this "vacation" complete?

* * *

Molly met with Justine Feldman, the seventy-year-old librarian, to clear the way for the ghost-hunting group to film in the old jailhouse.

Once the crew was set up, Molly retreated to the reference section of the library, specifically to the Cape Churn historical archives. The experience with the séance, before the chandelier had fallen, troubled her, like unfinished business.

She concentrated on the late eighteen hundreds. The records had been painstakingly scanned by local high-school students as part of their grade in history class, so all of the documents, old letters, maps and newspapers had been archived in a computer.

First she searched for Ian and Rose McGregor. In the archives, she found their marriage certificate and their certificates of death showing they both had died on the same day. Her chest tightened as she imagined the couple lying at the bottom of the cliff below where the house still stood.

With their date of death in mind, she scanned through letters and documents around that date, searching for any indication of another person who might have had a reason to kill Rose and Ian.

With so many documents to review, Molly soon realized her attempt could take days, maybe years, of painstaking research, reading everything in the years prior and the years after the couple's death.

After an hour, Molly rose from her seat at the computer and wandered down an aisle of antique books donated to the library at the end of the nineteenth century. She paused to read the lettering on the spine. As she bent to read one, something fell to the ground on the other side of the row of books.

Molly jumped, smothering a scream, her heart pounding. When nothing moved or made another sound, she eased around the shelf and peered down the aisles between two stacks.

A small book lay on the ground, bound in brown leather with gold lettering on the spine.

The Lady's Guide to Complete Etiquette.

Molly's mouth curved in a smile and she lifted the book from the floor, opening to the inside copyright page. The date listed was 1888.

Inside described the proper manners for a lady at home with family and in company, how to dress, how to make dresses, how to write letters and so much more. The book had a neatly handwritten inscription inside the first page.

Truth fears no inquiry.

The name beneath the quote was Elizabeth Slatington; the date written was one month past the date of Ian and Rose's deaths.

Molly paged through the book, searching for any other inscriptions but finding none. Near the end, a folded paper fell out into her lap.

She unfolded the old, yellowed paper and smoothed the creases.

The document was a bill of lading for the order and delivery of one rosewood music box from England. The company listed at the top was Gilmartin Trading Company, the item sold to E. Slatington.

Curious, Molly returned to the computer and searched for Elizabeth Slatington. The woman's name turned up in a number of newspaper articles concerning polite society of Cape Churn. One was about a quilting-circle meeting set for after church on Sunday a year before the McGregors' deaths. Another was a story about Elizabeth and her husband George's trip to San Francisco. And yet another about the birth of their first child. All of these happened in the years preceding Ian's and Rose's deaths. Scanning the court documents, she found the record of Elizabeth's death. Exactly one year following the deaths of Ian and Rose. Cause of death, strangulation; the town doctor ruled it as suicide.

Molly sat back in her chair, her heart battering the inside of her chest. One year to the day after the deaths of Ian and Rose. Coincidence?

Had she been murdered by the same person who'd pushed Rose from the cliff?

On a whim, she searched through the court records and newspapers for the name. She got a hit on an old court document fining one Vince Gilmartin one dollar for public drunkenness and sentencing him to two nights in jail to encourage sobriety.

Vince Gilmartin.

Molly's thoughts homed in on the name. She searched the scanned documents again and came up with nothing. Perhaps Rose's diary would shed some light. Her great-great-grandmother had been cryptic and sparing with her words in the journal, managing to record much of the local gossip in her short sentences.

Molly searched out the librarian and asked her if she found other documents related to Elizabeth Slatington or her husband to let her know.

"I know of some old letters and journals that did not get scanned in the big push to go digital. I'll check through those and see if I can find anything."

Molly thanked the librarian and went back to the computer to continue her own search through hundreds of documents.

"Hey." A hand touched her shoulder, making her jump.

Molly pressed her fingers against her chest and galloping heart. "You scared me."

"I'm sorry. I thought you might be ready to head back to the B&B."

"I am."

Nova peered over her shoulder at the screen. "Find anything interesting?"

"I was looking for information about the people of Cape Churn back when Ian and Rose were still alive. I didn't find much."

What else could she have said? For all she knew, Elizabeth Slatington was just another person who lived in Cape Churn back in the 1800s. That she died on the same date as Ian and Rose could mean something or, most likely, nothing. Without further investigation, she wouldn't know. "I'm ready. It will be nice getting back to the B&B before the rest of them return. I need to clean rooms and prepare for the evening meal."

"I meant to ask—if you're a B&B, why do you serve dinner, as well?"

"We're a good six miles out of town on a curvy highway. I figured it was worth the extra expense to offer dinner versus having my guests drive all the way back to Cape Churn. What did you learn about the woman they found?"

"Nothing."

"What did she look like?"

"Not pretty. Her face had been destroyed by whoever killed her."

"That's horrible. Why would he do that?"

"Could be a lot of reasons. The one that sticks out in my mind is that it takes longer to identify the body."

Chapter 15

After a brief stop at the local market, Nova drove Molly back to the B&B and helped her into the house, then carried the groceries into the kitchen.

"I'd like to start by cleaning the rooms upstairs," Molly said. "You don't have to help me."

"I know." He didn't have to help, but he couldn't stand around and do nothing while she limped from room to room, cleaning. "But I will. Want me to start on the bathrooms?"

"That would be great. I'll make beds."

Nova started work in Anita's room, cleaning the bathtub and sink. Molly quickly moved ahead, making the beds, plumping the pillows and arranging fresh towels in the baths. When Nova was halfway down the hallway, moving from one room to the next, he saw Molly enter Reed's room at the end of the hallway.

"Nova!" she called out.

His pulse pounding, he ran to her.

She stood just inside the room and pointed at something red sticking out from under the bed.

"If I'm not mistaken, that's one of the handles to the bolt cutter my dad kept hanging in the basement." She bent to pick it up.

Nova touched her arm. "Leave it."

The sound of the front door opening and closing reached them.

"Molly?" Anita White's voice called up the stairs. "We're back."

"I'm cleaning rooms," Molly called out.

Footsteps sounded, coming up the stairs.

"Let me handle this. Go on to the next room."

"I only have Talia's to finish," she said.

"Go."

Molly stepped out into the hallway. "Reed's coming." She crossed the hallway and entered Talia's room, leaving the door open a crack.

Nova stood inside and waited for Reed.

He didn't have long to wait.

Reed pushed the door open and stepped in while glancing back down the hall. "I'll see you at dinner."

A feminine voice answered, "See ya then."

Reed didn't turn to face the interior of the room and Nova until he'd closed the door. When he did, he stepped back, his fists up, eyes wide and wary. "What are you doing in my room?"

"Well, I came in to clean, but I found this." He nudged the bolt cutters with his foot, dragging it out from beneath the bed.

Reed's eyes narrowed. "What are they?"

"Bolt cutters."

"So? What are they doing under my bed?" He glanced from the cutters to Nova. "I didn't put them there."

"Any idea how they got here?"

"No." He bent to pick them up.

Something made Nova stop him. "Don't touch them."

"If they belong to Molly, she might be wondering where they are."

"You say you don't know how they got there?"

"Hell, no. What use would I have with a pair of bolt cutters?" His eyes widened, then narrowed again. "You don't think I cut that light down from the ceiling, do you?" He held up his hands. "I've got no beef with Molly or anyone else who was sittin' around that table last night. I'm trying to *make* friends, not hurt them."

"What about the skeleton key you've been carrying around?"

"Did you take that from my room and then leave it on the fireplace mantel?" Reed's cheeks flushed. "I found that key on the floor and thought it was cool. I'd have given it back if I thought anyone cared about it." Reed crossed his arms over his chest. "What's with all the questions? Are you accusin' me of something?"

"No, I'm not trying to accuse you of anything. We just want answers. Someone cut the chain the chandelier hung by. We want to know who and why."

"Well, it wasn't me." Reed tipped his head toward the door. "And what about the key?"

"It's the key to the cellar door. The one Molly was locked behind yesterday morning before you all went to the lighthouse."

"I like Molly. I wouldn't have locked her in the cellar."

"Then how do you account for the key?"

"I found it after we got back from the lighthouse. It was on the stairs."

Nova nodded. As much as he wanted to believe Reed was the one who'd cut the chandelier down from the ceiling, the man's surprise seemed genuine.

"That all you have to say?" Reed demanded.

"For now." He bent to retrieve the bolt cutters using one of the hand towels he'd taken from the bathroom. He wouldn't go into what he'd seen in Reed's phone photos. That was another conversation. Nova left Reed's room and waited in the hallway for Molly.

Molly came out carrying the soiled towels. "I heard. Do you believe him?"

"He appeared genuinely surprised by the bolt cutters."

"And the cellar key?"

Nova ran a hand through his hair. "I don't know who to believe anymore. Whoever has been causing the problems is right under our noses."

Preston climbed the stairs to the landing. "Everything all right?" he asked, glancing from Molly to Nova.

"So far," Molly answered with a cheerful smile that didn't quite reach her eyes.

Talia Dane arrived at the top of the stairs, as well. "Are we having a party in your room or mine?" She glanced from Preston to Molly.

"Nova and I just finished cleaning your rooms and bathrooms. You have fresh towels."

"And you need bolt cutters to make a bed?" Talia's brows rose.

Molly's cheeks reddened and her body stiffened. She made a terrible liar. Another thing Nova loved about her.

He stepped in with "I was cutting tree limbs away from the windows outside some of the rooms."

Molly visibly relaxed. "Now that the beds are all made, I can cook dinner. Anyone up for some clam chowder?"

"I am," Talia said. "Standing around an old jail cell all day reminded me how much I appreciate good food."

Nova steered Molly past the two guests and down the stairs to the kitchen. "Tonight after dinner, I want to collect all the glasses."

"Why?" Her eyes widened. "Fingerprints?"

He nodded.

"I think that can be arranged if you build a fire in the fireplace like you did last night. I have the makings for s'mores."

Nova worked alongside Molly preparing the dinner, chopping vegetables for the salad, stirring the stockpot of clam chowder and setting the table. The simple chores were accomplished in comfortable silence.

Occasionally, they bumped into each other and Nova stole a kiss. Tomorrow the ghost hunters were due to leave the B&B. If they didn't solve the mystery tonight, whoever had been terrorizing them would get away. Or worse, tonight would be the night he made one last move. If he was also the one who'd killed the woman in Cape Churn, he could be planning his next kill.

Nova glanced at Molly, his heart aching at the thought of someone hurting her. He wouldn't let that happen. No matter what.

Dinner didn't take nearly long enough. This would be her last night with Nova. The thought of cooking in her big kitchen after he left seemed sad and lonely. She found herself missing him even before he left. She loved the way he moved around her in the kitchen, accidentally bumping into her, although she suspected it was on purpose. He asked questions and anticipated her moves. He was there when she needed a hand pulling something out of the oven or stirring the chowder.

It wouldn't be the same after he left. She'd be back to cooking by herself. As much as it saddened her, she might as well get used to it. Their time together was coming to an end. Whoever had been playing tricks on them would soon be discovered or leave. Molly prayed whoever it was wasn't also the person who'd killed the woman with the bashed-in face.

When the chowder was ready, Molly poured it into two large tureens made of solid white porcelain from her mother's dinnerware. Nova had already taken out the salads, bread rolls and the condiments, arranging them on the table.

When Nova reentered the kitchen, Molly handed him a tureen. "It's time." Carrying one by herself, she hobbled into the dining room and set it on the table. She noted that he'd used the smooth water glasses instead of the cut crystal. Good, the fingerprints would be easier to lift.

Molly called the guests to the table. All of them came down except Reed.

"Reed?" she called up the stairs.

"Oh, I'm sorry," Talia said. "I thought he'd told you. He went for a walk and said not to wait dinner on him. Something about clearing his head."

Molly glanced out the front window. "I hope he comes back soon. Looks like it's getting foggy again." The fog was thickening. Not so much that he wouldn't be able to find his way back, but it would be that thick soon.

"I'm sure he'll be careful," Talia said. "He had really wanted to stay and explore the hills and coastline instead of going to town this morning."

Molly sat at the head of the table, worrying over Reed's disappearance. He wanted to clear his head? Her gaze met Nova's over her water glass. She could tell he wasn't too happy about Reed leaving. Especially when Nova wanted to get the fingerprints of all their guests.

What if Reed had taken offense at Nova's confronting him about the bolt cutters and key? Was he clearing his head of the anger? Or was he running away, afraid he'd been caught? Nova had the bolt cutters in the back of Molly's SUV to be taken to the police station when he had the glasses, as well.

Whatever Reed was doing, he needed to hurry back. Getting caught in the fog too close to the cliffs was far too dangerous.

At the dinner table, the conversation centered on the jailhouse and filming.

"I got some great infrared readings down there and caught it all on video," Josh exclaimed.

"We have a lot of footage to edit when we get back," Anita agreed. "But wow, this is going to be great."

Molly only half listened, staring at the candles burning in the middle of the table. Only one candelabra had been salvageable from the matching set that had been a wedding gift to her parents. She'd taken it to the cellar and placed it on the worktable beside the chandelier. Two of the things her mother and father loved about their old house.

There were so many. And so many responsibilities that came along with the care of such an old structure. Though she was happy to have the things her mother loved around her, they didn't seem quite as important now as having the *people* she cared about around her. Now she understood how a woman could leave her home to follow the man she loved around the world. Given the chance, she'd go with Nova exploring the world.

And he'd understand when she needed to return to her home. Her roots.

Her gaze kept going to Nova at the other end of the table, where he'd insisted on sitting to keep an eye on all those seated. He wanted to be sure he remembered which glass belonged to whom.

When dinner was over, Anita and Preston offered to help her clear the table and bring out the dessert. She insisted Nova could take care of the table while the other two helped gather the ingredients for s'mores to be made in the great room over the fire.

Molly loaded them with a tray of graham crackers, chocolate bars, marshmallows and long metal shish-kebab sticks. The group gathered around the fireplace, skewering marshmallows onto the metal rods.

Molly watched as the big white puffs were squished between chocolate and graham crackers. This would be their last night here. Possibly Nova's, as well.

"I have the glasses labeled and loaded into a box. Can you handle the cleanup? I want to run the glasses and bolt cutters to town and have them check fingerprints."

"Go. I can take care of myself for a little while."

Nova hesitated. "I'll hurry." He grabbed Molly's keys and left, planning on being back before dark. Already the sun was hidden behind a thin bank of clouds forming out in the Cape. He'd have to hurry. It might end up being another one of those foggy nights like the night before the last, when he'd nearly run off the road. Molly didn't want him to drive in that again.

Nova met Creed at the police station with the bolt cutters and drink glasses. Creed had come equipped with his laptop. One much like the one Nova had carried with him until it had been destroyed when his rental car took a flying leap off a foggy cliff.

Creed's laptop could link to the computers back at the SOS headquarters in D.C. Hopefully, Geek had something on the fingerprints of the driver of the abandoned car and the woman lying dead in the morgue.

He also hoped to find the owner of the fingerprints on the bolt cutters and match it to one of the glasses he'd brought with him.

Creed set up his computer on the police chief's desk and powered it up.

Nova handed the box of glasses to the chief, who, with the help of Gabe, went to work dusting for fingerprints, labeling them carefully.

As soon as they had the prints complete, they loaded them into their system. The chief sat at one desk running a print, while Gabe sat at another with a different one. They started with Preston and Reed.

Once Creed had his computer up, he said, "Call the boss."

Nova hit Royce's number and waited for him to answer.

"Oh, good, Valdez. I was about to call you."

"Do you have a match on either set of fingerprints?"

"I do on the set found in the abandoned vehicle."

"And?" Nova asked, his patience thinning with each passing minute.

"Adrianna Vega."

The name didn't ring any bells in Nova's mind. "Give me more."

"Found her fingerprints on the California DMV database. We ran a cross-check and found her on the U.S. Passport database, as well. She's been a regular between L.A. and, I'm sorry to say...Bolivia."

Nova let go of the breath he'd been holding and took another before he spoke. "Do you have a picture of her?"

"The DMV and passport pictures."

"Can you send them to Creed's email account?"

"Will do. Geek's loading them now."

"What about the dead woman?"

"Nothing in Washington, California and Nevada. Oregon is giving us fits. Geek tried going through channels. Now he's hacking to get in. Hopefully, it won't be much longer."

"Call me when you know something."

"I will." Royce hung up without saying goodbye. He was like that. All business. But he cared about his people and the job he'd been entrusted to do.

"Got a hit on Preston Todd," Gabe said. "He's in the Washington database for a conceal carry license."

"Any felonies?" Nova asked.

"None."

The chief had the prints from the bolt cutters and ran them through IAFIS. After thirty minutes it came up without a match.

With nine sets of prints to go through, it could take all night. Nova couldn't be away much longer from Molly. Every minute he was gone was too long. "Can we compare the prints from all the glasses just to the bolt cutters?"

"Send them to me," Creed said. "I'll run the compare while you continue the IAFIS scan."

A few minutes later, Creed looked up. "Got a match on the bolt cutters to the glass marked Talia Dane."

Nova frowned. "She's one of the guests who'd been pushed down the stairs at the jailhouse."

"Maybe she wasn't pushed, after all. She might have made it look like that to throw you off."

"I need to get back out to Molly." Nova lifted the phone. "What's the number out there?"

Gabe pulled his cell phone from his pocket, hit a number and handed it to Nova. "Calling the B&B."

Nova listened as the phone rang again and again until the answering machine picked up and Molly's sweet voice said, "You've reached the McGregor B&B. Leave a message at the tone and we'll return your call."

Gabe looked up from the screen on his desk. "No answer?"

"No." Nova handed him the phone.

"When she's sitting out on the porch," Gabe said, "she can't hear the phone ring."

"Maybe so, but I'm leaving."

"We'll let you know what we find," Creed assured him.

"I'll come with you." Gabe half rose from his seat.

"Let me call if I need backup."

"In the meantime," the chief said, "we'll keep running the prints until we find something new."

Nova turned to Creed. "Stay in touch with Fontaine. My cell phone may not have enough reception out at the B&B, especially if the fog worsens."

"You got it." Creed stood and shook Nova's hand. "If I can't contact you, I'll deliver the message myself."

"Thanks." Nova left the police station running, jumped into Molly's SUV and hit the highway headed out of town toward McGregor Manor and Molly. He prayed he was there before Talia tried anything else.

As he reached the edge of town, his cell phone buzzed. He checked the caller ID. It was Royce. "Valdez."

"Yeah, boss."

"We got a photo of Adrianna Vega. I sent it a minute ago. Should be hitting you about now."

His phone chirped. He slowed the vehicle and pulled to the side of the road so that he could study the photo of the woman who'd stolen the car. "Damn," he said, his blood growing cold.

"What?"

"I know who the dead woman is."

"Who is she?"

"Talia Dane."

Chapter 16

When she finished doing the dishes, Molly walked through the great room counting guests. Reed was still missing and it was getting darker and foggier by the minute.

She climbed the stairs by hanging on to the rail and limped down the hallway to Reed's room. After knocking twice, she used her key to open the door.

He wasn't in the room, and after knocking on the bathroom door, she checked the bathroom. Not there, either.

"He said he'd be back in thirty minutes." Talia stood at the door to Reed's bedroom. "You don't think he's lost, do you? I'm getting worried about him."

"I don't know." Molly eased around Talia, twisting the lock and closing the door behind her. She worked her way down the stairs, her foot starting to ache, Talia right behind her. Nova had been right—she needed to use the crutches a little longer, until her ankle was back to normal. She found one of the crutches leaning where she'd left it by the front door. Tucking it beneath her arm, she hopped out onto the porch and squinted in a hopeless attempt to see through the encroaching fog, wishing Nova would appear.

"We should go look for him," Talia said.

"I wanted to wait until Nova got back."

"We don't know how long he'll be. In the meantime, it's getting harder and harder to see," Talia argued.

"I know." After pacing the length of porch a few times, Molly came to a decision. The longer she waited, the less chance they had of finding Reed before the fog socked them in. "I'm going to have a look around."

"Miss McGregor?" A male voice called out behind her.

She stopped, turning hopefully, only to be disappointed. Preston hurried out onto the porch. "I'm missing an item from my luggage."

"What item is that?" she asked, remembering Nova had found a gun in the man's room.

He glanced around at Talia and lowered his voice so that only Molly could hear. "My personal handgun. I've got a conceal carry license and I brought my gun. But it's missing."

Molly touched his arm. "I know. With everything going on, I had the rooms searched for weapons. I put your gun away in my bedroom, just to be safe."

Preston's brows wrinkled. "I'd like it to be returned to me." He shot another look over his shoulder toward the house and whispered, "I know that chandelier was cut. If someone did that on purpose, I'd feel safer if I had my gun."

"I'll make sure you have it before we turn in tonight. I promise."

He frowned, apparently not satisfied with her answer.

Molly stared at the man, her eyes narrowed. He didn't look like a killer and her gut told her that he wasn't the one. "Look, if it makes you feel better, it's under the bed in my bedroom. Now, if you'll excuse me, I want to see if I can find Reed."

She knew she needed some kind of bread crumbs to follow if she was to leave the vicinity of the house and expect to make it back in thick fog. In the kitchen, she filled her skirt pocket with fat, dry lima beans. On her way back out the front door, she grabbed a flashlight off the wall-mounted battery charger and stepped out into the night.

Molly eased down the steps and onto the ground, heading toward the side of the house. "Reed!" she called out. She listened. No response.

"I'll check the other end of the house," Talia said as she stepped down from the porch with her own flashlight in hand.

"Stay right next to the house," Molly warned. "If you wander out in the fog, you can get disoriented and lose your way."

"I'll be careful." Talia strode off in the opposite direction.

"Ms. McGregor, do you want the rest of us to help?" Preston called out.

"No. The more people out here, the more chance of someone getting lost. I'll only be a few minutes. Stay put." Moving around to the side of the house, Molly yelled again, "Reed!"

Not until she was near the rear of the mansion did she hear something.

"Help meee…" For a moment, she thought she'd imagined it. Then she heard it again.

"Help meee…"

Hesitant to leave the safety of the house, Molly gauged the thickness of the fog. She could still see four or five feet in front of her. Enough that she could tell when she neared the edge of the cliffs. As quickly as the fog thickened, she wasn't taking any chances of getting lost.

"Reed?" she called out. "Keep talking so that I can find you."

"Here. I'm over here," he said.

Molly dropped a lima bean on the ground, took a step and dropped another. With each step she left a bean on the ground. After walking six steps, she turned and shone her light on the trail. The white beans were visible and left a path for her to find her way back to the house.

Feeling more confident, Molly kept going.

"Help me," Reed called out. "Please."

"I'm coming." Molly picked up the pace, careful to place her crutch on smooth ground. She didn't need another casualty lost in the fog. "Where are you?" she said when she hadn't heard his voice for a couple minutes.

"Here," he said, his voice growing weaker. "Over here."

Molly followed the voice. Why hadn't she come looking earlier? Reed could be hurt badly. And what could she do? She wasn't in any shape to help. The best she could hope for was to find him, go back to the house, call 9-1-1 and return with the first-aid kit.

"Here." The voice sounded as if it was getting closer.

Five more steps and Molly could see the edge of the cliffs ahead and hear the pounding of the surf against the rocks below. Had he fallen over?

"Reed?"

"Molly."

A dark lump lay near the edge of the cliff. It moved, a hand reaching out.

"Oh, thank God," Reed said.

Molly shone her light at his face and gasped.

"Oh, dear Lord." She rushed toward him, dropped her crutch and bent down beside him.

His face was bloody and bruised, his nose appeared broken and his lips were split. "What happened?"

"Hit from behind," he said, his voice garbled. "I fell. Blacked out. Whoever it was hit me again and again."

"Did you see him?"

"No." He lay back. "Pain."

"Can you walk?" Molly asked.

"Dizzy."

"I'm going for help."

He reached out and grabbed her arm, his grip weak but insistent. "Careful. Might get you."

"I'll watch out." Molly reached for her crutch, but it shot past her hand and fell over the cliff, the lightweight aluminum making clinking sounds as it bounced against the rocky ledges on its way to the bottom one hundred and fifty feet below.

"What the hell?"

"Oops, sorry."

Molly flashed her light upward into Talia's face.

Talia shone her light back in Molly's, the beam so bright Molly couldn't see the other woman's expression. "I didn't see it until I'd accidentally kicked it."

"It's okay. I can make it back to the house without it."

"I don't think so." Talia's tone didn't sound right to Molly.

She eased to her feet, balancing carefully on one foot to keep the pressure off her sore ankle. "I'm getting around better now on my ankle. I need you to stay with Reed while I go for help."

"Clever trail you left. It led me right to you." Talia moved closer, her light still pointing in Molly's face, her other hand behind her back, holding something Molly couldn't see.

The fog beside Talia seemed to shimmer, a form taking shape. A thought emerged, a sense of urgency along with it.

Move!

Molly limped backward away from Talia as the woman's other hand swung out from behind her back, wielding a long, dark metal object. A tire iron, aimed for Molly's face.

Molly ducked and leaped over Reed's body, away from Talia and the edge of the cliff. When she landed on her sore ankle, pain shot up her leg and she crumpled to the ground onto her knees, the flashlight tumbling across the ground and out of her reach.

"No!" Talia yelled. "You aren't going back to the house. I wanted to kill Casanova for what he did to my sister. But when I saw how much he cared for you, I knew I could hurt him worse by killing the one he loves. Casanova has to know what it feels like to lose someone he loves because of what he's done."

Molly scrambled to her feet, fighting to ignore the pain in her ankle. She took only a step before Talia threw her flashlight on the ground, grabbed her hair and yanked her backward, swinging her around and toward the edge. Below, Molly could hear the sound of the ocean.

"My father never loved me. Not like he loved Sophia." Talia shoved Molly closer toward the edge. "He blamed me for her death. I was aiming for Casanova because he betrayed my father. But I really wanted Sophia dead." With the lights shining around their ankles and fog blurring their faces, Molly almost didn't see Talia raise the tire iron again.

As the iron came down at Molly, she grabbed Talia's hand, wrestling for control of the weapon. Squeezing as hard as she could, she shook Talia's arm. When that didn't work, she kicked out sharply with her good foot, aiming for Talia's shin at the same time as she shook her wrist.

Talia grunted and the tire iron fell from her grip. Without the weapon, Talia broke away and took a step back. "Casanova Valdez is a liar. He wanted to bring my father down. He used my sister to get to him. And Sophia was stupid enough to fall in love with him."

"What does this have to do with me? I don't understand," Molly said, buying time as she inched away from the edge of the cliff.

"I wanted my father to love me. I'd gone after Casanova to kill him, to make my father proud of me." She pounded her fist against her chest.

"And you killed your sister instead."

"It was his fault!" she screamed. "I wanted to kill him for making me kill my sister. And I almost did that first night." Her voice lowered, her eyes narrowing, calculating. "But killing you is going to be so much more satisfying. I'm going to break his heart like he broke my father's. And knowing it was his fault will kill him a little more every day. A slow, painful death by guilt."

"You've got it wrong," Molly said. "He doesn't love me. We've only just met. He won't care if I'm gone." She had to talk this woman out of what she'd planned. Even if Talia didn't kill her, she would go after Nova.

Talia reached beneath her shirt and dragged something from the waistband of her jeans.

"Gun. She's got a gun," Reed croaked.

"This is for my father." Talia's voice shook and her eyes filled with tears. "I only wanted to be loved."

Molly had nowhere to run. Nothing to hide behind. She braced herself to lunge at Talia.

A shot rang out. The bullet slammed into Molly's shoulder, knocking her backward. She scrambled to keep her footing, but the force of being hit sent her over the edge of the cliff, the fog consuming her in darkness.

With his heart lodged in his throat, Nova drove Molly's SUV like a maniac on roads only an idiot would be out on in the Devil's Shroud. An idiot or someone desperate to save a remarkable woman from tragedy.

In his gut, he knew Adrianna was targeting Molly to get to him. He knew he'd seen her face before. In a picture on Sophia's dresser, the face obscured by shadows as they stood beneath a tree. He should have seen the resemblance. Now Molly could be the one paying for his oversight.

The fog had thickened so much he almost missed the turn for the McGregor B&B. He slammed on the brakes, backed up and raced down the drive, coming to a sliding halt in front of the house.

Six of the ghost hunters stood on the porch. Preston Todd and Anita White detached themselves from the others, running toward Nova as he climbed out of the car.

"Molly's out there somewhere and we heard a gunshot," Preston said.

"Where did it come from?"

Anita pointed into the fog. "I think toward the cliffs."

Nova touched Anita's arm. "Get on the phone, call 9-1-1. Tell them to send everyone—police, firemen, ambulances, the National Guard. I don't care—just send help." He grabbed the flashlight from beneath the driver's seat in Molly's car and ran to the edge of the house.

Preston followed. "What can I do to help?"

"Don't get lost in this fog."

"She went looking for Reed. He never came back from his walk."

"Where's Adrianna—Talia?" Nova asked.

"She was helping Molly look for Reed. She hasn't come back, either." Preston grabbed Nova's arm. "One other thing. Molly said she'd stored my gun in her room. I went to find it when she didn't come right back. I found the case under her bed, but my gun wasn't in it. The gun's gone."

Nova's chest tightened. That would explain the gunshot. Nova prayed Molly hadn't been hit.

With the flashlight pointed low to the ground, its beam reflecting off the fog, he jogged around the side of the house to the rear corner. The fog was dangerously thick. Four steps into it and he'd lose his way. He searched the ground, hoping to find footprints, something he could use to trace Molly's path.

At the back corner, the flashlight beam bounced off a single, dry, white bean.

At first Nova skipped past it. When he came back to it, he shone the light out farther and found another.

Preston pointed at the beans. "She left a trail."

Nova faced the man. "Stay here."

"I can't. That could be my gun. I want to help."

"Then stay close."

"I will."

They moved out, following the path of beans away from the manor.

"Molly?" Nova called out.

"Over here," a voice called out. It was faint, weak and male. Not Molly.

Nova followed the beans toward the voice. "Reed?"

"Here." A thump and a grunt was followed by silence.

"Stay behind me," Nova whispered to Preston. He eased forward, his light close to the ground and held out to the side, away from his body. If Adrianna used the glow of the flashlight as a target, he had a better chance of her missing him.

Nova noticed the abandoned flashlight on the ground first and almost tripped over Reed. The man lay like a pile of rags on the ground, his face in similar shape to the real, dead Talia Dane.

"Is he...?" Preston gulped, his Adam's apple bobbing.

Nova checked for a pulse. Reed had one, but it was weak. "He's alive. For now."

"Good God," Preston exclaimed. "Who did this?"

Nova's jaw tightened, his hands balling into fists. "Talia. Only she's not Talia. Her real name is Adrianna." He searched the immediate area looking for the woman. She had to be near. The ground around him was damp, jumbled footprints indicating a scuffle. He expanded his examination around Reed to the edge of the cliff only a few steps away. His heart pinched inside his chest as he forced himself to lean over and call out, "Molly?"

For a long moment, he heard nothing but the waves crashing against the rocks below. Then a sound drifted to him as if from the side of the cliff.

"Nova?" Molly's soft voice drifted up to him.

"Where are you?" he asked.

"Down here," she said, her voice shaking.

"Are you okay?"

"For now. But I don't know how long I can hang on."

"Are you on a ledge?"

"Yes. A very small one."

Nova grabbed the flashlight from the ground and handed it to Preston. "I need a rope."

Preston's eyes widened. "You want me to go get one?"

"There's one in the basement hanging on the far wall near the workbench where we placed the broken chandelier. Get it and the nylon seat harness hanging next to it. Follow the beans back."

When Preston hesitated, Nova yelled, "Run!"

The man took off running, his light bobbing away, swallowed by the fog.

"Molly?"

"I'm still hanging on. I don't think I can do it for long."

"Help is on its way. Please, *cariña,* don't let go. I have so much I want to say to you."

"I'll try," she said with what sounded suspiciously like a sob.

Laughter behind him made Nova spin.

Adrianna materialized out of the fog. "She was supposed to die. But this turned out even better." She held a pistol in her hand, pointed at his chest. "I've been waiting for this moment for two years."

"Why are you doing this?"

"When Sophia died, my father died with her." Adrianna's lips peeled back in a snarl. "I thought with her out of the way, he'd turn to me. Love me." She snorted. "Instead, he blamed me. It was my fault she died. I told him you were the one to blame. You were lying to him. You were going to take Sophia away from him."

"Killing me or Molly won't make your father love you."

"No, but it might make him respect me. He might finally look at me as his daughter and not the mistake he made with a woman at a resort in Mexico."

"Alfonzo is an animal. He doesn't care about anyone but himself."

"Liar! He'll care about me when I tell him I killed you."

Nova shook his head. "Adrianna, it won't make a difference. The man would just as soon trade his daughter for a brick of cocaine to sell. I wanted to get Sophia out of there. Take her away from that life."

"And all I wanted was a father. And you ruined it for me." Angry tears welled in her eyes and spilled down her cheeks. "I was aiming for you!" She pulled the trigger, the shot going wide of Nova.

He rolled to the side and back on his feet, lunging for Adrianna.

She fired again, nicking his thigh.

Nova barely flinched, throwing a side kick that knocked her in the gut. The gun dropped from her hand and she staggered backward, her arms waving as she teetered on the edge of the cliff. Her feet slipped and she grabbed for the edge as she fell over.

Holding on with one hand, she struggled to find something to hold on to with the other.

Nova raced forward. "Take my hand."

"It's over," she cried, sobs shaking her body. "Leave me to die."

Nova dropped the flashlight, threw himself on his belly and grabbed her wrist with one hand, refusing to let her plummet to her death.

"Let go," she pleaded.

"No," he said.

She reached up with her other hand and peeled his fingers loose, one at a time. "Just let me...die."

Nova tried to grab her with his other hand, but she shoved his fingers free of her wrist. She disappeared into the fog, the misery in her face the last image Nova had of her. He lay on his stomach, remembering how to breathe.

"Nova?" Molly's voice called out to him.

"I'm still here." He dragged himself to his feet.

"Am I going to die?" Molly asked.

"No, *cariña*." His voice caught on the lump in his throat. "I'm coming for you. Don't give up on me."

"I don't want to. But it's hard to hold on and stay awake."

"Then talk to me."

"I was shot."

His belly tightened. "Oh, baby, are you bleeding?"

"Yes."

"A lot?"

"I don't know," she said, her voice weak. "I'm tired."

"Stay with me, Molly."

For a moment, he worried she'd drifted off. He hated that he couldn't see her, couldn't reach out to her and bring her back to safety.

"I'll miss you," she finally said.

"I'm not going anywhere," he insisted. "And I'm bringing you home soon."

"And when you do, I'll miss you." She paused. "You won't have a reason to stay any longer."

Nova realized she was right. But oh, so wrong. "That's what I thought, too," he said. "Until I met one very strong-willed, beautiful McGregor who doesn't let anything get her down."

What sounded like a chuckle broke on a sob. "Anyone I know?"

"Her name's Molly. And by damn, I'm going to get to know her a whole lot better." He glanced behind him, shining the light back down the path of lima beans, praying for Preston to hurry. "I have something I've been meaning to ask you."

"I'm listening," she said.

"I know you love McGregor Manor, and I would never dream of taking you away from it. Do you think you could consider going out with someone who travels a lot for his job?" *Please, Preston, bring that rope before it's too late.*

For a long moment all he heard was the sound of the waves crashing against the rocks below.

"Molly?"

"I do."

Nova closed his eyes and prayed they'd get the chance.

"Nova!" a familiar voice called out in the fog behind him. Soon a flashlight beam penetrated the fog and Creed Thomas emerged, carrying the rope and seat harness Nova had been praying for.

"Thank God." Nova jumped to his feet and grabbed the harness, slipping his legs into the webbing.

Creed looped the rope around a giant boulder and secured it, then dropped the loose end over the side of the cliff. "You might want this." He slipped a headlamp on Nova's head and latched it in place. "The police and fire rescue are on their way. They should be right behind me."

"Thanks." All Nova had to do was get to Molly and stabilize her position. The professionals would complete the rescue.

Once he had the seat harness securely fastened, he looped the rope around the descent-control ring. Holding the rope out to his side, he backed to the edge of the cliff. "Molly?"

He held his breath for several long seconds before he heard a weak, "I'm...still...here."

"I'm coming down." He eased over the edge, careful not to disturb too many rocks to rain down on Molly's head. "Talk to me, *cariña.*"

"I'm tired."

"Talk to me so that I can find you," he urged.

After a short pause, she said, "I remember the first time I saw you."

"What? Two days ago?"

"Is that all? I feel like I've known you a lifetime."

"Me too, *bebe.*" He let the rope slide through the ring, easing himself down the cliff. "And yet, I want to get to know you a whole lot more."

"I almost spilled chowder on Gabe, I couldn't take my eyes off you."

"It's my swarthy good looks. Gets the girls every time."

She chuckled, her voice fading.

He was getting closer.

"I remember thinking you had the prettiest brown eyes," he teased, letting more rope out, descending as fast as he could without hitting her or missing her. He halted, waiting for her response.

"My eyes are green," she said.

"Just checking to see if you're coherent."

"Could you hurry it up, please?" Her voice was barely above a whisper, strained and breathless. "My fingers are cramping and I think I'm about to slip."

He glanced down, pointing his headlamp to where he'd heard her voice. His breath caught when he spotted her, three feet down on his left.

She clung to a crevice in the rocks, her face pressed to the smooth surface. How she'd managed to grab hold was a miracle.

Nova lowered himself a little more, then walked sideways against the escarpment until he reached her.

She didn't move her face away from the cliff.

"I'm right beside you and I'm going to step over you. Don't move a muscle. Let me." He secured his rope, freeing his hands.

Her shoulders shook with silent sobs. "I thought you wouldn't get here in time."

He reached for one of her hands. "I'm going to take your hand and place it on the rope. I won't let you fall."

"I trust you. It's this cliff I'm not so sure of."

"I told you I was coming," he said. "I don't stand up my dates. It's one of those things you should know about me."

"If this is a first date—" she laughed and sobbed, her fingers latching on to the rope "—I'd hate to see what you have in mind for a second date."

"Are you still hanging on?" he asked.

"I don't think I can," she whimpered. "I'm losing my grip—"

As Molly's hand slipped off the rocks, Nova reached out and swung her around, catching her in a leg lock around her middle. She clung to the rope, her eyes closed, her face white, a dark red stain on the shoulder of her blouse.

The motion had the rope swinging, the two of them swaying as they dangled over the sharp rocks below. Nova prayed that the knot he'd tied would hold long enough for the rescue team to get to them.

"You're bleeding," he said.

"Right now that's the least of my worries." She opened her eyes and stared straight into his. "Have I told you I'm afraid of heights?"

"I take it rock climbing wasn't your thing?"

She shook her head. "That would be Gabe."

"Nova?" Creed called out. "You got her?"

"We're both here," he called out.

"Molly?" Gabe's voice came to them.

Molly's eyes welled with tears. "I'm okay."

"The rescue team is on their way down."

"We're not going anywhere," Nova said, staring into Molly's eyes. "I'm not leaving."

Her eyes widened. "And when this is all said and done?"

"Quiero pasar mi tiempo contigo," he whispered. "I want to spend time with you. Get to know you. Cape Churn is growing on me." He laughed. "Must be that sense of family."

She sighed, leaning her head against him. "Family is everything."

"Sí." As he pressed his lips to her forehead, the rescue team arrived, taking control of the situation.

Before long, they lifted Molly up to the top and then helped Nova out.

Once on firm ground, Nova searched for Molly, his gaze scanning the crowd of police, firemen and EMTs that had gathered at the edge of the cliff.

Creed appeared beside him. "If you're looking for Molly, they're loading her into the ambulance. They're going to take her straight to the hospital to treat the gunshot wound. Gabe's going with her."

"Good." He wished he could have gone, too, but it had taken another twenty minutes to get him up to the top after they'd rescued Molly. "What about Schotzman?"

"They loaded him into an ambulance as soon as

they arrived. He's in bad shape, but they think he might make it."

Nova started around Creed. "I'll be at the hospital."

"Hey, buddy, you're bleeding," he said, pointing at the hole in his jeans where Adrianna had shot him in the thigh.

"It doesn't hurt." Or didn't until Creed pointed it out.

"You should let the medics check it out."

"It can wait until I get to the hospital."

"I'll take you." Creed jogged to catch up. "We'll take my car." He opened the door to his SUV and Nova climbed in.

Within fifteen minutes, they arrived at the Cape Churn Memorial Hospital.

"Drop me at the door," Nova said.

When Creed rolled up to the curb, Nova didn't wait for him to stop; he jumped out and ran inside.

The nurse at the counter smiled. "Can I help you?"

"Molly McGregor," he said. "Where is she?"

"She's in surgery. You can wait in the lobby. Someone will let you know when she's out."

Nova paced for what seemed like forever. When he checked the clock, thirty minutes had passed. He was ready to find her himself when a nurse pushed through the door marked Authorized Personnel Only.

"Molly's okay. She's out of surgery and in the recovery room. And she's asking for someone named Nova." The nurse smiled at him. "Is that you?"

He nodded.

The nurse stepped aside and he raced by.

"Molly!" he yelled.

"Nova?"

Emma Jenkins pushed open a door farther down a

long hallway. "She's in here." With a nod at the other nurse, she said, "It's okay. We'll take care of both of them in here."

Nova pushed past Emma and entered the room where Molly lay on a hospital bed with a clean white sheet pulled up over her breasts.

She smiled at him. "I'm okay. They got the bullet out. I might get to go home tonight."

He clasped her hand in his and pressed it to his cheek. "Good. I thought you might try to duck out before I got a chance to ask you out on a second date."

"Not a chance. What have you got in mind? Skydiving, hang gliding or race-car driving without brakes on foggy roads?" She laughed. "I'm game."

"Ah, *mi corazón*." He cupped her cheek and kissed her, his lips lingering over hers. When he broke it off, he brushed her hair back from her face. "Actually, I thought we'd go to Portland and shop for crystals to replace the broken ones on your *abuela*'s chandelier. Then I could hang it for you."

"That could take time. I didn't think you'd be around after this weekend."

"I'm thinking of relocating my home base to the West Coast, if my boss approves."

"Cape Churn?" She smiled up at him. "You don't want to travel the world and live in exotic places?"

He shook his head. "I can't think of a nicer place to live than here. It's beautiful, the people are genuine and care about each other. Like family, something I haven't had in so long, I hadn't remembered what it was like. You reminded me and I thank you for that." He grinned. "So, how about it?"

She smiled. "Which part?"

He spread his arms. "All of it."

Molly tugged his shirt, pulling him closer. She rested her fingers against the side of his face, brushing her thumb over his lips. "I do like the way you fit in my kitchen."

"I can make a mean omelet."

She curled her hand around the back of his neck and brought his mouth within kissing distance. "And in my bedroom."

"Don't you want to wait until after our second date?" he asked, his breath mingling with hers.

"No way. Who knows if we'll survive our second date?"

Epilogue

"And according to the suicide note found in Elizabeth Slatington's journal, she murdered the owners of McGregor Manor in 1888. Ian did not kill his wife." On the television, Josh Steiner stepped back, the video panning the front of McGregor B&B. "And now that his name is clear of all suspicion, he and his wife, Rose, can rest in peace." The video ended with music and the tintype photograph of Ian and Rose McGregor's wedding day.

"You knew?" Gabe turned to Molly.

"I was the one who told Josh about the note," Molly said.

"How did you find that information?" he asked.

She leaned against Nova, a smile teasing the corners of her lips. "I had my sources."

"Nova?" Gabe asked.

Nova shrugged, bouncing baby Tonya on his knee with a doting Kayla sitting next to them. "She told me Rose showed her the face of the woman in a vision, then led her to the book in the library. Who am I to refute a claim like that?"

Gabe's brows rose. "You believe all that mumbo jumbo?"

"I believe it was Rose and Ian who orchestrated my stay at McGregor Manor. Otherwise, I might not have spent the night and fallen in love with the woman of my dreams."

Molly slapped his shoulder playfully. "Adrianna cut your brakes, not Rose."

"I believe Rose told me when to jump out of the car." He tickled Tonya's chin and the baby giggled. "Nicole and I owe Rose our lives."

"Face it, Gabe," Molly said, leaning her back against the couch, more content than she'd ever been with all the people she loved most surrounding her. "It's all about family looking out for each other."

Gabe smiled. "Yeah. I guess so." He stuck his hand out to Nova. "And since you're soon to be my brother-in-law, welcome to this nutty family."

Nova shook his hand and handed Tonya back to Gabe's wife. Then he draped his arm around Molly's shoulders. "I can't think of a better family to belong to."

"Yeah, well, brace yourself, *mi amor*," Molly said, her heart so full it felt as if it would burst. "It's about to get bigger." She rubbed a hand across her flat belly, imagining it eight months from that day.

Nova's eyes rounded, his mouth falling open. "Are you?"

She nodded.

He pulled her into his arms and hugged her so tightly she thought the baby could feel it, too.

"Fantástico!"

* * * * *

Available May 6, 2014

#1799 CAVANAUGH UNDERCOVER
by Marie Ferrarella

Agent Brennan Cavanaugh's covert job in the seamy world of human trafficking turns personal when he meets the mysterious Tiana. Suddenly he's risking his life—and his heart—to save the undercover madam who's out to find her sister.

#1800 EXECUTIVE PROTECTION
The Adair Legacy • by Jennifer Morey

When his politician mother is shot, jaded cop Thad Winston gets more than he bargained for during the investigation with the spirited Lucy Sinclair, his mother's nurse. But keeping his desire at bay proves difficult when Lucy becomes the next target...and his to protect.

#1801 TRAITOROUS ATTRACTION
by C.J. Miller

To rescue the brother he believed dead, recluse Connor West will trust computer analyst Kate Squire. But the deeper they trek into the jungle, the hotter their attraction burns. Until the former spy realizes Kate knows more than she's telling...

#1802 LATIMER'S LAW
by Mel Sterling

Desperate young widow Abigail McMurray steals a pickup to flee an abusive relationship, never realizing the truck's owner, K-9 deputy Cade Latimer, is in the back. But rather than arrest her, the lawman takes her under his protection and into his arms.

HRSCNM0414

REQUEST YOUR FREE BOOKS!
2 FREE NOVELS PLUS 2 FREE GIFTS!

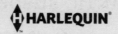

ROMANTIC suspense

Sparked by danger, fueled by passion

YES! Please send me 2 FREE Harlequin® Romantic Suspense novels and my 2 FREE gifts (gifts are worth about $10). After receiving them, if I don't wish to receive any more books, I can return the shipping statement marked "cancel." If I don't cancel, I will receive 4 brand-new novels every month and be billed just $4.74 per book in the U.S. or $5.24 per book in Canada. That's a savings of at least 14% off the cover price! It's quite a bargain! Shipping and handling is just 50¢ per book in the U.S. and 75¢ per book in Canada.* I understand that accepting the 2 free books and gifts places me under no obligation to buy anything. I can always return a shipment and cancel at any time. Even if I never buy another book, the two free books and gifts are mine to keep forever.

240/340 HDN F45N

Name _____ (PLEASE PRINT)

Address _____ Apt. #

City _____ State/Prov. _____ Zip/Postal Code

Signature (if under 18, a parent or guardian must sign)

Mail to the Harlequin® Reader Service:
IN U.S.A.: P.O. Box 1867, Buffalo, NY 14240-1867
IN CANADA: P.O. Box 609, Fort Erie, Ontario L2A 5X3

Want to try two free books from another line?
Call 1-800-873-8635 or visit www.ReaderService.com.

* Terms and prices subject to change without notice. Prices do not include applicable taxes. Sales tax applicable in N.Y. Canadian residents will be charged applicable taxes. Offer not valid in Quebec. This offer is limited to one order per household. Not valid for current subscribers to Harlequin Romantic Suspense books. All orders subject to credit approval. Credit or debit balances in a customer's account(s) may be offset by any other outstanding balance owed by or to the customer. Please allow 4 to 6 weeks for delivery. Offer available while quantities last.

Your Privacy—The Harlequin® Reader Service is committed to protecting your privacy. Our Privacy Policy is available online at www.ReaderService.com or upon request from the Harlequin Reader Service.

We make a portion of our mailing list available to reputable third parties that offer products we believe may interest you. If you prefer that we not exchange your name with third parties, or if you wish to clarify or modify your communication preferences, please visit us at www.ReaderService.com/consumerschoice or write to us at Harlequin Reader Service Preference Service, P.O. Box 9062, Buffalo, NY 14269. Include your complete name and address.

HRS13R

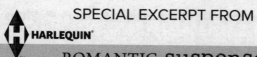
"Let me see, Abigail. I won't hurt you, but I need to know
bruises are the worst of it."

"That…that *crummy* button!" The words came out in
the most embarrassed, horrified tone Cade had ever heard a
woman use.

He couldn't tell whether the trembling that shook her entire
body was laughter, tears, fear, pain or all of the above. She
swayed on her feet like an exhausted toddler, and he realized
she might fall if she remained standing. He sank back onto
the picnic table bench and drew her down with him. She
drooped like a flower with a crushed stem, and it was the
most natural thing in the world to put an arm around her.
In all his thug-tracking days he'd never comforted a criminal
like this. How many of them had wept and gazed at him with
pitiful, wet eyes? How easily had he withstood those bids for
sympathy and lenience? How many of them ended up in the
back of the patrol car on the way to jail, where they belonged?

But how quickly, in just moments, had Abigail McMurray and her gigantic problem become the thing he most needed to fix in the world. He felt her stiffness melting away like snow in the Florida sun, and shortly she was leaning against his chest, her hands creeping up to hang on to his shoulders as if he were the only solid thing left on the planet.

Now I have the truth.

He had what he thought he wanted, yes. But knowing what had pushed Abigail to take his truck wasn't enough. Now he wanted the man who had done the damage, wanted him fiercely, with a dark, chill fury that was more vendetta than justice. He shouldn't feel this way—his law enforcement training should have kept him from the brink. He hardly knew Abigail, and the fact she'd stolen his truck didn't make her domestic abuse issues his problem.

But somehow they were.

He felt her tears soaking his shirt, her sobs shaking her body, and stared over her head toward the tea-dark river, where something had taken the lure on his fishing line and was merrily dragging his pole down the sandy bank into the water.

Aw, hell. You know it's bad when I choose a sobbing woman over the best reel I own. Goodbye, pole. Hello, trouble.

**Don't miss
LATIMER'S LAW
by Mel Sterling, coming May 2014 from
Harlequin® Romantic Suspense.**

HARLEQUIN®

ROMANTIC suspense

CAVANAUGH UNDERCOVER
by Marie Ferrarella

A thrilling new *Cavanaugh Justice* title from *USA TODAY* bestselling author Marie Ferrarella!

Agent Brennan Cavanaugh's covert job in the seamy world of human trafficking turns personal when he meets the mysterious Tiana. Suddenly he's risking his life—and his heart—to save the undercover madam who's out to find her sister.

Look for *CAVANAUGH UNDERCOVER*
by Marie Ferrarella in May 2014.

HARLEQUIN®

ROMANTIC suspense

EXECUTIVE PROTECTION
by Jennifer Morey
He's trained to be prepared for anything...but this

When his politician mother is shot, jaded cop Thad Winston gets more than he bargained for during the investigation with the spirited Lucy Sinclair, his mother's nurse. And when a stalker sets his sights on Lucy—possibly the same man who tried to kill his mother—Thad realizes just how much he has to lose.

Look for EXECUTIVE PROTECTION by Jennifer Morey in May 2014. Book 2 in *The Adair Legacy* miniseries. Available wherever books and ebooks are sold.

Also from *The Adair Legacy* miniseries:

HER SECRET, HIS DUTY by Carla Cassidy

Available wherever ebooks are sold.

Heart-racing romance, high-stakes suspense!

www.Harlequin.com

HRS27870

ROMANTIC suspense

TRAITOROUS ATTRACTION
by C.J. Miller

**From steamy jungles to opulent palaces...
it's nonstop action, danger...and passion!**

To find a "dead" agent, intelligence analyst Kate Squire
needs the man's brother—retired Sphere operative Connor
West. His skills as a trained assassin are essential for her
mission...but not so much her slamming, raw attraction for
the man himself....

For a loner like Connor, trekking into the jungle with a
secretive killer blonde at his side is not textbook. Caught
between armed insurgents and hungry predators, he fears
Kate may be his deadliest threat...until their very agency
turns on them. Stranded, outmanned and outgunned,
Connor has nowhere else to turn. Trusting Kate may be the
only way to get them out alive....

Look for the TRAITOROUS ATTRACTION
by C.J. Miller in May 2014.

Available wherever ebooks are sold.

Heart-racing romance, high-stakes suspense!

HRS27872

Love the Harlequin book you just read?

Your opinion matters.

Review this book on your favorite
book site, review site, blog or your own
social media properties and share
your opinion with other readers!

Be sure to connect with us at:
Harlequin.com/Newsletters
Facebook.com/HarlequinBooks
Twitter.com/HarlequinBooks